PRICE OF
STOLEN FLAME

S. S. NIGHTSHADE

Second edition paperback ISBN: 979-8-9913670-6-6
Nightshade's Writing Desk LLC

FOR

THE EMPATHS, THE ENRAGED, THE NEARLY UNHINGED

THE OVER-DRAMATICS AND OVERTHINKERS,

THE SOULS WHO ARE BOTH BURDENED AND BLESSED

TO FEEL

TRIGGER WARNING

Intended for readers 18+
All characters are 18+

- Religion: this text does not claim to represent accurate records or teachings of any religious histories or practices

- Kidnapping

- Explicit sexual scenes; allusions of rape

- Graphic violence; war; death; attempted suicide

- Substance abuse

- Violent/emotional outbursts

- Blood drinking

PROLOGUE

Starlight and flame is an intoxicating combination. Dimly, the flickering silver of the heavens fought against clouds of rising ash. Smoke covered everything, invading his senses as ruthless as it did the night, but he did not shut his eyes against the sting. Nor their screams. Witches, the lot of them, were his expertise by now. Finding them, seducing them, and of course, exterminating them.

White plumes of smoke stained the cloudless night as another's pitiful wail pierced the dark. Her sisters who were still being bound to their stakes, had begun chanting under their breaths. The sound was haunting, accusation and rage tainting the ancient spells.

But it was futile. Once receiving Gods Mark, they had lost their magic. Magic they shouldn't have in the first place.

"Twenty-three in total, Silvanus." A young Luminary Silvanus didn't know the name of, reigned his horse in to stop beside him. His face, like all the others, was half shaded by the blood red hood which symbolized their faction, The Luminaries of Repentance. "All to burn?" He sounded not much older than a boy. "Or shall some hang?"

"Burning is thorough," Silvanus mused, finally averting his gaze from the sky. He sat up, sliding his hood back, his shock of black hair being washed in moonlight and flame. A Devil in his own right, despite their noble cause. After a beat of silence he added, "And easier to clean up."

"Aye, Silvanus, as you wish." The Luminary bowed awkwardly in his saddle, before urging his horse on once again. Silvanus didn't watch him go, didn't watch the flames as they began swallowing his prey alive. Instead he draped himself across his own horses neck, threading his fingers through its mane, and inhaled deeply. Slowly recentering.

In another life, he hated this. But for his own self-preservation, he'd kill as many of these damned creatures that he was ordered to. After all, he was cleaning up his own mess.

"Another successful hunt I see." A voice of an annoying pitch interrupted Silvanus' thoughts, and he didn't need to turn to see who it was.

"Hello, Gabriel," he greeted, a hint of gravel gnawing at the edge of his words. He sat up, finding the Angel watching with a sick sort of fascination as the last stake was lit. A twisted smile had graced his otherwise blank face, sending a chill down Silvanus' spine. The final Witch, a girl, really, remained utterly silent as the flames licked at her skin. Like she was dead already.

"To what do I owe this intrusion?" Silvanus asked, unable to hide his disgust for the situation any longer. Gabriel though just released a hearty laugh, finally dragging his gaze to Silvanus.

"Just ensuring your error is corrected in due time. You understand the catastrophe that would ensue if Hell's power continued to spread further than the pit, more than most would." Silvanus nodded, momentarily swarmed by the memories of his time in the pit, and his transformation under the bloody fist of the King there.

"Hence why twenty-three souls are on their way down," he murmured, pulling his hood back into place. Gabriel watched him closely, the way his fingers fidgeted with the reins, the way he kept his gaze glued to the darkened night sky. He did not soften his words when he finally spoke.

"How many have you burned yourself?"

Silvanus visibly stiffened, but his voice remained serene as he said, "Just one. Their leader. Then I passed the torch." After moments pause he added, "It's good to make the boys burn most of them. They need to learn how to master their conflicting actions and emotions eventually, otherwise their dedication is an empty oath."

"And they're an easy scapegoat for you to keep your conscience clear." Gabriels voice had dropped to a dangerous pitch. With a snap of his fingers both men were on the ground, just a few feet from the raging fires. His grip dug into the back of Silvanus' neck, forcing him to watch the burning. "This is your retribution, not theirs. You will never be able to return as you once were if you do not do the job properly yourself."

Before Silvanus could reply, a commotion to their left drew their attention. From one of the ill-built cottages, a walking stick of a boy careened off the dilapidated porch and fell face first in the snow. Latin curses and spells were spewing from his lips in an enraged frenzy, immobilizing the Luminaries rushing out of the cottage behind him. Silvanus felt himself smirking at the boys fight, his eyes alighting on his unmarked neck.

"Well, I didn't know they could procreate," Gabriel muttered disdainfully. The boy cried out as another Luminary appeared from the darkened brush, intercepting him swiftly and slamming his spine to the dirt.

"Silence your hideous whispering!"

"Mori in flammas," the boy growled in response, before spitting in the Luminaries face. They raised a hand to strike him, but Silvanus began laughing, making them both freeze, gazes darting to him for the first time.

"My, my, you are a potent one, aren't you?" He extracted himself from Gabriels grip, crossing the trodden Earth to kneel before him. The child reeked of magic, enough so that Silvanus leaned closer, inhaling deeply.

"Where's my mother?" The boy asked, his lower lip trembling despite the rage in his eyes. Silvanus leveled his gaze on him, his humor dampening to a blank face.

"Burning, with the others." Tears shone in the boys eyes, but he did not scream nor turn to look. Silvanus leaned closer still, "Gods Mark does not have to be your fate. If you choose it, you may join me on my quest."

"What is the meaning of this?" Gabriels voice came from behind him, low with warning. Silvanus peered at him over his shoulders, his eyes glittering like ruby's in the flickering light.

"The problem with Hells magic seeping into the world is that Lucifer, nor us, have control over it." Gabriel's face contorted with annoyance, but he didn't argue, which just made Silvanus grin wider. "Don't fool yourself into believing that I'm unaware of your intentions with the fire. You want to purify this land. In my past life, I had the same goal."

"And in this one has your resolve wavered?" The question was poised like a blade. It was an assessment now, bordering on a threat.

"Even if it has, you need me," Silvanus reminded him. "You're incompatible with a magic like that. It will kill you if you try. So, unless you'd rather call out to your younger brother and see if he suddenly wants to join us, I'm your only tool to use to obtain it."

Gabriel continued to glare for a long moment, before begrudgingly relenting. His voice was coarse, "As long as you don't waver from our bargain, I see no reason why you can't keep the boy."

A flare of satisfaction went through Silvanus, his attention turning back to the boy on the ground in front of him. With a flick of his hand, the Luminary pinning him down released him. Silvanus approached slowly, crouching before him as he took him in fully.

He was in a pitiful state, half starved, and dirty as a dog. His nappy blonde hair was tied at the nape of his neck, where Silvanus could practically feel the blood rushing from his anxiety. But he did not cower.

"I do enjoy your spirit," Silvanus finally said, and the glare on the boy's face just turned more severe. Perfect. This child possessed more resolve, pride, and control over himself than some grown men, and Silvanus had to keep himself from praising him further. After all this time, the tables would turn as fate aligned. He sat back on his haunches, propping his chin in his hand and asked, "Tell me your name?"

"Finn." The boy held his gaze, refusing to let his voice shake even though he was clearly terrified.

Silvanus chuckled, shaking his head and clarified, "Your full name."

Finn jumped slightly as a stake cracked at its root, his gaze flickering to the dying fires for the first time.

"Finnegan Esmeraldas Hagan."

"Finnegan Esmeraldas Hagan," Silvanus purred. "How would you like to change the world?

CHAPTER 1

War is such a trivial thing at times. Glancing across the table, I catch my sister's eye, finding her equally as exasperated as I am. Becca's blue irises only thaw for a second, before she turns her icy gaze back to Aengus who has been trading verbal blows with Akashi for the past twenty minutes.

I was fairly certain the point they were trying to make had long passed, plus I stopped paying attention about ten minutes ago. I'd be willing to bet that they were just using the moment as an excuse to go for each other's throat, instead of talking about their obvious familial issues like functional adults. But I wasn't about to be a hypocrite and suggest it.

"You've been rephrasing the same topic for what feels like a decade," Becca drawls, her voice laced with *very* apparent aggravation. Her silver claws tap against the table making the arguing Hounds fall quiet, and I have to bite back a smile.

Hounds are strong, and proud, but after seeing how vicious my sister could be as a Hellcat they never dare to mess with her. Frankly, I don't blame them. She feigns a yawn before adding, "If you've made your point, some of us have better things to do."

"So, we're just going along with it then?" I feel Akashi bristle beside me, and don't have to glance up to know he's now glaring at my sister. A fresh wave of annoyance rolls through me as they take their turn to face off.

I know I should leave them to their own quarrels, but the temptation to grab them and bonk their heads together right there at the table was growing. This was not the time or place for whatever anger they still held for one another. We'd wasted enough time already.

As they began to bicker, my gaze drifted to the window at the far end of the room. The shattered constellation of stained glass welded into the stone cast an ethereal glow on all of us, burning in different shades of color and shadow.

This was once Lucifers throne room. A place to fear, a place to avoid. And if you found yourself dragged here, it was a place to beg. Just three months ago, this room was filled with blood and death. Below us, the dunes had been littered with corpses of Angels and Hounds. Above us, the sky filled with an army craving our blood. And now in the aftermath, the space seemed reserved for petty squabbling.

What I'd wanted it to serve as was a meeting hall, hence why the group of us sat here. In the space where Lucifer's gaudy throne once sat, I'd conjured a long, oval table which was surrounded on all sides by midnight cushioned pews. Rows of them lined the room in case a larger meeting was held, or, more frequently, if someone overheated and shifted into their Hound form, shattering the one being used.

The dips in the floor, which once ran with lava, were now filled with soil and night-blooming flowers. The wide double doors had been repaired, and accented with windows. Soundproof, but allowing for those outside to not feel shut out. And, of course, a few eccentric chandeliers with flame burning candles were added by a certain vampire with expensive taste.

The one luxury I allowed myself was the high-back chair I lounged in. The seat was the only visual indication that I was 'in charge', it's plum cushions the only source of color in the room besides the stained-glass window. I tried not to do much in that sense, avoiding the attention and air of importance even though I knew it was expected of me.

After the battle, the Hounds attention and demands were endless. I kept them at bay for a while by reorganizing the daily functionalities and duties they had, ensuring that they would actually have some time to themselves for rest or enjoyment. That was the easy part. The hard part was the handful of packs who were unwilling to accept me as the new... boss... master... whatever. It all made my skin crawl.

Aengus had called for execution. Luna, banishment. And Becca, I'd rather not describe the things she'd threatened to do. Before things could grow more hostile, I decided to release the Hounds who wished for complete independence to purgatory. The only effort they owed me in exchange was to protect the people and creatures dwelling there.

It was a middle ground, which they thankfully agreed on with little argument. So, as long as they defended the defenseless, I'd leave them be. Not that I ever checked in on their behaviors, or if they even stayed there as requested. They were just free.

I didn't take this throne with the intention of ruling or controlling anyone, so I didn't understand or appreciate the visceral reactions that were 'on my behalf'. I didn't take this throne expecting to be thrust into this position or with these duties. I hadn't intended to take the throne at all to begin with.

Now bitter, I fiddled with the lace choker on my neck. It was the only thing I never took off, the thin shield between the world and my scar from the move which cost me my life in this very room. I didn't even know the cut had scarred at first, not until Akashi finally asked me if it hurt at all.

I dropped my hand to the table with a light slap, wishing my restless thoughts would cease, and instantly everyone fell silent. Except my sister of course, who finished saying whatever inappropriate 'dog' comment she was making. I rolled my eyes again.

"For hell's sake," I murmured, sitting up straight. My gaze swept across the few Hounds in the room who were not of my pack, each of them displaying a varying degree of curiosity tinged with apprehension. I swallowed the bile rising in the back of my throat, trying to soften my voice and muster a smile. "How many times must I assure you that you may speak freely? Please continue where you left off, preferably about the actual issue at hand." I added the last part with a pointed look between Becca and Akashi, the latter who finally retook his seat.

"Apologies, my lady." My Commander, Aengus, amongst other things, drew my attention again as he sat forward. His fiery red hair was pulled back in a Viking style braid, so nothing sheltered me from his striking green eyes, the same shade of the man's at my side. He folded his hands neatly in front of him, the picture of formality. "You'll need to forgive us while we adapt to having a seat at the table, so to speak. It's not that we are ungrateful. We just..." he trailed off, looking lost.

"Don't know how to be," Luna finished for him. From his side, the woman who raised me and filled the void my birth mother left, reached out to press one of her hands firmly over her mates. I felt Akashi bristle beside me once again as he tracked his mother's move. Threads of tension, his anger and confusion, were palpable while he silently studied his parents.

To their left, Hikari whispered with Kuma, the pins and needles of their gazes digging into my skin as I mulled over her words. A foot bumped mine under the table and I fought the urge to turn and look at Silas.

After the battle he rarely left my side, hovering over me more than my sister and Akashi combined. I was unsure if he felt obligated since I saved his life and welcomed him into my pack, or because his own brother was locked in the dungeon far below us. A traitor and a killer, but alive.

His foot knocked mine again, harder this time, insistent that I don't remain silent. I pinched the bridge of my nose, releasing a sigh.

"I believe that feeling is the only thing we could collectively agree on." Murmured agreements and fragmented apologies echoed through the space as I stood, the familiar prickle of power under my skin urging me to wrap this up.

"In summary, we're at war, we're regrouping, and there's a lot of shit I gotta figure out. I don't have nearly enough answers for you all, and while I work on that end of things, please just go about your daily lives. If you're tired, rest. If you're hurt, heal. I won't send for any of you and expect unconditional obedience. We're trying to get away from that type of lifestyle. Aengus, I'll consider your plan overnight, but today's meeting is over."

I turned away from the table, ignoring my churning stomach when the only protests I received were from my pack. If they wanted to remain there and continue to plan or argue I wasn't going to stop them, but the walls were closing in on me and I needed to let them crack. I closed the door softly behind me, only continuing down the hallway a few paces before pausing, sliding the tapestry Silas had hung in the main hall to 'add some color' to the side.

The stone behind the draping maroon fabric was microscopically different, dipping away from the curve of the hall into a secret tunnel. Inside was a maze of passageways and stairs which only the pair of us knew existed, hence the tapestry's placement.

The corridor was only a few inches wider than my shoulders, making it next to impossible to navigate with my wings. It took a few weeks, but I'd learned to summon and dismiss them at will, and now these passages became my favorite way to traverse this place, and occasionally hide.

Small lanterns hanging from the ceiling light the way, flickering with the violet flames of my magic. After a few turns and one steep downhill, the tunnel widens and opens to a small cavern. I slow my steps as I enter, eventually stopping and pressing my forehead to the damp stone. My breath leaves me painfully as I slowly exhale, and for the first time in two weeks I allow the chains clamped around my magic to loosen.

My body hums as power floods me, and a pearly glow graces my skin. Instantly, moss blooms against the stone beneath my fingertips, and a nonexistent breeze ruffled the feathers of my wings as they appeared out of the shadows swirling at my back.

You lasted longer than last time, Angel-born.

I felt my muscles coil as the now familiar presence perched on my shoulder. It was this which made me keep my magic under wraps. This which disallowed me to unleash it, unless in complete privacy. This… thing within the Hellfire I had stolen. A Devil hearing voices was not a reassuring feat.

"Hello, Vallen," I whispered, feeling it curl against my neck appreciatively.

It had been insistent on a name, any name. Insistent on talking at all times of day. It behaved like a teenage boy. Full of energy and curiosity, and behaving unnecessarily vulgar at times.

Why must you neglect me so? I thought we were becoming well acquainted with each other last time.

Last time.

I failed to block out the memory of my fangs in a young Hound's throat. I didn't know them. I didn't realize what I was doing until Akashi's voice rang in my ears, panic in his eyes as he pulled me off the other male who willingly allowed his Master to almost drain him dry.

"You have no control over your urges, and the repercussions will only fall to me," I say through gritted teeth. I feel my tail, a leathery whip ending in a point, lashing back and forth behind me in annoyance.

Repercussions, it let the word roll over an invisible tongue. *We have no need to adhere to such things. We only have need for power.*

I felt the ghost of a fingertip trace down the back of my neck and goosebumps sprang to life on my skin.

You are full of power, Angel-born. We would love to devour it.

The invisible chain on my power went taut, yanking it back into the depths of my soul. The moss on the rock in front of me dried and crumbled, the glowing of my skin shut off like a light, and I staggered backwards from the sudden weight loss as my wings disappeared.

The thrum of my magic vanished. Vallen's presence no longer haunted me.

I never felt so empty.

CHAPTER 2

I emerged from the walls only slightly late for dinner. Unlike the enchanting stage of the meeting hall, the dining rooms were quite modern, and designed to house an army.

The main room was filled with long oak tables, stained nearly black against the slate floors. One of the first things I did was hire a full kitchen staff from Atlantis, moving them here full-time to feed everyone. At first, the Hounds ate like starved animals. Whatever my father had provided them with before was inadequate, to say the least.

Three times a day, a buffet style meal was served, and the Hounds had a full hour off from their normal duties to relax and eat. Each pack had a set rotation to stand guard during these hours and was immediately relieved to eat after the others had finished.

A set of double doors connected the (new) private dining space to the main room. Occasionally, Luna, Akashi, Hikari and Kuma would eat in the main hall with the other Hounds, taking the opportunity to find old friends of theirs and introduce themselves to the new packs. From the Hounds who stayed, they were met with reverence, especially Luna, as her bravery was the only thing which made this future possible.

Wherever Luna went, Aengus would follow. The two of them had been inseparable, and considering their time apart I didn't blame them. Though I couldn't completely block out the awkwardness and pain radiating in my chest– Akashi's not my own.

I don't know if it has something to do with the imprinting bond, but I didn't dare ask. Whatever he was feeling, I wanted him to be able to process it, and not block it out just because I could feel it too.

Even if the Hounds were absent, Silas and Becca always joined me for dinner. Though I appreciated their company, I was undoubtedly third wheeling. I never paid their flirtations any mind, and studiously avoided noticing any wandering hands beneath the table.

I did, however, draw a firm line at blood sucking on one of the nights the three of us were in there alone. At my squawks of protest, Becca had offered to share him, Silas grinning with a wicked gleam in his eye. Their laughter told me that the embarrassed heat I felt in my face probably rivaled the fire in my veins.

I nodded to the Hounds who spotted me as I passed through the main hall, successfully avoiding being caught up in a conversation and slipped through the doors to my family's dining space. An oak table identical to the ones outside sat in the center of the room, draped with an indigo runner. Silver candlesticks and glass roses functioned as centerpieces, and a glittering chandelier of frost white diamonds hung from the ceiling. Despite the table being set for eight, it was empty.

Panic flared in my belly, and I fought to keep it down. They were probably socializing. Perhaps Silas and Becca opted for complete privacy tonight. There was a reasonable explanation for this. I plucked my glass off the corner of the table, I never sat at the head of it, hoping whatever alcohol that was served would be enough to take the edge off my anxiety. Before the liquid even touched my tongue, I froze.

Seems like someone cares for us.

Vallen was all but purring as the scent of blood flooded my nose. And not just any blood, but the beautiful, delicious, intoxicating scent of a certain Hounds.

My fangs pressed to my lower lip, and I flung the glass across the room like it was a ticking bomb. It shattered when it hit the wall, the pieces skidding across the floor like shards of ice. Then the doors to the main dining hall slammed open on a rush of wind, all the laughter and pleasant conversation dropping dead.

"Where is he?" I growled out the whisper. Desire and hunger flared to life in my belly, at odds with the panic coursing through my limbs. The room began to blur as I fought to breathe through it and I clenched my fists, trying to remain calm.

"I'm right here, Raven." The scent of pine and rain washed over me just as his hand caressed my cheek. Instantly, the panic and rage dissipated, giving way to just the wanting. I leaned into his touch, and he pulled me deeper, letting me drown against the scent of his skin.

I felt his muscles shifting against me as he gestured to the Hounds at his back, and immediately the conversation picked up again, the clanking of dishes seeming extra apparent. I was frozen in embarrassment and shame, realizing my lack of control probably eliminated any trust I'd gained from our audience. Akashi though just lifted me against his chest, and a moment later the double doors to the dining room swooshed shut, finally giving me some reprieve.

"Why didn't you drink it?" There was a hint of disappointment in his tone which made me wince as I untangled myself from his arms.

"I didn't realize you left it," I said, not daring to voice the thought in my head. The fear of someone draining and leaving his blood for me to find. Someone who already tortured my sister, and was undoubtedly planning their next move against me.

We'd be stronger when that time comes if you just gave in, Vallen murmured in my ear, making my skin begin to hum once more. I shook my head roughly before I could stop myself and heard Akashi sigh.

"Your reaction out there is why I did," he said. "I realize you're not going to tell me what's been going on with you, but don't expect me to pretend I don't see you struggling. I want to be there for you, even if I don't understand."

"And you think your blood will help me?" With Vallen chuckling in my ear I couldn't help but hiss the question. Akashi's eyes widened in shock before he resumed the blank face Luna taught us how to master.

"Sorry. I assumed you were craving a drink since I found your fangs in Talum's throat the other day." The accusation hit its mark.

"I already apologized for that," I said, averting my gaze.

"I'm well aware." He took a step toward me, as if his body remembered exactly how I apologized and wanted my legs wrapped around him in similar fashion right here right now. "And while I accepted it, apologies are only going to get us so far. You're my–"

"Stop." I couldn't bear to hear the words again. "Just stop."

"I can't stop," he growled, his next step fully closing the distance between us.

"Even if I wanted to– which I don't by the way. This," his finger landed lightly on my sternum, tapping atop my imprinting mark beneath the fabric, "is just a symbol. Does it change some shit for me? Yea. But I'm not by your side just because I chose to imprint on you. You accepted the mark. You accepted me."

His lips pressed to my temple, kissing me lightly. I wanted to hug him. I wanted to bite him. But what I wanted to do the most, was run.

And yet, I did nothing, remaining frozen in place like a statue. He sighed into my hair, completely relaxed against me, blissfully unaware of my inner turmoil.

"You're my mate, Raven. I'll say it over and over, until you can stomach hearing it."

I bit my tongue. I knew his words were true. I'd said as much to my sister, thought it to myself. I'd felt it down to the core of my soul for decades before the mark on my chest was put there.

But I couldn't trust it. I couldn't trust anything anymore. If I trusted it I'd somehow ruin or lose it, now that I'd become what I was.

It was agonizing to pull away from him, but somehow, I forced myself to. Before I gave in to the thrumming relief in my mark which I'm sure echoed in his. Before I gave into the strength and safety of his body. Before I gave into my urges.

You're just prolonging the pain for all three of us, you know? Vallen chastised but I ignored them. Just like I ignored the stabbing pain in my chest as I left Akashi alone and slipped into a shadow to disappear.

CHAPTER 3

"You realize you let perfectly good blood go to waste, yes?"

"Go away, Silas," I grumble, burrowing deeper under the blankets piled over me. I don't know how long I've been locked away in my room, but Becca's persistent knocking at the door faded a while ago. I slunk in here shortly after my conversation with Akashi, wanting comfort I didn't deserve, so settled for burrowing under every blanket I owned.

"I have better things to do then babysit you, or alleviate your self-inflicted tantrums." Silas tsked, annoyance dripping off each word.

"Since you're not being paid to, then don't," I retort, rolling my back to him. A string of curses left his lips as he began ripping the blankets off of me.

"What do you think you're—"

"Your mate may be content with respecting your space and allowing you to drown out the world, but I myself have grown quite bored of the soap opera you've been putting on."

With a flourish the final blanket was yanked from me, and I blinked against the light which he of course had turned on.

"What if I had been–"

"Naked?" He cut me off a second time, an asinine grin twisting onto his face. "As always, it would have been my lucky day."

He snickered while I glared, and then began preening himself, using my mirror to 'fix' his midnight hair before picking invisible lint off his jacket. As usual he was dressed to the nines. His midnight blue suit– with an excessive lace collar– was tapered to fit his slender frame, and his shoes were so shiny I could practically see my reflection.

He looks satiating.

I didn't acknowledge Vallen, but also couldn't disagree. Silas was nothing short of stunning, to the point where even the elves or high fae mistook him for one of their own. Porcelain skin, glossy hair, and impossibly rosy lips, full enough to hide the fangs hidden inside that clever mouth. Interrupting my thoughts, he clucked his tongue, and began to loosen his tie.

"I truly don't think I'll ever understand why you refuse your mate's blood." He was still chastising me as he bared his neck, but his tone had softened with sympathy. "Especially when it's clear to everyone you're starving."

"Do you want me to explain myself?" I ask, even though we both know I won't. He released a dramatic sigh before beckoning me forward. Against my will, I'm on my feet in a second. I have to grab the bedpost to keep myself from launching at him like an animal, gritting my teeth hard to remain composed. He looked like he wanted to laugh at my struggle.

"You need to drink at least three genuine gulps, so that maybe we can get something productive done tomorrow." Unable to come up with an argument, I just continue to glare at him.

His eyes held mine, glittering intensely with humor, before dulling empathetically when I relent. I dip my chin, the only sign to my agreement, and Silas crosses the space between us in a flash. Cradling my head, he urges me forward until my mouth presses against the crook of his neck and my fangs bare over his pulse.

Finally, Vallen all but moans in my head and shivers erupt through my body.

I keep it fast, short, but take enough. Silas says nothing, only smooths my hair reassuringly while I drink as a sign that he's just fine. When I finally release him I flop back onto the bed, my breathing ragged as I fight the swell of power coursing through me to remain contained.

"Very regal," he muses, pulling a kerchief from his pocket to press against the bite. I'm too exhausted to reply.

With the taste of Silas' blood lingering on my tongue, it's easier to pay attention in the meetings the next morning than it was the past few days. The chains wrapping my magic are loose, but secure, and Vallen has remained silent all day.

Aengus and I had finally reached an agreement which the remainder of the Hounds at the table seemed satisfied with, and we broke off early for lunch. As the group exited, I caught Akashi's hand, squeezing in a silent plea for him to wait for a moment.

"About yesterday–"

"Why did you agree with Aengus's plan?" I blink, shocked by his tone, and annoyed that I've been getting cut off so much recently. But I bite my tongue, and lean back to sit against the table.

"Because I think it's a good plan." At least, I think it would be safer to catch them off guard and counterstrike, rather than wait for them to attack again. The only question was, where?

"Did you not hear my reasons against it?" Akashi's eyes search mine with an intensity that threatened to scorch me, so I match it. He may be an alpha, he may be my mate, but if he thought I would buckle under the pressure of those two things just because the other Hounds seemed to, he was only kidding himself.

"Oh I heard you." I arched a brow, "But I think they're mostly fueled by paranoia."

"Paranoia?" He barked a laugh, shaking his head incredulously. "Attacking Heaven in two months really sounded like a great idea to you?"

"Would you rather we squat here until they come back?" I challenged, "Because it's not if they come back Akashi. It's when." And I would rather not be taken by surprise like last time. Or given another ultimatum between family members dying.

Since Becca was abducted, I took extra precautions with my family. They were not allowed to go anywhere alone, always needing to travel with at least two other Hounds. Weekly, they were given a finite amount of my blood to amplify their own powers and strengths.

Their bedroom doors were heavily warded with both mine and Becca's magic, which would instantly react to anyone entering outside of our pack. Anyone who wasn't a welcomed guest, or stupidly tried to break in, would be subjected to the full brunt of mine and my sisters power coming down on them. It felt all types of wrong and controlling, but I would not lose one of them to the Angels again. Anzen was enough.

"I would rather you have more time to properly heal and adjust to your new powers." Akashi's voice cut through my thoughts. "Until you have them under control, we shouldn't make any attack plans."

"Control?" I heard my voice lower, felt Vallen's invisible hands caressing up my sides as the chains on my power shuddered. "You have no idea how much control I'm wielding every day."

"Then show me."

"I am."

Resistance is not control. I ignored Vallen.

"I'm not spewing fire, turning into a demon, or bringing this cave down on top of us." My voice was a whisper.

"You are randomly sucking the life out of people though," Akashi countered, the alpha in him still refusing to back down.

"I'm not running away from the throne– that the rest of you practically forced me onto by the way." I switched tactics, pushing off the table and invading his space. "I'm stepping up in order to keep us all alive. My powers aren't rampant, and my emotions are numbed to keep them that way. So, you tell me," I was close enough to feel his heartbeat reverberate against my chest as I asked, "how should I be showing you I'm in control of myself?"

"Sorry to break up the latest lovers quarrel." Becca's voice, laced with unshed laughter, rang from behind me. "But unfortunately, this can't wait."

"I was just leaving." Akashi's voice was gruff as he turned, not sparing me another glance as he exited the room. Becca's eyes met mine, the blue irises dancing in question but I just shook my head.

"What is it?"

"You got a letter," she said, tilting her head. "Actually, Finn got a letter. But there's no way in hell I'm giving it to him first."

I released a long sigh, chains on my power clicking back into place.

"Let's go."

CHAPTER 4

The dungeon was the one place Silas did not follow me. Though I was hoping we would find a few living Angels after the battle, all we came up with was pieces of corpses and their fallen weapons. The Hounds' rage and threat to their territory had left no survivors on Heavens side once they were grounded.

Finn's cell was twice as large as the ones around it, and crammed full of shit he didn't deserve. It was reinforced with silver holy metal, as well as melted down gold from the Angel's swords. The construction was a necessity, but glamorizing it was too good of me.

A piece of me still had yet to release the sparks between us, or ignore the goodness he had in him. The girl inside me was long dead, but her feelings were still very much alive. That was the only reason he found himself with such amenities.

A comfortable bed with thick blankets to ward off the dungeon's chill lay pressed against the wall. There was an array of books and records to pass the time, stacked neatly in the corner. The latest addition was a small desk at his bedside, so that he wouldn't have to eat his meals on the mattress or the floor.

"To what do I owe the pleasure, Angel?" His honey-smooth voice, so hot it nearly permeated my skin, echoed off the walls. I knew now that like his brother's gift, the heat I felt wasn't my body reacting to him. He was trying to paralyze me with his magic, not seduce me.

I analyzed him slowly in the firelight. The three torches on the wall burned with my violet flames, making his usual golden hair bank to almost silver. The gold chains on his ankles and wrists clinked together as he stood from where he perched on the edge of his bed, and he smoothed some of the wrinkles out of his cream button-down shirt.

"Just checking in to make sure your accessory is still in perfect condition." I smiled, reaching my upturned hand between the silver bars as he approached. He flashed that sunbeam smile at the two Hounds stationed behind me, as if he were bragging about lowering his chin into my palm.

"Are you sure you're not here to check on my wounds once more? You were quite guilty after that show of brutality."

Aware of our audience, I ignored the sting the reminder brought. My fingers reached up to brush the hair off his forehead, carefully not lingering on his skin. Slowly, I traced the golden halo locked around his temple. It was only this which kept him from manipulating everyone in the room.

"Devils have no need to feel guilt," I replied, voice dulling as I dropped my hold on him and reached into my back pocket. I waved the crinkled envelope in front of his face.

"Gabriel continues to seem convinced you're alive. Even though I sent him an ashen corpse last month." I let the letter fall to the floor, melting into the shadow at my feet, the contents not mattering. Finn chuckled, leaning against the bars of his cage, not acknowledging the hum of holy metal against his skin.

"I thought for sure that would work. My apologies, Angel darling." His smile was tight. "I shall come up with a better tactic to convince him."

"That's not necessary. I think I'll just send him your head instead."

It took a moment for my comment to register, him blinking slowly in surprise before rage made his red eyes glow like embers. He fisted the bars of his cell, knuckles going white. This is who he was, I reminded myself. Vengeful. Not the beautiful sunshine man who I believed in once upon a time.

"You could never kill me, Angel. Deep down, you still love me." A shocked laugh bubbled from my lips, and I took a step back.

"Love? If I loved you, don't you think it would have been you I chose that night?" I will never forget that it was Finn who came for me first, after my return from Heaven. His hands were on me, his voice the promise of pleasure in my ears, but I had refused him.

"I think you chose what you deemed as the safest option." His words now rang annoyingly in my ears, and he pressed forward until his face filled the gap between the bars in front of me. "I think you're afraid of letting yourself loose. Your decision had nothing to do with me or Akashi. It was all about how much of a good girl you wanted to stay, or how free you might have been."

I turned on my heel, feigning a bored expression. I nodded to the pair of Hounds on either side of the doors, who straightened to attention.

"See to it that he gets his daily dosage of blood and a proper meal. Then leave him in silence."

"You won't be able to kill me Raven!" Finn shouted at my back. Slowly, I turned, feeling a truly dark smile curving my lips.

"You're right Finn. I won't be able to kill you. I already held back when I wanted to." I laced each word with venom, knowing my eyes shifted to black pits when I added, "But after what you did to your brother, I'm sure Rebecca would love to."

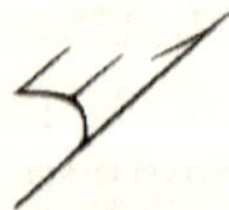

"Don't actually kill him," I said as I entered the main hall, the dungeon door swinging shut behind me with a groan. Throughout the interaction, I could feel

Becca's presence vibrating across the shadow realm, watching while remaining out of sight and scent of Finn.

"I wouldn't bother wasting my energy on something so trivial." She materialized at my side, the metallic pleats of her black bodysuit catching the lamplight as she fell into step with me.

I'd conjured several for myself, as well as a few low-backed shirts to mitigate the amount of tearing fabric should I need to call on my wings quickly. Becca had taken to the jumpsuits almost instantly, and after a ridiculous amount of whining I finally shoved some in her own closet.

Growing up, my brothers never seemed to care about how much clothing they destroyed each time they shifted, but my sister preferred being able to salvage her glamour. Now, she could simply unclasp the hook at the nape of her neck, and transform into her Hellcat after the fabric pooled around her ankles. I on the other hand was just happy to no longer be harassed to replace her fancy clothes.

"So, who's the letter actually from?" Becca nods her head toward the envelope, which had reappeared in my clenched fist. "Not actually Gabriel, I hope?" I snorted and shook my head.

Though the ruse she'd come up with hadn't made Finn talk as much as we'd wanted, pretending to get letters from Gabriel had been a smart tactic. Turns out, as noble as Finn had been to their cause, he was still willing to share information in order to save his own skin. Unfortunately for us, it wasn't very valuable information. Over time, it was clear that he knew very little, even if he pretended otherwise.

"The letters from Jesibelle," I mumbled, hoping none of the Hounds in the corridor would hear. Becca wrinkled her nose.

"Again?"

Jesibelle was the head of the only female Hellhound den, the Night Howlers. And she was not a fan of me to say the least.

"She's requested an audience with me at her den, again. Refused to aid our cause, again. And has demanded the alphas start returning to their beds, again." Becca's disdain grew with each thing I rattled off.

Before everything went down, I knew very little about the Hellhound's way of life. My pack had sacrificed it and left it in the past in order to save me, so little information was shared. I knew alphas were rare, females rarer, and one's like Luna were the rarest, but that was all. Jesibelle was intent I get a 'proper education' on their livelihoods and expectations before recognizing me as their new master. Which at this point, I was fairly certain I didn't want if it meant dealing with her on a regular basis.

"I hate to say it, but you might as well go and get it over with. We don't exactly have limitless time," Becca mumbled.

I grunted in agreement, trying to roll away the building itch and ache in my shoulders. Lately, a new, constant weight settled on me, even when my wings were absent. It often felt as if my body was being crushed between two stones.

"Don't send her a reply. I'll go tomorrow."

"Can I suggest that you take Hikari?" She snickered at my arched brow, clarifying, "He has the best temperament and is a beta, so the horn-dogs won't ignore you or try to drag him off to bed." Another good point. I stopped walking.

"Are you sure you don't want my seat at the table?" I asked, and she released that shrill canary laugh.

"Respectfully, Your Majesty. Hell no. I prefer my freedom." The teasing smile was off her face before she even finished the sentence. "Rave I'm sorry. I need to think more before I talk."

"It's fine." I forced a smile onto my face even though a familiar, aching numbness crept through me again. "I'll see you at dinner?"

She nodded, worry still lingering in her eyes when I turned to walk away, but I didn't dwell on it. Just like I didn't dwell on her words. After all, it wasn't like I could feel the pain of losing something I never had.

CHAPTER 5

"Kuma will come with me." It was the first statement I made at the next morning's meeting, starting us off in a frenzy.

"Huh?" He gaped at me.

"He's like, the worst option of all of us," Hikari said, quickly adding, "no offense."

"No, I agree," Kuma said with a shake of his head.

"He has no diplomacy skills and still has yet to make rank," Aengus chimed in from the other end of the table. "The second issue I have no doubt will be resolved in a few days' time. He's only been delayed due to your packs... delay," he repeated the word awkwardly. "Also, you'll find most female Hellhounds are the polar opposite of your mother. They won't appreciate his frankness."

"Which is why he's perfect," I counter. "They'll hate his attitude, and he has no rank. Other than drooling over his muscles for a few minutes, they'll be forced to focus on me because he's of no use to them."

"Ouch." Kuma slouched in his chair, his hand clutching at his heart and I rolled my eyes.

"Seriously?" I grumbled earning a roguish smirk from him.

"Raven's right." I, along with everyone else, whipped my gaze toward Akashi in shock. Though his face was a neutral, blank mask, he was clearly annoyed, sitting with his arms crossed and his eyes glued to the table. We hadn't had time to talk since our mini argument, so it was a reassuring surprise to have him on my side. Especially since this was specifically a Hellhound issue. He cleared his throat, voice gruff.

"If I went with her they'd want to breed, despite me not being able to. Same with Aengus. They can't breed with Mom, but they can tear her apart for abandoning their so-called duty. And even though he's a Beta, Hikari would be too much of a distraction. Kuma should go."

"I could go," Becca quipped from across the table, ice blue eyes glittering with feline mischief.

"No." Akashi dragged out the word, the corner of his mouth turning up in a half grin. "We're trying to prepare for an ongoing war, not start a new one." Becca snickered.

"Family jokes can take place at the dinner table. Can we please stay on topic?" I asked, my annoyance flaring. I was more stressed and anxious about this meeting than I was willing to admit, and if this didn't wrap up soon I was worried I'd have no time to calm myself.

"Kuma will join me. The rest of you can see to your typical duties. And Becca, for hells sake, don't let Silas follow me to the den. No matter how pretty he is, he's still a vampire with a massive ego. Not a good combination with an aggravated she-wolf." My sister mocked a salute as Silas began sputtering appalled protests in defense of his character, but that was that.

After a few minutes Kuma, Akashi and I were the only three remaining at the table, the former looking between the two of us uncomfortably.

"I can wait outside."

"You can wait here. Akashi's the one who needs to go," I say with a pointed look at the door. Again, he had switched from supportive to stubborn in a millisecond, and I refused to look at him.

"Family jokes can take place at the dinner table?" Akashi's tone was incredulous. "What the fuck was that?" I grit my teeth, shrugging.

"That was the woman in charge of this place needing everyone to focus, so her brain doesn't explode trying to play Queen, and daughter, and sister and lover all at once." My heart was slamming in my chest as a rush of adrenaline shot through me. All I needed was for him to leave, all I needed was two damn minutes to myself and everything would be fine.

"You don't need to *play* anything," he shot back. His voice had lowered to a pitch I only hear him use with the Hounds, and reflexively I bristled. "You just have to *be*. Exist. Live. That's all any of us ask of you."

"Thanks for simplifying my plight." I sighed, forcing my face to adapt the neutral expression Luna taught me as I pushed back my chair to stand. If he wasn't going to give me space, I was going to take it and leave before I snapped. "Now if you excuse me, I need to go talk to the women who wanna beat me up because they want to have your babies and I'm in the way."

"Of course you're in the way." I shot a wide-eyed look at him, unable to stop the spear of shock and hurt that went through me.

"Yea, I'm definitely waiting outside," Kuma muttered, rising from the table.

"Don't you fucking dare leave me here Kuma Nightshade!" He froze, his body literally locking up halfway out of his seat from my command. Mortified, I raised a hand to my mouth. "I didn't mean to... go ahead Kuma."

"It happens. I don't take it personally." Kuma groaned, rolling his neck out of the odd angle it was set at before disappearing out the double doors. Once they shut, Akashi whistled, clapping twice in mock applause.

"Banning family jokes from all but one table. Commanding your brothers. The thrones really gone to your head hasn't it, Little Bird?"

My power erupted through the room as any sense of control I had over myself disappeared. Violet flames encircled the floor around the table, trapping us inside. Then thornless vines bloomed from my wrists to pin Akashi's hands to his sides as I lunged forwards, yanking him towards me by the collar of his shirt.

Please, please, please, can we just have a tiny taste? Fuck. Off.

I struggled with myself, arms shaking, breaths coming in ragged pants, but Akashi just leaned in closer.

"There you are," he said gently, suddenly nothing but warmth and love resounding in his tone despite the raging chaos around him. My power hummed under his attention, and was subdued slightly. When his hands were free, he sealed me between his arms. "Now that's the women I want to enter their den. Stay in their way, and make sure they know my mate isn't to be fucked with."

"You're an asshole," I muttered against his chest, fisting the back of his shirt as he tucked my head under his chin.

"It's much simpler than that really." His hands caressed the length of my spine. "I'm yours."

Blessedly, Kuma said nothing about what happened in the meeting hall. He just fell into step beside me, and began listing off the various vulgarities he wished to see in the Night Howlers den. I tuned him out at the mention of pantyhose, not wanting all of my brain cells to be fried before we even arrived.

It wasn't a far walk, just across the valley where the lake once stood. After Becca had melted the ice, and I stole the hellfire, all that had been left was a steep canyon in the Earth. There had been a few close calls of someone falling into it, mostly the adolescents who had created a game of lingering near the edge, so I'd used my magic to slope it into a more gradual dip.

Jesibelle made her den known about a week after we arrived here. Her first letter chastised me for my incompetence of not learning of them myself. And my honest reply that the other Hounds had said nothing about them, not even the females who were present amongst my ranks, hadn't sat well with her.

Hellhounds functioned in packs, and though hundreds of packs existed here, they all coexisted and functioned as a single unit. Except for the Night Howlers. They were completely independent, functioning even outside of Lucifers' orders since they had a perfect track record of producing at least one alpha pup per litter. That's all I knew of them before knocking on their door.

Their iridescent, moonstone door.

Kuma just shrugged at my raised brow, mouth splitting into a grin. After a moment, the door opened with a soft woosh, and the scent of all things floral wafted out towards us. The woman standing in the frame was a few inches shorter than me, barefoot, and in a long gown that shimmered like rippling water.

"Hello, my lady."

"Hi," I choke out, a tsunami of self-consciousness momentarily obliterating any formality I could hope to portray. She raised a perfectly plucked eyebrow, just a shade darker than her skin. Her hair was glossed and pinned back from her face with glittering star cut clips, and diamonds hung off her slender neck and wrists. As her golden eyes slid from me to latch on Kuma, her rose painted lips spread into a dazzling smile.

"Well, hello to you as well." The sultry tone to her voice had me fighting the urge to gag. Kuma though bent at the waist, bringing his face close enough to hers to make her blush.

"I'm rankless with a shit mouth. So settle down sweetheart," he cooed.

Instantly the flowery scent permeating the air dulled, as did the intensity of her smile. I felt myself blushing as I realized that was probably the scent of her heat. For hells sake.

"Jesibelle has been requesting an audience with me," I said, regaining my voice. "I haven't meant to keep her waiting, but there have been many pressing matters to attend to." The she-wolf waved a hand flippantly.
"Just come in. I will make her aware of your arrival." I forced a tight smile, already able to tell this visit was going to be as painful as I'd imagined.

The entry hall was plain, yet elegant. Cream walls boasted a few artistic tapestries, and the marble floors were scrubbed to shine. The she-wolf led us to a parlor filled with an assortment of plush chairs and fainting couches. Gesturing to a silver teacart she insisted we helped ourselves, before she disappeared down a corridor in the back.

"You could have warned me," I growled, suddenly self-conscious. I perched on the edge of a couch the same color as buttercream frosting, and tried to ignore the fact that it was trimmed in flaked gold. Kuma had plopped himself down in a navy chair, the high back ending a few inches beneath his shoulders. He held up his hands in mock surrender, still grinning like a dumbass.

"I heard rumors sure, but didn't know they were this excessive. Besides, you spending the morning panicking and primping and plucking yourself wouldn't have mattered anyway." I frowned, glancing down at my frayed grey jeans and leather jacket. This one was new, with studded diamonds on the shoulder caps, but I still felt dirty and cheap after seeing the first she-wolfs dress. And when Jesibelle entered, she made me feel like a kid dressed up in a crappy Halloween costume.

I knew it was her as soon as she walked in. The shimmering whites and sage of her gown complimented the honey glow of her skin. Her soft blonde hair was divided into two Dutch braids resting over her shoulders, dotted with shattering emerald hair pieces and silver threads woven intricately between the locks. Her eyes bore a shocking similarity to Hikari's, sparkling an ocean blue, but the pretentious glint they held more so resembled my sister.

She was flanked by a group of she-wolves, each wearing their own luxurious garments and jeweled pieces. I felt like a rat. A wet rat.

"Welcome, my lady." Her voice was like a violin, sweet and high. "I've been waiting for this moment since the Master learned of your existence, all those decades ago."

"You're speaking to the Master," Kuma growled low from my side.

Jesibelles sultry gaze slid to him, nose wrinkling at his scent. But then she blinked, jaw slackening momentarily before quickly averting her gaze back to mine.

"Of course. My apologies."

"None necessary," I reassure. "It's an adjustment we are all having to make." I quickly gestured for them to take a seat, feeling awkward with them all standing in front of me.

As the she-wolves settled themselves I poured a glass of tea for Kuma, handing it to my brother wordlessly. He took it, eyes catching mine with begrudging understanding. He'd keep his mouth shut, for now at least.

"I was beginning to think you were ignoring my letters, having not received one back from you in the past month." Jesibelles voice tinkled into my ears again and I sighed.

"I didn't exactly have the time to pay a house call right away. But now that I've found time, what do you want?" I asked, getting straight to the point. Jesibelle seemed inclined to draw this out, pouring her own cup of tea and smoothing her skirt.

"We had a previously existing arrangement with your father." A quiet growl rumbled from Kuma, but she continued without even glancing his way, "I would like to negotiate, so that my den does not get dragged into your war." I cocked a brow.

"I'm listening."

"Just how much do you know of my den?" Jesibelle asked, eyes traveling over me in clear assessment.

"You were breeders, exclusively." It wasn't easy, keeping the judgment from my voice. "You could guarantee a new alpha pup born to each litter, many of which blessed with powers similar to my mothers and my... boyfriends." Looks of disdain and a few snickers echoed around the room but I ignored them. "In exchange, Lucifer granted you your own den and a life of luxury. Is it wrong to guess you intend to keep things as they are?"

"Yes, we have always succeeded in producing powerful alphas." Her smile sent a chill down my spine. "I'll speak plainly, my lady. I have no intention of sending my girls to war on your behalf. But if we were once again provided suitable partners, we could continue to produce alpha Hounds for you to utilize as you wished."

The room was so silent you could hear a pin drop. I felt like she was baiting me, trying to force my hand in some way, but at the same time, sincerity dripped off her every word. And it made me feel like I was going to puke on her polished floors.

There was zero doubt in my mind that this woman would readily exchange the lives of their pups, if it meant they could maintain their lifestyle. I took a moment to compose myself, my voice empty when I finally spoke.

"First of all, I am not my father. I am not interested in maintaining any system he had previously set up with anyone." I pronounce each word perfectly, unwilling to let them be twisted. "Which brings me to my issue with your proposition."

"Whatever issue you may have, I will do everything in my power to alleviate it." Jesibelle remains poised and bright, but the smile on her face wavers as I lean forwards, resting my elbows on my knees.

"Secondly, I have lived around Hellhounds all my life. Was even raised by a very powerful, female alpha. So don't begin our relationship by trying to manipulate which alphas you are willing to give me, when we both know there's two in the room with us besides yourself."

All the she-wolves stilled, the previous judgement on their faces replaced by shock, and fear. I grinned. "I know exactly which two, by the way. And right now, it would be more beneficial to have a grown Hounds help, instead of breeding more children to fight." At this, Jesibelle shot to her feet.

"We did not breed to produce fighters. We bred to produce alphas."

"You've been exchanging your children for your own freedom." I let a shackle on my power slip a bit, shadows creeping in at the edges of the glittering room as I said, "I don't like that arrangement one bit, so here's my deal. If you want your freedom, take it. But if you want to stay here, then behave with some honor and fight alongside your kids this time."

"You have no idea what you're saying." Jesibelles voice went shrill.

"I know exactly what I'm saying." I rose, crossing the few feet between us. Every Hound in the room bristled, poised to react if necessary as I crowded Jesibelle so much that she was forced to retake her seat. Bracing my hands on either arm of her chair I leaned over her, caging her in.

"Akashi is the alpha of my pack, and he was lucky enough to know his mother. The rest of my brothers were bred and trained to be killing machines, and you knew it and did nothing to stop it. They didn't get to know a parent's loving embrace, until Luna swept us away and provided them with what you withheld." Tears shone in Jesibelles eyes, but I didn't stop,

"You may think you're doing me a favor by dragging my alphas into your beds to sire more power, but you're not. I have enough power. What I lack is a united front. Loyalty built on bonds, rather than fear." I leaned closer, lowering my voice to a whisper only she could pick up. "And by the way. Your son is one of the best males I know. It's a pity he doesn't even know you."

"S-son?" Her hands had begun shaking in her lap and I nodded.

"There were visual similarities right away. Your eyes, and how you carry yourself. But your scent confirms it. For his sake, I hope you stay."

I pushed back from her, shadows retreating to the corners of the room. Having said my piece I began striding for the door, and heard Kuma's chair scrape the floor as he stood to follow me. Jesibelle and her ladies remained silent as together we exited the den.

We walked in uncomfortable silence, and I began to regret my tactic. If I had hurt Jesibelles feelings, that was tough luck. But I didn't know if Kuma was faring well with the blunt description of his life.

We got about halfway across the valley before I slowed my steps. I was about to ask if he was okay, but he suddenly jerked to a stop. Quickly he turned his back to me, before he was bending to double over and heave up the contents of his stomach.

"What's wrong?" My hand flew to his back, rubbing soothing circles as he retched again. My brain was racing, trying to find out what was done to him. Was the scent of their heat too much for him? Had they poisoned the tea?

"That was Hikari's mother?" He asked hoarsely, and I snapped out of my panic as clarity settled in. Of course he heard that. His hearing was the best out of our whole pack. And having spent more years with Hikari than I had, he probably suspected it as soon as he saw her too.

"I'm fairly certain, yes," I replied softly. He nodded once, before instantly retching again.

"Oh, fantastic." Sarcasm and panic laced his voice when he finally stopped heaving. He pulled away from me, dragging his palms through his long hair, then down his face, through his hair again.

"Kuma you're scaring me," I said, eyes searching his.

"That was Hikari's mother," he repeated, laughing, the sound empty. "And she's my mate."

CHAPTER 6

Hikari's mother was a jarring surprise, one that I could tell Kuma wanted to bellow out as soon as we returned. He said it was too important for Hikari not to know. I said I didn't want any more interior fights to happen. It was his birth mother, who he didn't know, and on top of it his brother was suddenly her mate.

Begrudgingly, with the promise that we would talk about it once all of this was over, Kuma agreed to keep his trap shut. For now, at least. I sent him to train for the remainder of the day with Aengus, hoping the physical strain would keep his shock at bay. Then I immediately searched for my mother.

"Hi," I said, plopping in the grass beside her.

"You don't usually venture up here," Luna commented, but given that her eyes were glowing a faint blue, I could tell she wasn't quite with me yet. While she soul searched, I reached forwards and brushed my fingers across the headstone we sat beside.

After the battle, the Hounds buried our dead on the cliffs which rose above the cave, and this is where my brother Anzen lay. The sprawling grassland above the sea existed on the edge of our side of the veil and the human world. In spring flowers bloomed, filling the space with color and life. I seldom came here, hardly able to bear the weight in my chest. But my mother visited daily, making sure to clear the graves and spend some time with her son.

"Oh, Raven." Luna's voice held a note of surprise, and I gave her a reassuring smile as she looked me over, her eyes back to their normal woodland brown. Her voice though, was apologetic. "I thought you were your... Akashi. Your scents are so entwined now, sometimes it's difficult to isolate the two."

No one called him my brother anymore, and Luna was the only one who never referred to him as my mate. It's like she was waiting until I did first.

"That's actually kind of what I wanted to talk to you about," I said with a sigh. "I don't know nearly enough about

Hellhounds. Your way of life, all of this stuff with mates and imprinting. I need someone to fill me in with blunt details. Akashi won't tell me anything. He says it's not a big deal and doesn't want me to overthink it, but not knowing makes me look like an idiot. And I haven't asked the others because they might be tempted to gloss over certain topics because I'm their... Queen." The word tasted like lead on my tongue.

"I take it you finally visited with Jesibelle?" Luna asked, voice wry. I nodded and she groaned, pinching the bridge of her nose. "Well, my sister was never known for her gentle hospitality. What did she say that caused you concern?"

"Sister?" I gawked at her.

"By many centuries I assure you," she said with a sad smile. I pursed my lips.

"So then, Hikari? He's really your nephew?" Lunas gaze grew far away.

"Yes. I was able to save my son, and my nephew. Kuma and Anzen, they were the children of friends of mine who sadly, are no longer with us."

"Does Hikari know?"

"He does not." Her eyes flashed blue. "I would prefer to keep it that way."

"I already discussed that with Kuma. We'll wait until we actually have the time." My fingers tightened on the grass beneath me, part of me beginning to agree with Kuma. If it were me, I'd want to know.

Instead of adding another brick to the guilt castle I was building, I shifted back to the topic which had me seeking her out in the first place.

"Since you haven't sent me packing, does that mean you'll tell me all the itty-bitty Hellhound secrets so maybe I understand what's going on for once?" Luna chuckled, but I could tell by the look on her face that she would– and wouldn't sugarcoat it. A wave of relief went through me and I lay back, releasing the tension from my muscles as best I could. Finally, I was going to get some answers.

"When I was young, I was a member of the Night Howler den," she started, voice soft and faraway. "The belief there is that a war cannot be won without soldiers, and sacrifice. Not all female Hounds are suited for the mentality which battle demands. Being soldiers was out of the question for most of them, so they pledged to honor the second half of the belief, and sacrifice what they could."

"Their children?" I guessed, unable to hide my disdain as Luna nodded.

"The reason they can produce strong, alpha pups so consistently is because they do not take more than three males to their bed within a century. This gives their bodies time to familiarize themselves with the bloodlines, and instead of fighting off their partners' DNA, it learns to accept it. Paired with that, each male must be ranked a Beta or higher. Some of them only breed with Alphas exclusively. They are the rarest, so when their genes manifest they're dominant not recessive. This ensures strong offspring, regardless of what rank they receive in the future.

"After their birth, pups don't stay with their mothers longer than they are nursing. This helps alleviate emotional distress for both the pups and mothers, as the less time they share the less likely they develop a bond with one another.

"They're then placed in the care of Omega Hounds to be raised and given basic training. Pups of the same litter are always kept together until they receive their rank, usually under the guidance of a Sigma about a decade after their maturity. Only in special circumstances, such as a delay in training like Kuma's, does the timeline of receiving rank alter. If that's the case they're placed under the guidance of a Beta or Alpha.

"Hikari was the only one of your brothers who received their rank before we fled. I knew Akashi would be an Alpha since he was born, it was just a matter of time. A part of me also suspected that Anzen would be able to match that strength. Kuma though, I can genuinely say I'm unsure of which rank he'll receive, as his strength and character are fit for multiple roles."

The sky was a mirage of blue, pink, and gold in the evening light, and a soft breeze kissed my skin. My mother's scent was a reassuring blanket wrapping around my shoulders as she spoke, and I fought the urge to curl against her legs like when I was little. I remember a time she withheld everything to protect me, but here, just the two of us, she was finally speaking freely. Must I ruin it for myself by pushing for more?

Yes.

"And the difference between imprinting and mates?" She went slightly rigid beside me, debating.

"Please, Luna." I didn't want to beg, but here I was.

"I know you want to tell me to ask Akashi. I have. He's brushed it off every single time. In fact, the only thing he's said about it is that the Night Howlers can't breed with him. I don't understand how that's possible. I don't understand what he did or how it's different than Becca and Silas, and I don't think I can fully accept him unless I do."

"Akashi was always your mate." My eyes shot to hers, finding them apologetic, if not a little afraid.

"Some greater power ensures that we are not alone throughout the long lives we live, so mates are not an uncommon occurrence in the immortal world. However, imprinting bonds, if nurtured correctly, extend beyond loyalty or choice. It's not only a companion for life, but a bond between souls. The very essence of what makes us individuals merges, and becomes one entity." She pauses, as if the words hurt her to say.

"You being Akashi's mate wouldn't stop my sister and her den from demanding he warm their beds. He's an Alpha. His power, his genes... that's what carries our kind forward. By imprinting on you, they're forbidden them from pursuing him."

"How?" I ask, feeling my brows knit together. "It's just a mark on my skin."

"It's a mark on your *soul*," she corrects, a hand coming to rest on my shoulder. "You sense what he can, and feel what he does. And as your soul is entwined with a Hound, a Hound is forbidden to do you harm. That's why when you foolishly stormed down here without our aid, no one touched you. Even if Lucifer ordered them to, they couldn't." She sighed, releasing her hold on me.

"Furthermore, Akashi did not imprint on you only for your safety. You are his mate, and he wanted nothing to come between you. Thus, the Night Howlers are prevented from pursuing him to breed."

I was unsure of what shocked me most. I'd assumed my heightened senses and emotions had something to do with Vallen, or were due to the surge of demonic power, similar as my Reformation earlier this year. But I never would have suspected that imprinting on me was a living shield between him and the Night Howlers.

My gut rolled recalling the night he did it. I was adamant he didn't waste it, and thought his insistence was because he wanted *me*. Now, the move also proved selfish.

"What does it do to Akashi?" My voice came out airy, throat tight. If it was true that I'd been feeling his emotions in my chest, then could he also feel mine? Could it go deep enough that he might be suspicious of Vallen? That thought had me bolting upright, forcing Luna to release me.

"As far as I can tell, right now your imprint is a one-way bond. You can sense what he has given to you, but as you are not a Hound, you haven't left your mark on him. It doesn't lessen the potency of his actions though. But Raven," her change in tone instantly had me bracing.

"When a Hound imprints, they are only fertile for the one whose soul is tied to theirs. And..." She trailed off for the first time in the conversation, her expression going blank the way she trained us to.

"What Luna?" My voice serrated the silence between us, piercing like an arrow. A silence that shattered completely as she said,

"And as your souls are tied, so are your lives."

I jumped to my feet with a cry I wasn't expecting to feel erupting from my throat.

"He loves you, Raven!" Luna called, voice raising over the storm brewing above us. "His choices have always been because of that!"

Thunder rolled with my rage and lightning crackled alongside my fear. Above us, the clouds billowed like smoke from a forest fire as the two halves of me collided.

The first was vicious, and defensive. Doubt manifested as a cyclone inside my head. Did he truly care for me that much as his mate, or was imprinting on me while I was naïve to the true depth of it just a way to ensure a future where he kept his freedom? Akashi was not one to be held down. He did as he pleased, even when we were children. The possibility of him using me as a shield from the expectations of the Night Howlers, and a chess piece against my father, had me spiraling with both a sense of possessiveness and betrayal.

But the other half of me was howling louder. Panic, guilt, pain, and fear, all whipping acid and threatening to melt down the shackles in my mind. That half had me dropping to my knees in the mud, and gasping for breath as lightning began striking the ground. High pillars of glass rose around me, encapsuling me, trying to block me out from what I could not run from.

Akashi would never have children. He would never truly be free, or safe, or live a full, satisfying life.

Because of me.

CHAPTER 7

The club was just as I remembered it. All bass, sweat, and neon lights. A scene I never would have found comfort in during my previous life.

I had quelled my storm just enough for Luna to not be hurt by my rampant feelings. I didn't dare look at her as I commanded her to return to Aengus, knowing I would shatter in an instant as I forced her to obey me. It was unnatural, a daughter being the Master of her mother, but if Luna had any negative views about it, she kept them to herself.

Once she was gone, I fled, slipping into the shadow realm and crossing the veil back into Purgatory. The air was hot and moist, so different from the dry cold of Hell. And the *color.* I nearly wept when I collapsed in my garden of glass roses.

Hell was all ash blue and rust red. No variation. No true sunlight or warmth. The citrusy lemon-lime of the air here would indeed give me a headache, but it helped clear the rushing panic from my mind. And the will-o-wisps, already

singing and playing in my hair, were
enough to ground me, recentering myself
enough so that I could breathe without
gasping. Color. Life.

Our house was still wrecked. We
hadn't returned to fix the glass or outer
walls since Heaven abducted my sister.
Our timeframe was too short to do much
else besides board up the windows and
reset the wards. But inside was exactly
how I remembered it, all elegant marble
and gothic accents. I didn't linger, taking
only a moment to reform my clothes
before stepping out onto the street.

The walk was a blur of sound and
people. Most recognized me, and it was
still a shock to me that they didn't run. It
was actually quite difficult to get to the
club with the number of people flocking
after me. I had to pay one of the bouncers
a hefty tip just to be able to gain a
moments peace.

Now, I sat in the sanctuary of a
private booth on the bar level of the club,
my back to the dance floor and it's erotic
tendencies two floors below. My jeans and
jacket were gone, replaced by a sheer,
backless bodysuit. Clusters of sapphires
and opals, ranging from fiery red to the
purest of blues, weaved across the thin

fabric to barely keep my modesty intact.
The mask on my face was made of twisted
black silk, with teardrop cut gems
dangling against my cheeks. And four
empty glasses of a green apple-y tasting
drink were lined up in a neat row in front
of me as I bobbed my head to the music.

"Bloody hell." A hand slid along my
jaw, before yanking my face up. Through
my blurry vision I was able to make out
Silas, one of his perfect brows arched in
clear judgement. "So, this is where you
ran off to, to throw your latest fit."

He waved a hand, motioning for me
to scoot over, and didn't wait for me to
comply before cramming himself in the
booth next to me. He raised one of the
empty glasses, nose flaring as the scent of
the drinks hit him.

"How many of these did you have?"

"Enough for Vallen to shut up."

"Vallen?"

"The man gunning for Akashi's
position in my life," I drawled, flagging
down a waiter for more drinks.

"Oh, is that so? Do tell," Silas
muttered, pinning the waiter with a glare

that promised a slow death if they brought me any more drinks. The short fey male quickly scurried away, tucking his shimmering wings in tightly as if he feared Silas would tear them off. I sulked.

"You're never any fun."

"Oh, I'm plenty fun. I just keep my head on my shoulders in the process. Now let's go." Silas reached for my hand, but I yanked away.

"I didn't even get to dance yet!" My voice rose to a whine, and he stared at me incredulously.

"That would be unwise."

"Would it though?" I scrambled over the table on all fours, nearly falling on my ass as the alcohol made my head spin. Once I got my balance, I had enough motor control to rise, and curtsy with a giggle. Silas ran a hand through his hair, exasperated.

"If your mate learns I condoned this type of behavior he'll have my head," he muttered. I turned, leaving him no choice but to follow me as I began strutting toward the spiral staircase leading down to the lower levels.

"Ough, my *mate*." I spun again, walking backwards. "So loyal, so HONEST. Hah! My mates a secretive little shit, you know that?" Silas opened his mouth to reply, but his gaze latched onto something over my shoulder.

"She's been drinking fae-brewed vodka laced with blood," he blurted, before snapping his mouth shut.

"Huh?" I stumbled, and my backwards retreat came to a halt as I bumped into a wall of muscle. I slid my hands behind my back, running my fingers across the man's thin shirt and feeling rock hard abs flex beneath my touch.

"Oh, those are nice. Do you wanna dance with me?" I giggled again, turning against the man, and throwing my arms around his neck.

"Hmm, I don't know." He lifted a hand to brush a few stray hairs away from my face. "Sounded like you were pretty pissed at me a few seconds ago."

I blinked, squinting up to familiar green eyes piercing me from beneath a black Mardi Gras mask. I raised up on my tippy toes, inhaling against his neck.

"Fuck…" I groaned, tongue darting out to taste his skin. Anticipation lit up my nerves. His scent, his taste, his everything, was exactly what I wanted.

"We could do that." The hand which had been playing with my hair slowly drifted lower, cupping the back of my neck as I poised my fangs to bite. "But I'm *much* more interested in hearing what my mate has to say about this Vallen character."

I froze, snapping out of the daze my bloodlust threw me into. Rearing back, I reached up to yank the mask off of him. I was vaguely aware of my mouth hanging open as Akashi slowly reached forward, taking his mask back and replacing it on his face.

Akashi was here. And he was pissed.

"I-I think you have me confused with someone else!" I blurted, turning on my heel. His dark laugh was right behind me as I careened down the stairs, all but throwing myself into the swell of bodies swaying and grinding on the dance floor.

Hands reached for me, caressing, beckoning, but didn't hold me against my will as I maneuvered through the crowd.

This whole affair was based on unbiased, unchallenged consent. There was nothing forced, just enjoyed. So as long as I kept moving, I would be fine. What I didn't bet on was Akashi walking straight into the fray after me.

"So, this is the kind of thing you're into?" His growl drowned out the rest of the noise. I managed to side-step his embrace, placing a pair of female harpies between us.

"The idea's crossed my mind," I shot back, my anger getting the best of me. How dare he track me down, and have the audacity to be mad on top of it! He was the one keeping secrets, telling half-truths, leaving out the most important pieces of fucking information!

"I don't know if I should be offended by that, or turned on."

"Fuck off!"

"No." His hand slid into my hair again, yanking me to a halt and he snickered. "I seriously can't believe someone hasn't used this tactic in a fight yet."

"They'll throw you out if they think this isn't consensual," I threatened, glaring up at him. "Especially since I'm their Queen."

A slow, wolfish grin spread over his features. He dropped my hair, fingers working at the buttons of his shirt and within a second his chest was bare. I couldn't stop my eyes from traveling over each muscle hungrily, appreciating the view despite everything.

Then my eyes snagged on his imprint mark. It was paler than his natural shade, and sliced across his left hipbone. Wordlessly, he swiveled me so that my back was pressed to the wall. My protests died in my throat as a single claw replaced his pointer finger, resting on the dip between my collarbones. Despite the music and bodies crashing around us, everything turned slow-motion and quiet as he slowly tore the neck of my top into a scandalously low V, revealing my matching mark which rested on the center of my chest.

"Now there won't be any misunderstandings," he murmured low enough so that only I could hear. He pressed closer, his breath hitting my neck as he asked, "So, who'll it be, Little Bird? Me, or Vallen?"

A growl ripped from my throat, but he ignored it, leaning in to sink his own teeth into my neck and sucking hard. My hands fisted his hair trying to yank him back, but he paid me no mind. Instead he lowered his mouth between my breasts, tracing the mark with the tip of his tongue. The move made my legs buckle and I cursed again.

"I want to rip this sorry excuse of an outfit off you and fuck you till you can't walk. Right here. In front of all these people." He smirked up at me, "Don't believe me?"

Say yes, Vallen purred. The ghost of a caress went down both my ribs, invisible fingers clenching tightly to my hips. *You and I both know that's exactly what you want, so stop fighting your mate, and give in.*

I don't know what I would have said. I don't know if Akashi would have actually done it. Because right at that moment, Silas burst through the crowd, slamming into the two of us.

"We need to go, right now!"

CHAPTER 8

Three Angels were in the club.

The partygoers fled, as most of them were creatures born from dark magic or, like my sister, other Gods. The trio paid them no mind, forming a V formation to keep us where we stood. Though none of their wings were visible, mine appeared over my shoulders with a rush of wind.

The one in the center had two long, golden swords strapped across his back, and was studying me with a smug smile. His companions each had their bows raised, silver arrows notched and aimed at us. Their weapons might be useless against me, but Holy Metal was deadly to both of the men at my side, so I kept my mouth firmly shut.

As if reading my thoughts, the one on the left adjusted their aim, before suddenly releasing their arrow. Automatically my wings flared outwards, shielding Akashi and Silas as the second Angel took their shot as well. Painlessly, I felt the arrows ricochet off, dropping harmlessly to the floor.

"So, the rumors were true. After all this time, you have finally risen." The Angel in the center spoke, a hint of approval in his tone.

"You're trespassing on my territory," I said, grimly. "This is your one chance to leave alive." The Angel released an unbothered laugh, smooth and easy.

"Relax, we didn't come to fight."

"Your friends taking a shot prove otherwise."

"A test," he replied, smiling as if all was fine and dandy.

"What do you want?" I asked, ignoring Akashi pushing against my wing. I had accidentally pinned him and Silas to the wall, but frankly I didn't care. It was the safest place for them to be.

"I believe Gabriel has already made you aware of our wishes." I bristled as the Angel stepped forwards. His face was lit with fascination as he studied my wings, but when sparks leapt from my fingertips his gaze quickly met mine again.

"I'll admit he's not the best at breaking things gently, or giving a true sense of motivation. Though kidnapping your sister was both a reckless and impressive act, I'll give him that."

"Keep beating around the bush and I'll take your tongue as a trophy." Shadows pulled from the corner of the room, dulling the glow radiating from their skin and their weapons. Thorny vines twisted from my fingertips, each a serpent preparing to strike. The Angel's smile turned cold.

"Now if you do that, you wouldn't be able to hear me promise to reunite you with your mother."

I blinked, my shadows halting their advance as panic rushed through me. The image of Luna with that spiked collar through her throat had me on the brink of unleashing literal Hellfire before he clarified, "Not the Hellhound."

As the words hung in the air, I felt as if water was rushing away from shore, building into the impending tsunami which was coming to crash down and drown me.

Not the Hellhound, Vallen cooed in my ear. *Uriel speaks the truth.*

"Uriel?" I asked aloud, unable to contain the sudden sense of recognition. The Angels brows furrowed.

"How did you know my name? I had not told you." Uriel eyed me with renewed apprehension, his body stiffening in subtle defense. I took a sharp breath as I placed the name, a new wave of sickness hitting me as I recalled my father's words.

'I did not kill Bastet. I believe Uriel had that pleasure.'

Yes, he should burn for that sin alone. Vallen's voice was dripping with malice, their emotions matching my own. But, I didn't show the only card I had to play.

Instead, I pitched the room into darkness. The lights exploded, sending glass and sparks raining down on us. Fire burning candles went out with a sharp hiss of smoke. The Angels flanking Uriel cried out, but all he did was squint, as if trying to see me through the gloom, but we were already gone.

I used the momentum of a single wingbeat to push all three of us into the shadow realm, my hands catching one of Akashi's and Silas' so that they would not be lost in the darkness. Silas' grip on mine was so tight it was cutting off the circulation, his arm vibrating as he tried to contain his own rage. I could feel the urge for him to rip from my grasp, to go to Becca's side. Or maybe to teleport back to the club and drain the Angel for what he did to her. Luckily, he held fast until we stepped out of the shadows in the dining room.

The conversation died, our family looking up at us in various states of shock and alarm. Becca took one look at her mate and dragged him off before he went into a feeding frenzy. Luna was on her feet next, hands gently wiping at my cheeks and it was only then that I realized I was crying.

"I picked the worst time to come calling I see."

All heads turned to see Jesibelle standing in the open French doors, the Night Howler den behind her.

Ten minutes later, I was perched in Akashi's lap, gaze flipping between Jesibelle and the Hounds behind her. For the time being, I capped my rampant emotions. I couldn't afford to have a meltdown about what just happened, or entertain the fresh stab of betrayal in front of these females. Especially not if they intended to join forces with us. Right now, we needed to get through this, and I was more than willing to be Akashi's shield if he needed me to be.

Rather than moving to the throne room, we retreated to my quarters. My 'room' alone consisted of 5 individual rooms, making it more of a wing, I guess. Tucked away in the back, my bedroom was a blank canvas, holding little other than the largest four poster bed I had ever seen and a single floor to ceiling mirror. The mattress put a California-king to shame, and was covered with lush layers of buttery soft blankets and sheets, the same shade of midnight as the sky. The matching drapes cascading from the posts were encrusted with clusters of diamonds and pale pearls, giving it a galaxy affect.

Two of the other rooms consisted of my own library, and a private training space. The library was stuffed with texts all bound in the same plain, black hardcover, but all of the books held different stories ranging from folk tales to war strategies. In the rare moments I had to myself, I fought through the process of identifying and organizing the maze of information.

The athletic equipment (and walls) in the training area were reinforced with a titanium steel alloy, making it near impossible to break anything unless I was trying to. There was a sparring pit, as well as a steam room, which I would probably never use.

Then I had my guest rooms. The only one we'd used at this point was an entertainment space. Pool tables, a wet bar, movie theater accommodations, and various other sorts of games were tastefully stored or displayed in the space.

But we were in the formal guest space today. Unlike the Night Howlers parlor, it did not reek of luxury and glamour. This was very much Lucifers visitor space, sporting stiff backed chairs and leather couches.

Akashi's hand had been a hot iron in mine as we led the pack here, unrelenting in his immediate move to the centermost of those couches. I hadn't even been able to change out of my skimpy bodysuit before he maneuvered me to sit fully in his lap rather than beside him. The immediate relief that coursed through his body was physically reciprocated in mine.

Luna sat in a chair beside us, rigid as a statue. Flanking her stood Kuma and Hikari. This was the first time Aengus had left her side, not wanting to add to the tension in the room. Jesibelle didn't even glance in their direction, her sister, her son, her mate. I wanted to punch her.

Like the rest of the female Hellhounds, her eyes remained focused on Akashi, curious, and wanting. He in turn did nothing to suppress his aura. If anything, the steady pulse of dominance drifting off him intensified enough to make even my skin flush. Jesibelle though remained poised, displaying a sense of control that a few of her companions lacked.

"They reek." Akashi was smirking with amusement, and disgust. "If they

can't control themselves, they aren't
welcome in this meeting."

"I don't believe you're the one who's
orders I'll be listening to." Jesibelle
answered with a polite smile, but she
arched a brow, looking to me.

"Your preference?"

"They leave," I said flatly.
Immediately two young Hounds, twins by
the looks of it, all but fled from the room.
I made a show of sniffing the air, unable
to keep the grin from sliding on my face.
"That's better."

Slowly, Akashi's grip on me
loosened. For a moment, I wondered if he
wanted me to move now that the two
Hounds in heat had left. But then he
rocked his hips beneath mine, and made a
show of spreading his arms across the
back of the couch as he got comfortable
underneath me.

Clarity set in as I realized he
wasn't using me as a shield. If anything,
he was letting me use him as a throne—
and he wanted them to see it. There he
was, an Alpha Hound, bare from the
waist up and showing complete
submission. And they couldn't touch him.

He didn't bother muffling his pleased groan as I shifted in his lap to face them more fully, and my stomach flipped in response to the bolt of desire that radiated through the mark on my chest. I wasn't sure if it was that or the alcohol still in my system, but my voice was edged with sultriness when I finally said, "Let's get to the point Jesibelle. Why are you here?"

"You were crying earlier," she comments, ignoring my question. She rose from her seat, pale blue skirts hushing against the floor as she came to stand in front of me. Slowly, she cupped my chin in her palm to study me.

I heard Hikari snarl and take a step forward, but I held up my hand, silencing him as I held her gaze. If he had any inkling that this woman was his mother, he didn't show it. And Kuma said and did nothing, probably trying to pretend she wasn't even in the room. Jesibelles dainty fingers traced my jawline, her eyes unreadable as she studied me. After another beat of silence her lips, painted a wicked shade of red, tilted up into a smile.

"I thought I saw it before, but now, I'm sure. You have the light in your eyes." I blinked.

"Huh?" The undoubtedly un-queenly response left my lips before I could control it, and she laughed. But not unkindly.

"As you breath shadows, you also shed light. It's easier to see now that the tears have cleared your eyes."

"Jesibelle is what we call a seer." Luna's voice shattered whatever bubble the two of us were currently in, and I jerked away from her touch. Akashi instantly pressed a hand to my back, steadying me as Luna continued. "Her ability not only shows glimpses of the future, but also reads a person's character and intentions. This allows her to make accurate interpretations about their future. Usually."

Neither of the she-wolves looked towards each other, but the bridge of prickling tension between the two grew more tangible by the second. Luna had tricked her, I realized. She had kept her sister, the one who should have been able to predict her mutiny, completely in the dark.

I didn't want to imagine the aftermath for Jesibelle. My father's undoubted rage must have rained an excruciating punishment down on her and the rest of the Night Howlers. My respect for her grew slightly in that moment, acknowledging the strength it took to endure him, and some of my disdain for her began to wane.

"Why are you here, Jesibelle?" I repeated my question, voice cutting through whatever unspoken war was brewing between the sisters. She straightened, hand falling back to her side.

"I have not pledged myself to a new master since my banishment. I believe my ladies and I are the last Hounds here with the choice to do so." At that Kuma glanced our way. His face revealed nothing, but his eyes burned with a bridled anxiety.

"Banishment?" I prompted, shifting my gaze back to her, unsure of what she meant.

"Lucifer banished me when I failed to foresee Lunas betrayal." And there it was, out in the open. Neither of them batted an eye.

"So, did you come to pledge yourself and your ladies to me, or not?" I asked, breezing past the topic, not allowing a single one of them to linger on it. Now was not the time to settle old scores. Currently, time was not a luxury any of us had to waste. We would have to counterstrike sooner rather than later, and I needed to know what arsenal I'd have available.

"We cannot fight," Jesibelle said, tucking a platinum curl behind her ear as she regained her seat. "We are untrained, and mentally unsuited for a battlefield."

"I know," I tried to speak calmly, but my frustration was building. "I wouldn't expect any of you to go one-on-one with an Angel, but it would be beneficial to us all if we had someone on the ground dedicated to retrieving and tending to our wounded, rather than leave them to bleed out."

"The wounded which are our children." Her tone sharpened, her usual grace dissolving for the first time.

"I feel it imperative to clarify our separation was the punishment for my failure. We did not willingly serve our sons to the Devil keep our freedom.

Though there is nothing I can do to correct that sin, I can protect what I have now. There are some girls in my den who have never been outside its walls. So, I would like to offer myself, in exchange for their freedom."

"But you're already free," I said, unable to keep the shock from my voice as I studied each she-wolf anew. "I wouldn't force or subject you to anything you wouldn't wish for yourselves. I just want your help." Jesibelle smiled again, but this time it held pity.

"We would never be truly free, should we acknowledge you as our master. Even your own family and mate are bound to your command. Should you wield it with purpose or accident it does not matter. So again, I offer myself, in exchange for their freedom."

The silence was deafening. Because she was right.

CHAPTER 9

After Jesibelles harsh revelation, I didn't know where to go. I couldn't look at Akashi as I left, afraid he would try to rectify my guilt and my shame. I tried to wave off my sister's attempts of company, but she only relented after a boom of thunder shook the castle.

Blindly I stalked halls, my father's ghost haunting me from the shadows. This place may be filled with and commanded by my power, but it was still scarred by his presence. I knew the wounds left were deep, but for the first time I considered they may actually be irreparable. Silas may have redecorated the building. I may have restructured the lifestyle. But there was nothing in this blasted castle I actually created myself.

Now is this wise?

Vallen was hovering round my shoulders as I descended the stairs into the dungeon. The Hounds currently guarding Finn's cage were squatted on the floor, playing some type of dice game when I threw open the door.

"Leave us," I said, ignoring their sputtered apologies and quick exit.

"Well, this is an unexpected surprise." Finn's smile was sultry, and the familiar sensation of his spell rippled the air. I was loathe to admit the heat of it made every broken thing in me hurt a tiny bit less.

I genuinely believed I caught him by surprise, as he was shirtless and bent over the sink with water slowly leaking from his cupped hands. His ruby eyes gleamed, raking over me hungrily. It dawned on me that I was still in my damn bodysuit from the club. At one time, I might have been embarrassed, but now I just felt a sick sort of satisfaction.

I had perched on my half naked mates lap, looking like this in front of the female Hounds who were willing to do anything to bed him. And now, my enemy was gazing at me as if he wanted to worship me. I could use this.

With a twist of my wrist the shining bars of his cage contorted outward, and I stepped through. Aware enough, Finn took a step back, gaze drifting up to the violet candlelight as it shifted to a molten red.

I took him in fully, eyes traveling the expanse of his exposed skin, his muscles shaded in the dancing light. Once, that body had been smooth and clear, but after what he did, I had left my mark.

Pale scars of weaving vines climbed up his torso and fell down his arms, matching the route my flames had twisted through his body. Truth be told, I'm still not sure how I threaded my fire through him. It was a frustrating fact, which was a highlighted research point in my library. His golden chains delicately clicked together as he dried his face, the matching halo glinting as he dipped his head in my direction.

"You're staring at me like a woman starved."

"Just thought you would like to know how discomforting the look felt," I mumbled, finally averting my gaze. He released a heavy sigh and plopped on the edge of his bed.

"Does he know?"

I slid my gaze back to him and regretted it immediately. Finn lounged like a king. It was an inviting picture, him relaxing back onto his elbows with his legs stretched out lazily. He reached to his bedside table, retrieving a cherry from the dish there and popped it into his mouth without a care in the world.

"Does who know what?" I finally asked, ignoring the building wave of emotion inside me. His answering grin was smug, the points of his fangs digging into his lower lip.

"Does Akashi know how miserable you are?"

I didn't so much as blink, but my magic gave me away. Whips of shadows snared Finn's wrists and ankles, dragging him upright. He just continued to grin. And talk.

"Does he know how pent up you are? Would he be willing to help this half of you find release?"

I felt the stroke of Vallen's fingertips skimming up the sides of my thighs, the touch so real it sent electric shocks through me.

Had I known this was all it would have taken, I would have persuaded you to come to this male ages ago.

"No," I mumbled, shaking my head roughly, bracing a hand up against the wall as I fought against Vallen's advances. Their touches were on my spine now, sliding between the slits for my wings, making the sensitive flesh sing. Finn chuckled just as my fangs began aching in my mouth and I realized I had spoken aloud.

"No, young Akashi wouldn't, would he?" My bloodlust only grew with Finn's taunting, the room growing too cramped, too *hot*. "Oh Angel, let me help you," Finn whispered, voice full of longing.

Let us help ourselves, Vallen moaned in agreement.

I don't recall moving but I was suddenly straddling him. Finn's skin was as warm and smooth as I'd remembered, the heady scent of cloves and honey making my mouth water. He openly moaned when I sank my teeth into the crook of his neck, releasing heavy, unchecked breaths as I drank my fill. His blood, like his scent, was sickeningly sweet. I can't remember the last time I drank this much blood. It had to be weeks, if not months.

And then his teeth were in my neck
as well. I released my bite with a hiss,
tilting my head back, overwhelmed in
sensation. I felt my shadows slip from
him and then his hands were roaming
me, palms caressing up from my hips to
my breasts.

He released the bite with a long
lick, before digging his fangs in again
above my collarbone. One of his hands
deftly slid between my legs, the thin
material of my bodysuit doing nothing to
dull the sensation of his fingers coaxing
my clit in soft circles until I cried out. My
nervous system was dancing, and I felt
like I was floating.

*Angel-born, you're getting too
carried away.*

Vallen's touch coasted over the still
throbbing bitemarks before migrating
higher, dipping beneath the fabric of my
choker to trace my scar. The sensation
jerked me out of my head, and I threw
myself backwards, landing on the stone
floor with a painful smack.

Finn fell with me, catching himself
on his knees in front of the bed.
Immediately he reached for me, but

paused when I summoned a blade from the shadows and held it to his throat.

"This did not happen." I wanted to growl, but my voice came out in a shaking whisper. "I did not come here. You did not touch me." A smirk twisted onto his swollen lips, still glistening with my blood.

"You would have cum, had I more time."

"Finnegan," I begged, my carefully nonchalant façade withering to nothing. His smirk did not waver, nor did the challenge in his eyes as he nodded.

"You did not come here, my Queen."

CHAPTER 10

A tempest would not have produced enough water to cleanse me of what I've done. I was so mortified that I could barely manage to remove myself from the room, let alone drag myself up the staircase. At the first sound of voices, I slipped into the shadows, disappearing to the naked eye, my existence now hovering between my world and the darkness.

I waded through space and time, walking through the walls, emerging through the stone, until I was in a full sprint across the barren pit which stretched the length of this never-ending cave. Red sand heaved in bursts under my feet, the blue mist curling around me in a taunting embrace as I pierced through it. The air was crisp like a winter's day, fresh and painful as I gasped for more of it. I longed for darkness, for cover, for trees providing scribbled routes between their trunks and places to hide.

I felt the ground vibrating beneath my footfalls long before I heard the heavy strides of a Hound chasing me down. A hiccupped laugh came out of me, sounding scared and strangled and stupid. What must this look like to them? Their queen, covered in blood, streaking across this cursed Sahara at God knows what time while still in this blasted slutty bodysuit.

And I was indeed covered in blood. I had done nothing to clean myself, nothing to hide the evidence before I fled. The crystals on my bodysuit were stained with the ruby remains of Finns blood, a dried trail of it leading from the corner of my mouth down the column of my throat. My own blood, dried in glittering gold patches, stained my collarbone and chest.

I stopped running, fully aware that even with all my powers I could not outrun a Hellhound. Sand sprayed outward as I leaned into a skidded stop. Producing two twin daggers from the shadows around my hips I whirled around, arms poised to throw the blades.

The Hound who was chasing me mimicked my quick halt. I did not recognize him; amber eyes flickering like flames, and a coat of ashen white fur.

"Can I help you?" I asked.

He snorted, tossing his head in an incredulous way as he side eyed me.

"I simply wished to confirm you were well, my Lady." His tail whipped back and forth, more like my sisters than a Hounds. "How am I to assess your given state?"

"You can simply not assess and leave me to my devices." I flipped one dagger in a lazy arch, catching the blade by the tip while trying to appear bored.

"I cannot do that." There was an undercut to his tone that I didn't like.

"You can't obey your master?" I dared to growl the title, ignoring the sickening waves of guilt and glee thrashing within me. The Hound snorted again and began to tread a slow circle around me. I shifted my daggers to an angle easier to strike, not moving an inch.

"Truthfully, I thought I was mistaken the first time I saw your blood." His voice echoed in my head, inquisitive yet taunting. "But it appears you have another's stained on you as well."

"Congratulations. Would you like a promotion for pointing out the obvious?" I muttered sarcastically.

"The obvious is that you refuse to drink from accessible sources. That's something which hurts us both." He did not flinch when I embedded the first of my blades into his shoulder. Just snorted again, the tip of his tail whipping my thigh gently before he sat in front of me.

"Who the fuck are you?" I hissed, vines curling around my wrists and shadows rising from the ground. The Hound tilted his head, smug as anything.

"I'm yours." And then he was gone. Just, *dissolved,* in front of me into open air.

And my dagger forged from shadows disappeared with him.

I hadn't heard a peep from Vallen since Finns cell. Nothing about the dagger. Nothing about Akashi sleeping (naked) in my bed when I returned. Nothing as I washed all the blood from my body and healed the bite marks on my skin. I was utterly alone with my guilt and fear. And I forgot how much it sucked to feel that way.

I retreated to my library, unable to bear lying beside Akashi with all of this fresh in my head. Just hours ago, he had had me pinned to the wall in, frankly, my favorite place in the world. He had been persistent, wanting. And then we were attacked, and then Jesibelle showed up, and then I allowed Finn to... what time was it? Did that even matter anymore?

I tore books from the shelves at random, desperate to find any explanation about the Ashen Hound. Hours later, I was buried inside a fortress of stacked books, and still had no answers.

The last time I was like this was when I had been researching Vallen. There was nothing about them in these books either, so the only information I'd been able to obtain was what they decided to share. So now I had a voice in my head, and a Hound I was hallucinating well enough to touch... yea, I was doing great.

Wearily, I rose from the table and pulled my robe around me to ward off a sudden chill. Perhaps I was going about this all wrong. The answers I sought were not in the Devils library, but I knew of another library holding records dating back to the beginning.

Now that is certainly unwise, Angel-born. Ah, so he was around, and just not bothering to help. Typical.

"And what makes you say that?" Alone for once, I allowed myself to freely ask rather than compete in a mental game of tennis with Vallen.

You are the Light Walker, yes. But Gabriel knows of the gift now. He would have taken precautions. I sighed.

"Is that supposed to scare me?"

It should.

I raise my palm, willing a small, silver flame to appear. It pops and sizzles for a moment, before growing steady, curling like a cat around my skin until my whole hand glows with Hellfire.

"You won't answer my questions, but you don't deny when I guess right," I mumble, turning my hand over. "You're

Hellfire. You're sentient. I can hold you, yet you're not real. That Hound was one of the same. A sibling?" I ask.

No. I clenched my hand shut, dousing the flames.

"Then there you have it. I have a multitude of questions, and scraps for answers. I will do what I must, and you won't argue about it with me further."

"Arguing with you has rarely gotten me anywhere." I freeze, goosebumps littering my skin at the new voice. I'm too afraid to turn around as I hear Silas ask, "More importantly, who have you been talking to?"

CHAPTER 11

Silas made a show of peering around the room, ruby eyes glistening with disappointment after he kicked a stack of books over and no one was hiding behind it. Then those eyes narrowed and snapped back to me. In a flash he was at my neck, inhaling sharply.

"Is my blood no longer enough to satiate you, my lady?" His voice came out grave, the restrained anger and pain making me ache. He straightened to glare down at me. "Perhaps you disallow yourself to drink to your fill? Is that the reason you ran to drain a rat in its cage?"

"I didn't drain him," I said softly, closing my eyes against his heavy gaze. "I just didn't know where else to go." At that Silas released a haughty laugh.

"Oh? Your mate and your sister failed to cross your mind as suitable options?"

"You don't get it. I'd hurt them—"

"I get it better than anyone else in this cursed place!" His fingers locked on my shoulders, nails digging in as he lowered his face to be level with mine.

"You don't want to scare him? You don't want to kill him? Those are just fronts you're using to avoid the fact that you don't trust him." I try to push away but he holds fast, lowering his voice.

"And believe me, you will kill him if you don't trust him. Beings like us can only endure starvation for so long."

"Stop." The plea came out in a whisper, and I dropped my forehead to his chest as I fought against waves of nausea. "Silas, please. I can't take it. I can't deal with this right now. There are more important things I must handle before focusing any attention on what I may or may not need."

"And that's where you're wrong again." His tone was unforgiving. "This war is but a moment in time. If we all survive, what's important then?"

Satisfied enough by my silence he releases me, stepping back. Pulling a flask I'd never seen before from his jacket he tilted his head back, and I was stunned further by the scent of my own blood hitting my nose.

"So that's where you keep your rations?" I ask dumbly, not knowing what else to say. He grunted.

"Forgive me, Your Majesty. Though I can tell you showered, that does little to cover the fact you've been bitten tonight." I wince, but find myself unable to defend myself once again.

Silas seats himself in the chair I'd abandoned, yanking the closest book to him and began to flip through its contents. "What have you been looking for in here?"

"Information on rare magicks," I mumble, bracing myself as I add, "like Hellfire, and disappearing Hellhounds." Silas stills completely, head cocked, eyes boring into me, and I relent.

I tell him everything that's been going on with my magic since falling into that frozen lake. I explain the conundrum with Vallen, and how often they're in my head. That the random bursts of bloodlust are from their influence, and I can do nothing but lock down my magic and endure.

Then I described my reaction to Finn, how he played me with my doubts about Akashi's feelings, and Vallen used that to their advantage to satiate their cravings. Finally, when I get to the part about the Ashen Hound, Silas raises a hand.

"Does anybody know?"

"What do you mean?" I asked. If possible, his eyes narrow even further.

"Have you let anyone know what you have been enduring for the past three months, or have you stubbornly tried to balance this on your own as well as plan for war?" At my silence he curses, slamming the book in front of him shut.

"There is nothing any of you can do to help me. To soothe this," I say, feeling the ache in my chest building towards a precipice.

"We could find a way," he argues, hands running through his hair. "I found a way with Rebecca. I would aid Akashi in finding a way to help with you."

"I don't want his help." At this, Silas' gaze turns bemused.

"While I realize that our relationship has grown over the past few months, you can't just leave your mate and sister out of this because you're afraid of what may be said." He lowers his voice, leveling a serious gaze on me. "Especially Akashi. I see how complicated your relationship with him is, but you cannot outright refuse him. He's your mate, regardless of the bond you share."

"I'm protecting them," I say, adamantly. "Anzen is already dead. Rebecca was already kidnapped once. Now, Akashi is bound to me for eternity. However I live, he lives. However I die, he dies. I won't make him bear this too."

Silas sat there quietly for several long moments, before silently rising from the desk. I thought he was going to reprimand me, or frown at the very least. But when he paused in the doorway, he just sounded sad as he asked,

"Raven, how long will it take you to realize you have never made him do anything?"

CHAPTER 12

Silas refused me his blood for an entire week, a smile on his lips each time he directed me to seek the help of others. Not wanting to distract anyone else with my wellbeing, I refused to. It was already risky enough spilling as much as I did about my current state to him, and I found myself bracing for when he would inevitably run his mouth. To whom, was my biggest concern.

Luna couldn't know. She'd spent decades of her life trying to keep this from happening to me, and was still grieving the death of her son. For the same reason I couldn't tell Hikari or Kuma. I could tell Becca, who surely would mock me for it. It was she who once said we don't need to drink blood to survive, but the longer I go without it, the less likely I feel that to be true.

And Akashi, well, he'd react one of two ways. He would either swamp me with questions and hover, monitoring my every craving to ensure I don't become more devilish than I already am. Or he would play a fool, and let me suck him dry in the name of love until all I had left were his bones. I don't know which option I feared more.

I paced before the stained-glass window in the meeting hall, the air around me ebbing and flowing with magic as I moved. My fangs had been out for a full two days, and last night I could no longer dampen the ethereal glow to my skin. My tail reappeared this morning, the stubborn thing making jeans impossible with its constant flipping about. Because of this I had to make the rare public appearance in a skirt.

I'd donned one of my jumpsuits, a violet silk which mimicked my fire, and altered the back to cut scandalously low to accommodate my tail. Then I conjured a matching overskirt, agape in the front so I wouldn't trip, to tie around my hips. The weight of it dragging behind me was enough to pin most of the insistent flicks of my tail, and the lace beading even dampened some of the glow on my skin.

Smartly, everyone had kept their mouths shut about it when I entered the meeting hall. Kuma was the only one who outright gaped at me, and I thought I caught a glimpse of a grin from my sister, but she kept her comments to herself. Beside her, Akashi sat with a lazy, burning desire in his eyes even though he kept his gaze on the table. I focused on ignoring the heat his attention ignited, which became surprisingly easy when Jesibelle decided to join us.

The she-wolf sat across from Luna, and I took a moment to study the pair with painfully un-subtle stares. Luna was clad head to toe in black fighting leathers, and chose to stand behind Aengus, rather than take her normal seat beside him. Jesibelle was the polar opposite of her sister. Today her blonde hair was pinned in an extravagant array of pink clips and bows, and she wore a flowing peony gown adorned with opals. She looked completely out of place beside the battle-ready Hounds seated at the table, but sat with her head high, nonetheless.

"Remind me again, what I'm doing here?" She asked, the question echoing in the silence of the room.

"Two reasons, actually." I, finally ceased my pacing, coming to rest a hip against the tables edge. There was enough bitterness between the two of us already, and I'm sure what I was about to tell her would only make it blossom further.

"One, I was testing you. I was genuinely curious if you would come to a meeting if I summoned you directly. Since you don't recognize me as your Master and all, it's reassuring to see you choosing to be here."

There were a few quiet chuckles, and a smirk from Kuma, but other than her lips pressing together in annoyance Jesibelle did not react.

"And the second reason?" She quipped. I grinned, my tone easing.

"I may not be your Master, but as you reside in my domain, I am responsible for you. I thought you would like to be informed of our future plans, since the outcome will affect you regardless."

"I appreciate the thought," she said, a flare of surprise crossing her features. I nodded to Aengus, who stood and slid a few hand-drawn maps and plans across the table towards her.

"We plan to attack on the sixteenth day of July. In the mortal world, that's just shy of a year away."

"Yet here it is but a month and two weeks," Jesibelle said, interestingly perceptive. "Will the battle commence here as it did last time?"

"If all goes according to plan, the battle will commence across the border, in Purgatory." Aengus glanced at me, and I flashed a quick smile, hoping it was reassuring enough for him to keep the reigns. "It's not our intention to put anyone at risk who does not wish to participate."

At that, Jesibelle visibly relaxed, eyes shifting to me as she said, "I appreciate that very much."

"You made your wishes clear," I said, voice softening. "I'm doing my best to respect them."

"But there is only so much grace Lady Nightshade can give during a time of war such as this," Aengus continued, hardening his gaze at her. As Lunas mate, I was assuming he had zero intention on being around Jesibelle for longer than necessary, so I allowed him to continue getting her up to speed as fast as possible.

"On this day, the majority of us will leave. Only a few Omegas will remain with the pups and adolescents who are not yet fit to fight. We would appreciate it if the Night Howler den would consider helping care for them until we return. They are, after all, your children.”

The room was so silent I could hear my own blood rushing in my ears.

“I have no issue with tending to the young,” Jesibelle replied, folding her hands on the table. “And I’d like to take this opportunity to clarify, that offer extends beyond just this one day.”

She was playing chess now, and that was a strategic move. Kuma was fully grinning at this point, the whites of his teeth showing. He looked like he was contemplating rising and crossing the room to her, but it was Hikari who made the next move. I watched as my eldest brother leaned across the table, sounding terrifyingly like Luna as he said,

“Your children have no need for such belated generosity. One day will do. We shan’t need you any longer than that.”

I felt a rock drop in my stomach. He was glaring at Jesibelle with a flavor of malice I recognized, the same intensity of hate I had turned on my father. I don’t know when or how he figured it out, but he just leaned back in his seat with a practiced smile as if he didn't care his mother looked like she was about to weep.

I hadn't realized I'd moved to be by her side, until her hand reached up to clasp mine which now rested on her shoulder. Her fingers were trembling, and I found myself suddenly wanting to comfort her.

She'd made it clear that having no contact with their pups was not a decision they had made easily. Frankly, it wasn't even a choice if it was something Lucifer demanded. Their den literally called it a sacrifice, and I could see now how heavily that weighed on her.

"I believe it would be best if you were spared the remaining details," I said offering her my other hand to help her stand from her seat. "The rest will be quite vicious, I'm afraid."

"Again, I thank you. I shall take my leave and inform my ladies of our expected duties." Jesibelle released my hands, finding the strength to raise her chin as she exited the room, a Queen in her own right. After the doors swished shut behind her, I addressed the room as a whole.

"You will treat the Night Howler den with respect, not contempt. None of you were spared from my Fathers greed, including them. Am I understood?" There was a soft chorus of agreements, and I let the subject drop.

Turning my back to the table, I crossed the room to the large trunk I had a few of them carry up here earlier. "Now, let's discuss our fighting tactics. I have a proposition for you."

"Tactics? But we already planned our ambush?" My eyes shifted to the Hound who spoke, recognizing him as the one I had bitten. Talum, Akashi said his name was Talum. Though his hands were shaking with veiled anxiety, he held my gaze. I bit back a smile.

"You're right. We have a date and time. Formations. But we don't have a wild card." I flipped open the two brass locks on the trunk. "Do you want to ask me what that is?"

"I wouldn't want to question you," he says automatically. Despite myself, I released a laugh, knowing I must look like a woman going mad.

"Oh, but you must," I insist, turning around to face him fully. "I know what I am to you. I know you will obey my every word should I actually command you. But you need to know I don't intend to abuse that privilege. I didn't make this table for show," I said gesturing round to the group. "If you have questions, ask. If you have concerns, state them. I assure you I will be far more displeased if I find you are purposely withholding things out of fear of bruising my ego. So, Talum, on behalf of everyone else who is curious, I encourage you to ask your question."

He looked taken aback by my words, or maybe by the simple fact that I knew his name, I wasn't sure. But I remained patient, let him squirm for a minute, let him exchange a series of looks with Aengus. Then his brown eyes shifted back to me, and he sat up a little straighter.

"What's in the trunk?" He asked, fully serious and confident.

At one time in my life, I might have laughed, it was such a simple question. But I understood the magnitude of this moment for the Hounds. For centuries they blindly obeyed, regardless if they understood or agreed. My father would have shared nothing about his plans, expecting them to react flawlessly with the new weapons I was about to share.

"Coming from a different generation and world, there's a few things I've noticed which puts us at a permanent disadvantage. You all fight strong, I'm not trying to undermine that. But your strength only gets you so far." I lifted open the trunks lid, pulling a large plastic case from it which I hauled onto the table.

"You have twice the advantage on the ground now with mine and Rebecca's shadows. However, if the Angels remain in the air, there is little you can do. I believe these will remedy the issue."

I opened the case, pulling out a series of metal parts. It had been years since I pieced one together, and I felt Lunas assessing stare as my arms went through the motions of assembling the gun.

"This is a military grade AR-15. Human military, but powerful, nonetheless. Its range is thousands of that of your claws and teeth." My voice carried through the room as I placed the assembled weapon on the table. "I'm not banning you from fighting in your Hound form. I just thought that the more distance you can keep between yourselves and the enemy, the safer you would be."

There was a range of reactions and emotions. I allowed the Hounds to discuss amongst themselves as I produced five more cases from the trunk, and quietly assembled the guns they held. Aengus picked up one of them, turning it over in his hands, passing it to a few of the others to assess and familiarize themselves with. There were a few uneasy glances towards me during some of the disagreements, but I remained passive, taking my seat at the middle of the table again.

"I have a concern," Luna said, and all eyes turned to her. She wasn't one to typically speak here, other than during a group vote.

"Go ahead Mom." I bit my tongue, hoping I didn't accidentally undermine her in some way, but the corners of her mouth turned up in a smile.

"I understand the thought process behind this weapon choice, and I do agree. Yet, I feel the need to ask: did you think of what to replace the normal bullets with?"

A few of the Hounds paled. Yes, I had just let Talum question me, but Luna just flew miles beyond him with hers. I grinned.

"Yep. Quite a neat fix actually." I crossed to the trunk again and lifted a small box of ammunition from the bottom. After pulling out a few bullets, I passed them around for the Hounds to see.

"These are my shadows, mixed with cursed obsidian to retain a solid form. They should do no permanent harm to you, if you misfire."

And if they struck true, an Angel would be downed, if not dead from the shot alone.

Excitement replaced hesitance as the Hounds rose, the hall vibrating with their energy as they passed around the weapons and began speaking over one another with new plans and ideas. I felt myself truly smiling for the first time in months, the tease of relief coasting through me. Finally, the distance between us all closed a little bit.

CHAPTER 13

"Can I ask about the dress now? Or did you come up with another stupid rule for us?" Becca's voice came from behind me, and I glanced to see her striding onto the balcony I'd secluded myself on with a bottle of wine extended in her hand.

"It's not exactly a dress, so don't get too excited over it." I heave a sigh and begrudgingly add, "Though I have been making a few stupid rules recently, haven't I?"

"You mean like literally commanding the Hounds to not make jokes anywhere but a specific table?" I cringed at the memory, and made a mental note to verbally correct that for my brothers later, as well as mind my tone in the future. Becca all but forced the bottle into my hands, before hopping up to sit on the balcony rail beside me.

"You're more stressed out about it than them," she added, reading my mind. I didn't reply, just popped the cork on the bottle and took a whiff.

Bittersweet cherry and blackberry greeted me, the liquid dark enough to stain my teeth. I took a swig while she pressed, "I'm curious though. You're never in a skirt, so why now?"

"Bodily malfunction," I mutter and toss back another mouthful. "One that would heavily discourage their comfort zones expanding."

"The Hounds?" I looked at her flatly.

"Yes."

"Who gives a shit about their comfort zones?" I forget sometimes just how candid my sister can be. I offer the bottle back to her and she takes it, helping herself to a long sip.

"Unfortunately for me, I care. And for now I don't want them to know about this." I brace myself as I reach for my skirt, unsure of how she would react. As soon as I lift the fabric wide, my tail darts into freedom. I barley catch the triangular tip before it slaps her in the face. "This has been driving me literally insane."

So, I'm coming in second to a scaled appendage? Please, not right now.

I flinch at the unexpected touch of Becca's fingers, holding my breath as she too grabs hold of the straining muscle.

"Can't you hold it still?"

"Oh wow, I didn't think of that," I grumbled, my voice thick with sarcasm. Before she can ogle me further, I move the overskirt back into place, capturing the damned thing beneath it once more.

"How long has it been out like that? I didn't see it yesterday." Becca's eyes assess me coolly, tracking my clenched jaw and forced swallow.

This was exactly what I had been worried about. She was keen, and far more manipulative than I. If I didn't watch my words carefully, I'd soon be vomiting everything up to her as I had done with Silas.

And yet, I couldn't deny that it felt good, like some of the weight had been lifted from my shoulders. The problem was that relief is temporary, and soon Silas knowing about my predicament would not be enough. I would seek comfort elsewhere and he knew it, which was why the dick was icing me out.

"Earth to Raven." Becca waved her hand in front of my face.

"Sorry," I said, taking the bottle back from her too quickly.

"Silas smelled like you when he came to bed last week." I choked on the wine, bending over the banister and coughing. Becca remained stoic, her gaze piercing me relentlessly. "You know he and I don't forbid each other from seeking out another's company, but I would appreciate a heads up if it were to happen again. I wouldn't just go and bite Akashi without telling you."

A bolt of possessiveness, hot and wailing, flared through me at the thought. Though it quickly ebbed, logic overpowering instinct, her point had been made.

"It's not like that," I started. "I didn't even suck his blood that night. But he did drink mine— not a bite just the rations." She cut my rambling off with ease.

"Then why did he stumble in, stressed and reeking of you but refusing to speak?" She asked. Damn. It. I glanced at her side long.

"How likely are my chances of getting you to drop this?"

"Why are you so insistent on hiding it?" My chances are zero it seems. I don't look at her when I reply, placing the bottle of wine between us on the railing.

"This adjustment hasn't been going well for me. It's harder than my Reformation was. More demanding. More… everything." As if to amplify my point my tail suddenly lengthened a few more inches, now wagging against the stones beneath my feet.

"Does Akashi know?" Becca asked and I groaned.

"I don't ask for much, sister to sister. So please fucking listen to me when I say to keep this between us." My grip on the banister was so tight my knuckles were white.

"Okay jeez," Becca held up her hands in mock surrender. "If it's gonna get this stressy let me keep the wine then." I barked a laugh.

"It's all yours."

I gazed out across the empty expanse of the cave-land below us. The endless red sand. The hanging blue mist. The sheer rock walls climbing upwards in every direction.

"I miss Purgatory," I breath out, finally admitting it aloud. "I want us to move back to our mansion in Atlantis."

"Can you even do that?" Becca asked, voice softening in a way that had me knowing her next words were going to cut. "Truthfully, Silas and I have wanted to go back for a while now, but I wasn't going to leave you to clean up this mess alone. And hey we have a castle now, so that's pretty cool right?"

Her attempt at humor did nothing to soothe the weight crashing back down on me, but I just smiled a reassuring smile, and nodded.

"I would be able to handle it, I think. Though I'd prefer to have you here until the war's over at least, so that I know your safe."

"I'm safe," she said, voice taking on a serious tone. "All of us are safe, because of you."

I knew my answering smile was weak, but it was all I could manage. My focus was on not fleeing from that balcony, screaming and crying like a madwoman, because this conversation was just confirmation that two more people were trapped here because of me.

I spent the majority of the next day training the Hounds. Though I would have preferred to be in fighting leathers, and maybe get an opportunity to get to work off some steam with good-old-fashioned violence, my tail was determined to make it impossible. Irritatingly, it kept wrapping toward the front of my body to slip out from under the edge of any overskirt I tried, so I was forced to be out here in a full dress to hide it. It took three layers of heavy navy velvet to pin it down, but at the very least, the fabric was thick enough to ward off the damp chill in the air.

Luna and Becca assisted me as the two of them were the only others here with any experience handling firearms. We broke off into three groups, Luna with the Sigma's, Becca with the Betas, and I worked with the Alphas. By the end of the day, each group was shown how to

assemble and shoot four different
firearms.

We had only gone through the
motions with rubber bullets today, which
was a decidedly good call since one of the
Sigma's misfired directly into another's
calf. The rubber bullet thankfully
bounced off, not leaving much more than
a bruise.

After spending another full night
in the library, I didn't have enough time
to conjure that many targets. The Hounds
though didn't complain, and each were
able to practice shooting with at least two
different guns before the day was over. I
wasn't overly worried about that though.
They would get plenty of target practice
over the course of the next few weeks, and
were adept at picking up new skills.
Today they just needed to learn the
basics: assemble, load, and most
importantly, reload. It was enough of a
good start in my book, so I sent them to
dinner early.

As their whoops and hollers began
to fade off with their retreat toward the
dining hall, Kuma weaved his way out of
the back of the group. He had the biggest
grin on his face, and a few of the Hounds
he passed clapped his shoulder good

naturedly or shook his hand. I shared a look with Luna, the two of us heading towards him with equal excitement.

"You did it, didn't you? You've received your rank?" Luna asked as we reached him, hands gripping his. Kuma's chest swelled with pride.

"I'm about to go tell Hikari to start working harder, cuz I'm gunning for his job."

"You're a Beta!?" I exclaimed, sparks of excitement popping off my fingertips. I threw my arms around my brother, and he easily caught me in one arm while drawing Luna to him with the other. I could smell it now that I was so close, the new tangy musk clinging to his skin.

"A shocker, I know." He grinned down at us. Luna raised a hand to cup his cheek.

"And are you satisfied with it?"

"Ma, I've been waiting my whole life for a rank. Some moron coulda declared me an Omega and I wouldn't have said shit about it."

"Now *that's* unbelievable," I tease, swatting at his arm.

Kuma scoffs and quick as anything tosses me over his shoulder, spinning us fast enough to make my hair whip around me. Suddenly, I feel like a little kid again, playing with my brothers behind the cottage until dinner. For a second I thought I might cry, but then I'm laughing, truly laughing as I cling to his back and kick my feet.

After some nonserious chastising from Luna, he placed me back on my feet. After one more hug, she departs with his enthusiastic permission to find the rest of our pack and start planning a small celebration. Only after she retreats does the brightness of Kuma's smile fade.

"Do you think she'll accept me? As just a Beta?" I reached for his hand, squeezing it once.

"I know I have no room to talk, since Akashi and I aren't exactly a secret," I say, ignoring the warmth in my cheeks and his knowing grin. "But take it from me: don't do anything while we're on the cusp of another battle. It will be rushed, and you won't have time to solidify the bond. And besides that, you really should talk to Hikari before you even think about pursuing her."

"It's not as if I need his permission."

"No," I concede, "but I don't think you want his anger either." I smirk, before nodding towards the castle entrance. "At the very least take a shower. She'll definitely reject you if you approach her smelling like that."

He grins again, and I can feel his reassurance through the lone pat he leaves on my head. I stand there and watch him go, and that overwhelming sense of nostalgia threatens to drown me once more.

I don't fight it this time. I just stand there, breathe, let it crash and rumble and flow, before it recedes on its own, faster than I expected. When the ball in my throat dislodges, I lift my skirt, breaking into a jog after him.

"Kuma?!" I call, and he pauses in the doorway, head cocked, and eyebrows knitted. So many things have changed or have been taken from me, but this has remained the same. I feel my heart beating in my chest, rampant like a wild animal as I run to my big brother before I can talk myself out of it.

"Uh, what happened between a minute ago and now?" He asks, a mix of puzzled concern. I gulp for a breath, eyes flashing to his.

"I really, really need to talk to you."

CHAPTER 14

I felt anxious after confiding in Kuma, but it had been a healthy choice. I didn't tell him much, keeping it to my growing powers and asking if he could help by giving me some blood. He had a few concerns for my well-being, but oddly seemed happy that I'd asked this of him. The only thing he wasn't thrilled about was keeping it a secret from Akashi. He only settled when I told him that Silas knew, and this was my first step in asking for help.

Now, the two of them check on me in shifts. They each would meet me in the library once a week, so I'd get refreshed every couple of days. Initially, I'd wanted it to function like the rations they were getting from me, but Silas was adamant that I drank directly from the source. Something about satiating the 'experience' and not just my stomach.

I in turn kept myself in check even more. I didn't indulge in bloody drinks if I grew stressed, and set aside time to practice my new magic, hidden from view in the belly of the lake. I figured it was high time to strengthen it rather than suppress it. And Vallen remained on a very, very, short leash.

I had made Becca aware of the arrangement, since I was now biting her mate weekly. Though she thanked me for telling her, her relentless teasing hadn't failed to make me blush. For being mates, the two of them never seemed bothered by the other's activities unless they were caught off guard. My own relationship though would most likely be the polar opposite, which was why Akashi didn't know at all.

I promised myself I'd tell him about what's been going on, and about the night with Finn. I hadn't intended for it to be a secret this long, and I certainly wasn't going to prolong it past tonight. It was a singular slip up, nearly three weeks ago now, and only happened because I was being stubborn and trying to handle these urges on my own. I knew he wouldn't be pleased with my arrangement with Silas and Kuma, but I hoped he would agree that it was better than the alternative.

What he would hate the most would be Vallen. Silas and I had gotten nowhere with research, and though I was piecing together a plan to rob Heaven for a second time, I decided a Hellhound being aware of sentient Hellfire was probably a smart thing. That, and I had to address the Ashen Hound at some point.

But instead of telling Akashi, I told Kuma. He already knew about my bloodlust, so it was an easier conversation. He didn't have much to offer on the subject of Hellfire, as Lucifer kept those secrets closely guarded, but the Ashen Hound sparked a few things from his memory.

When they were adolescents in the years before me, Luna heavily quizzed them on the lore and fading magicks of their kind. He said their magicks faded because of Lucifer draining the land, and his greed to keep what remained under his control.

It was that reason why so few Hounds were born with gifts like Luna. Akashi's case had been different, as Gabriel blessed him directly. Briefly, we both worried if that meant the Angel could take that power away, but we set that aside with my growing pile of secrets and concerns.

Kuma believed this Ashen Hound could be one of these fading magicks, or a runaway Hound who possessed one. He encouraged me to speak to Luna about it, but I declined.

My days were already impossibly packed, and now that I've added the two weekly feedings and my trainings, I rarely had a moment to myself. Akashi and I only see each other in passing, like ships in the night. I usually don't return from the library until after he's asleep, and he rises long before I do to head to the training grounds and wake up the adolescents. During the day, we're surrounded by company. Whether it be family, the army as a whole, or small meetings around the oval table, we never get a moment alone.

"The puppies are complaining about not getting to use real bullets." Becca drops her bodyweight against my shoulders, quite literally knocking me out of my thoughts as I lurched forwards.

The two cauldrons on my worktable tip and spill their contents, making me curse lightly. I'd found this little study while building Finns cell in the dungeon. It was small, and dark except for the fireplace, but it was private, and quiet. Perfect for alchemy and mental breakdowns.

"Well, thanks to that, now they're gonna have to wait even longer," I mutter, cupping my palm under the table edge and gently sweeping the powdered obsidian into it.

"What the hell is that?"

"Drugs."

"Very funny." She shook her head and pointed to the black ink staining the table from the other cauldron. "I meant that one."

"Demon blood." I dumped the powder back into its container, before wiping the residue on my skirt. Despite the regular feedings, it was a regular thing now to have my tail or wings randomly appear for as long as they pleased. Today, my tail was wreaking havoc again, which meant I was wearing another dress. Vallen often complained when I was finally able to will the appendages away.

"Demon blood? You mean we gotta deal with those now too?" I sighed, measuring out the powder and liquid again, before pouring it into a small glass globe hovering above a group of candles to simmer.

"Demon is a relative term, I guess." Yea, that's definitely how to tell her that the right side of my body still bleeds gold while the left, I've recently discovered, now bleeds black. A discovery I was beyond thankful Finn did not make. "No new creatures have popped out of the rocks planning to cause a problem. Don't worry about it."

"It smells vaguely familiar," she comments, pupils narrowing to slits like a cat as she watches the mixture begin to boil. I arch a brow, stunned to realize I'm not the only one withholding changes. That makes me feel a little bit better.

"That's because technically the Hounds, and us, are types of demon," I say, refocusing on my work. "Everything that lives down here is demonic, to some degree. The scents kind of blur after a while, especially since I have more than one creature's blood mixed together here. So, like I said, it's a relative term. And no, I'm not taking blood donations." I grin up at her, and she returns it.

"Aww you don't want mine? I mean it's red, but it still counts, right?"

"No," I say, forcing my voice to remain light and not panicky as I form an excuse. "You're half God, so despite being Lucifers kid, that half would win in this case. Hence, red blood." She sighs dramatically.

"And yours is gold, otherwise you'd be on a drip while you were working." I wince, making a mental note to lock my tourniquet and needles away somewhere more secretive than the top drawer of my library desk.

"Can you actually take over for a bit? I need to go find Akashi," I say, moving to stand. "It's simple enough. Mix an ounce and a half of powder with two ounces of blood and bring it to a boil. Then let it set in any of the iron tins behind you. Yes, you have to measure each one individually or it won't work." She snorted.

"Are you sure you're not just making it more tedious for me so that I'm here longer, and you get more private time with your wolf?" She arches a brow, a shit eating grin on her face.

I wonder how hard she would hit me if I told her that I tested the bullets on myself in order to get those measurements. My growing pile of secrets is threatening to break my bones, but I manage to smirk back at her.

"And if I said that was the case?"

"I'd say run before your brain catches up to your intentions." She nudges me aside and takes my seat.

"Just remember, one and—"

"One and a half powder, two blood. Now go, get, scram," she says with a wave over her shoulder.

The stone of the castle floor is cold under my bare feet as I walk down the hidden tunnels. Typically, I would use my magic to light the torches as I went, but my skin is glowing bright enough to light the passageway ahead of me. I had almost normalized that one, as it interfered with my daily life the least. Almost.

I emerged from a hidden doorway set in a bookshelf, the glow to my skin less apparent in the warm lights of my library. Lights I had not left on.

Akashi was standing behind my desk. All the drawers were open, their contents spread across the dark oak surface. There wasn't much I was trying to hide, but he had found all of it, including the tourniquet and syringe. His eyes were pulsing with restrained power, veins bulging in his neck as he fought to hold back whatever angry or scared outburst I could tell he was on the brink of having as he slowly raised his head to look at me.

"What have you been up to behind my back, Little Bird?" I tense. The nickname was once affectionate, but now it's seldom used.

"Akashi, you can be as mad as you want but let me explain first," I said, slowly sliding the bookcase behind me back into place. His eyes tracked the movement, wells of confusion and anger as he pieced together yet another secret I'd been keeping from him.

"You're sneaking through the walls, feasting on our brother, and sticking yourself with needles. It had better be one hell of an explanation."

Though I shouldn't feel it, a small wave of relief hits me. He didn't know about Vallen then, didn't get that far through my stuff to find my notes, or bully Kuma enough to make him spill.

"I sneak through the walls to avoid being bombarded with questions day in and day out. I'm avoiding everyone, not just you." I didn't sugarcoat it. "It's exhausting being in charge of all of this. And the passageways offer me moments of privacy."

"If it's so exhausting you could just order us to leave you alone. I know working as a team is a foreign concept to you." His words stung but I let it go, remaining calm.

"I will not rule as my father had." Some of the rage in his eyes ebbed at that and he dipped his head, relenting slightly.

"Which is worse, to you?" I ask, shifting to sit in one of the velvet armchairs. "Kuma or the syringe? Which do you need explained first?"

"The syringe." I was surprised. I thought he would be more bothered by Kuma.

"That one is painfully simple, actually," I said, averting my gaze. "We need bullets that kill Angels. My blood is an ingredient for that." I was dipping my toes in dangerous waters now, having just told Becca it was generic demon blood. If the two of them wound up discussing the topic… I didn't wanna think about that.

"And that's why you're drinking Kuma's blood. For energy," Akashi said, drawing his own conclusion and releasing a heavy breath. "Fuck, that makes sense. I'm sorry."

"*I'm* sorry," I said, pointing at myself. "I'm the one doing all this behind your back."

"Apologize to Kuma, not me," he muttered, flopping down in the desks chair and running his hands through his hair. I furrowed my eyebrows.

"What do you mean?" He leveled his gaze at me.

"You put him in a tough spot. Between his Alpha and his Master."

My breath hitches. I hadn't thought of that. By confiding in him and begging him to keep my secrets, that meant he was forced to withhold information from Akashi. All of this was so complicated, my web of lies beginning to tangle into threads sharp enough to cut.

"I will," I say, pinching the bridge of my nose. I hear the chair creak, followed by the few steps it takes him to cross the room to me. He sinks to the floor before me, arms sliding around the thick velvet of my skirt, red today, to hug my legs to his chest.

"You've been dressing prettily. Any particular reason?" He asks, voice softening, no longer angry.

"Hmm?" My mind is distracted, half paranoid about his hands rubbing down the backs of my calves and feeling my quivering tail.

"Luna would have actually needed to beat you into this," he says, fingers skimming to my ankles. "And even if she succeeded you would have found a knife to slice it off."

There was a sudden tear of fabric and then a short silence, before I realized he did exactly as he described with his claws. And with sudden freedom, my tail whipped out to curl around his wrist, yanking him closer to me.

CHAPTER 15

Both of us sat there, frozen for a moment. I could see the gears in Akashi's mind turning. See his eyes placing my hands, one clamped over my mouth in horror and the other fisted into my skirt, before his gaze fell to the floor. To my tail which coiled around his arm like a snake.

"Jesus Christ!" I hiss, finally breaking out of my mortified trance and yanking on the damn thing. With fumbling hands, I unravel it from his arm, before pushing up and stumbling a few feet away. "I-I'm sorry. I can't exactly control it."

"Why were you hiding it?" His question catches me off guard, enough for the gag I have on Vallen to slip.

Yes, why ARE you hiding it, Angel-born? Why do you suppress your own self as you suppress me. Shut up. *It's completely unnatural.* Shut up! *You should really let yourself relax. You know that sister of yours is right, I'm surprised*

*you don't leave a trail of diamonds
everywhere you–* SHUT UP!

Blessedly he fell silent, but that
didn't solve the present scenario of me
standing backed up against the desk,
devil tail whipping around me while
panting like I had just run ten miles.

"Raven." Akashi's voice is gentle as
he closes the distance, but his grip on my
wrist was firm as he repeats, "Why were
you hiding it?"

"I didn't want it to scare anybody,"
I admit, breathless. I hadn't been working
my ass off to gain the Hounds trust just
to flaunt in their face that I am in fact
still a Devil. Akashi's hand glides up to
my elbow, head tilting as he rakes his
gaze over me.

"And now the real answer."

"That is a real answer," I insist.

"You terrify them by existing," he
says bluntly, free hand tilting my face up
toward him. "Having a tail won't make or
break that fact. They have centuries of
trauma to heal, and patterns to unlearn.
Don't wear a dress for their benefit." He

154

leans forward, voice lowering as his nose knocks against mine. "So, what's the real answer?"

His hand skims down my neck, down my side, before coming to a halt at my hip. I feel his fingers curl, bunching the fabric, lifting it a few inches.

"Akashi," I warn. Feeling my cheeks heat I quickly turn my face away.

"I told you I never wanted you to hold yourself back with me, didn't I?" His breath was hot on my neck. "So why are you trying so hard to hide from me, mate?"

Cool air passes over my legs as he continued to slowly work the skirt up my legs. I was shaking now, with the effort not to lash out, with the effort not to run. At the first touch of his fingers my hips bucked of their own accord. He chuckled low in my ear, pressing a single open-mouthed kiss just below my jaw.

"I can make this torturous for you, or you could just be honest with me." There was another short rip, and I felt my panties fall to the floor seconds before his finger lazily slides between my slick folds, circles my entrance, and withdraws. I feel all his muscles tense as he groans against my skin. "You're dripping."

"You won't like my honesty," I managed to choke out, keeping my face turned away from him. "You'll overrule it. You won't understand."

"Try me." His finger stalled atop my clit, making me growl out with frustration.

"It's a Devil tail." My voice cracks and I hate that it does. I hate that I'm shaking from just a few touches. "I don't want anyone to look at me and think of him, especially not you." A moan slips from me involuntarily as his finger plunges into me, a delicious, slow pumping reward for my honesty that has me rolling my hips in earnest.

"Little Bird, don't get so worked up just yet. This is an important conversation we're having." His finger disappears and I shake harder in frustration. He grins, lifting me to sit on the edge of the desk, claws appearing in place of fingers. I can only watch as he tears a slit up the center of my skirt, tossing it open and baring me to him.

"You might be able to ignore that I've changed, but I can't." I have no idea how I'm still able to breath, let alone argue. He just shrugs, before dropping to his knees before me. My breath catches in my throat as he lifts each of my legs over his shoulders, placing gentle kisses on the inside of my thigh.

"Can't ignore what I'm not aware of now, can I?" My tail has way too much range in this position, and I can feel when it caresses the hard planes of his abs and chest through his shirt. He groans again. "If you had any control over that thing, I'd ask you to rub it against me lower."

Before I can reply his mouth is on me, slow and hot, tongue lapping me in leisure. My own body reacts the opposite. I'm a wildfire sparked to life, a firework seconds before it burst, a writhing tangling mess of want and can't do anything but lay there and take what he's giving.

Just before I tip over the edge he pulls back again. I curse, but he's coming for me now. His hands go to his belt, and my tail follows the movement eagerly. As soon as he's free, the triangular tip drags along the bottom of his length, urging him towards me. He all but moans into my mouth as he drives home, hips colliding with mine and keeping me pinned to the desk as he buries into me again and again.

I cry out, shattering almost instantly as the effects of his teasing catch up in one big burst of honey-edged pleasure. I throw my legs around his hips, sinching him closer, hooking my arms around his neck. Thornless vines are wrapping around us loosely, growing from the desk beneath us. I arch my back, willing the growth under me to hold me up, craving a deeper angle.

Akashi pauses, watching me squirm, resisting the pull of my legs, my silent pleas for him to keep going. Wordlessly he presses back on my thighs, the intensity in his eyes being the only thing keeping me from fighting him as he slowly turns me over.

On shaking legs I'm bent over the desk, and he makes quick work of removing the torn dress from me completely. I'm panting. I'm dizzy. I can't distinguish if it's anxiety or anticipation I feel as his palm closes around the base of my tail, giving it a gentle tug.

"Let's give you a positive experience to associate with this piece of you." As he says it, my tail once again curls around his arm, tugging him forward as he pulls me back to sink onto his length.

I draw in a sharp gasp. The fit is so snug, so perfect I actually whine when he withdraws. That earns me another, quicker thrust forward and I feel like I'm melting from the inside out.

"Akashi, please," I finally whimper, my face burning. He releases a rough laugh.

"Are you begging me, Little Bird?" He's trying to draw this out even longer, but I can hear the edge of desperation in his voice now too. I rock my hips back and feel his whole body go rigid, hear the air rush from his lungs, so I do it again, a third time, and then his hands slam down on my hips holding me still.

"Do that one more time and I'm gonna end up spilling inside you in the next two seconds."

"You're the one edging me," I pant, hands curling into fists. "After all the bickering, the least you can do is ruin me."

"You want me to ruin you?" The words drip with praise as he tugs me impossibly closer, seating himself at a deeper angle. "Baby, I'll worship you until you break."

We crash together like storm and sea, soaking salt and thrumming power. The desk becomes ruined, completely overgrown in my ecstasy, and eventually we're in the bed. All darkness and touch and magic and need, twisting together under the galaxies bursting to life in my room as we come undone again and again.

I'm drunk on sensation and high on power, my reality reduced to this bed and my mate and this feeling. Those thoughts are still bewitching me as we finally curl against one another, completely spent.

I've come to recognize a sense of wholeness that I only feel in his presence, and I can already feel the ache of loss in my chest returning. It's as if my soul is in mourning, knowing that come tomorrow the distance between us will return until I can find a way to keep him safe.

From me.

CHAPTER 16

It was an effort not to scream when I woke up. The Ashen Hound was seated at the foot of my bed, looking every bit bored as I scrambled to cover myself and Akashi with the blankets.

"What the fuck?!" I hissed, tail whipping angrily.

"Is that how you greet all your guests?" He asked, huffing a breath. In the half-light of my bedroom, he appeared to flicker slightly, as if he weren't completely here.

"Who are you?" I growled. I didn't repeat my mistake from last time and summon another shadow dagger. Instead, I withdrew my sword, once my mother's. The earring cuffs I wore doubled as weapon and shield, and now the long golden point, etched with silver and bleeding obsidian, was poised against the Hounds throat. If a Hound could, he grinned.

"I'm. Yours."

The urge to stab him multiplied.

"That's not what she asked." I broke into a cold sweat then, refusing to glance down at Akashi as he stirred, and slowly pushed up to his elbows. I could feel his tension threading through the bond on my chest as he took in the Hound before us.

"But it's a true answer, nonetheless." The Hound bared its teeth. "In her soul she knows what I am. Should she finally cease suppressing me, we could fight together. We would *win* together."

At that Akashi snarled, a menacing sound which promised a torturous death. It should have made me recoil, but instead I just leaned back into him.

"Stop speaking in riddles." I drag the flat of my blade slowly down across its shoulder. "Either tell me who you are, and what you want, or disappear exactly as you have before. Prove that what I saw was real, and that I'm not going as insane as I think I am."

"You see me can you not?" The Hound countered, "You feel me, too. You know I am just as real as you. How I come and how I go does not change that aspect."

"You dodged the questions," Akashi growled. I could feel him restraining himself behind me, waiting for my permission to strike. More so, I felt his eyes searing into the back of my head, demanding how I knew this Hound and for how long.

"My name," the Hound said, standing despite me turning the edge of the blade against his jugular, "is Vallen. That should be enough for you to figure out the rest on your own."

I jerked my sword, but was too slow. Just like last time, the Ashen Hound disappeared on the spot, not even a flicker of magic hanging in his wake.

I was breathing hard, the panic I'd been burying for the past few months all rushing to the surface. Vallen!? That was impossible, a coincidence only. The voice in my head was something I named, not something that was real. Well, at least not more real than the fire I now possessed but refused to use.

Akashi rose from the bed, and a new ripple of fear went through me. He crossed the room, putting as much space between the two of us as possible before sliding to sit on the floor, back braced against the wall. He was silent for what seemed like years, which only gave my screaming mind more time to turn on me. By the time he spoke, I felt like I was going to faint.

"So, that's the guy vying for my position, is it?" His voice was quiet, weak.

"What are you talking about?" I purposely never mentioned Vallen in front of Akashi. I didn't want him to panic about my new powers. I didn't want him hovering. I didn't want him involved as I unraveled faster and faster.

"At the club. The night Uriel showed up," he muttered.

My mind raced through the nights events. The arrow flying through the air, ricocheting off my wing instead of piercing it. The feel of my bodysuit being torn beneath Akashi's touch. Silas pulling my bloody drinks away from me. Silas' face when he noticed Akashi leaning over my shoulder, as I complained about his and Vallen's behavior and–

I dropped my sword, stunned. Akashi leaned his head back against the wall, shutting his eyes against the sight of me.

"I can understand why you're drinking Kuma's blood. Plus, it's making him feel useful, finally being able to be directly involved. I can even understand your secret rendezvouses with Silas– don't think I didn't know. After Finn and Anzen, he and I have grown pretty close too. After all, he's the one who took me to the club that night to find you. But another Hound... that I didn't see coming."

"Akashi it's not what you think. I'm not–"

"You'll always have your secrets," he cut me off, eyes opening with a fresh spark of anger. "But I didn't expect you to have lies, too."

"I'm not the only one with secrets and lies," I said, my anger finally awakening to shield me from the pain coursing through me. "I may be your mate, but you used my naivety against me. You knew if I understood what imprinting was, I wouldn't have let you."

Akashi jolted as if I shot him. We stared at each other in silence, our pain and anger ebbing and flowing in the space around us. Finally, face grim, he stood.

"No, I guess you wouldn't have."

I've made a lot of mistakes in my life. But none quite as stupid as this one.

I've sparred with my brothers till we were bloody pulps. Goaded others into fistfights just so I would not be blamed for releasing my rage. I've snuck out, stolen cars and magazines, and argued with Luna over trivial things.

I've pursued men I shouldn't want. Letting them touch me and pretending I was still clean after, as though I did not kiss the blood of my brother's murderer off my fingertips.

I've lied for decades. About who I was. About what I could do. About what I couldn't do as well.

I've tried to kill innocent people.

I've let guilty people live.

I've left my mate to wake alone, again. In the past he was probably confused, and scared. This time I feared he wouldn't care.

As I slipped through the shadows of my castle, I ignored the pleading voice in my head. Ignored its wailing to return to him, that if he was still sleeping beside me, we would make it. Because the other voice, the one who has never been kind, said he was only there because he had nowhere else to go. After his choices, he had to save face. He couldn't share the bed of another female and get anything out of it, so sleeping with me was better than sleeping alone.

I walked through my halls naked at first, completely uncaring. The cords on my control didn't snap, they just ceased to exist. Shadows clung to me as I walked, manipulating themselves to cover me in comfortable black leathers, and glossy plated armor.

There was a gap in my pants for my tail to come through. My top was cut low in the back, so when my wings appeared they could do so with ease. And though I didn't dwell on it, I could feel the cool kiss of scales down the length of my spine. The only weapons I carried were my sword and shield. Mine. The sword had already been changed from what Mary wielded, and my shield was never something I needed for myself but kept with my always. Plus one more item, less fanciful.

I sent away each Hound I came across with the order to forget they saw me. So, when Uriel took a seat next to me at the bar, bass thumping around us, I was completely on my own.

"Welcome back," I said, not sparing the Angel a glance or even a moment to reply before pressing the handgun into his ribs. "I believe you said something about reuniting me with my mother."

CHAPTER 17

"Tell me you're not seriously considering using that party trick to pry answers from me?" Uriel had a bemused smile on his face, his gaze flicking to the gun for only a second before holding mine.

"Consider it a friendly test of my own," I said, a vicious smirk gracing my lips. Then I squeezed the trigger. With the combination of alcohol and music thumping in the club, it wasn't a shock when barely anyone noticed.

Uriel doubled over, his fist coming down on the bar so hard the marble cracked. I made a show of patting his back, throwing my head back and laughing as if he simply drank something too hard to handle.

"Fuck," I sucked a gulp of air in between clenched teeth, "that felt so much better than I was expecting."

"Devil," Uriel ground out from between grit teeth.

"Aww." I met his eyes, mocking a pout. "Don't say that about your niece. It's only rubber, you'll live just fine. But I do have a full clip of live rounds to experiment with, if you think of playing a game with me." I smiled, and his eyes snagged on my fangs.

"You wouldn't..." he started, but trailed off, gaze darting between my bared teeth and the gun still pressed to his side, trying to decide which of the two would be worse.

"Tsk tsk Uncle, I knew the church had some dirty secrets, but I would have never expected a real Angel to consider something like that." Uriel flushed straight to scarlet, and I turned up my nose. "You'd probably taste rotten anyways."

"You belong to your father," he seethed, "the Devil. And you want to carry out his desires." I arch a brow.

"Throwing bible verses at me now? That's boring." I toss my hair over my shoulder, the long tresses having been set in a million little braids at some point. Probably by the pixies.

"Here's one for you though," I eased back a little, the barrel sliding up to his armpit. "It's from the book of Zephaniah, I believe:

> *"They will do no wrong; they will tell no lies. A deceitful tongue will not be found in their mouths."*

I pause, and grin. "Perhaps I really should pluck out your lying tongue. Bartender, pass me a knife," I cooed.

"I have not lied about your mother. Mary lives," Uriel insists. The look on his face is deadly serious so I sat back, giving him a full once over for the first time.

All Angels are similar looking in the face, though unlike Gabriel, he has forsaken his robes today. His outfit of choice consists of jeans, a muscle tee and a loose-fitting sports jacket. Black vans are on his feet, quite similar to a pair I have in my own closet. His straight black hair is cropped short, and brown eyes study me intensely from beneath a silver mask he didn't bother with last time.

"I didn't insinuate you lied about my mother," I finally respond and motion for Jefferson, the bartender, to come over. "Just to the entire population of humanity who you seem hell-bent on converting to Christianity, that's all."

"And how exactly did we lie to them?" He asks, frowning as two steaming cups of glittering blue liquid are placed in front of us.

"By not practicing as you preach," I say, taking my cup and raising it to my lips with a smile. "Relax, poison isn't my style. It's Baby's Breath, fit for a Cherub," I say, pressing a hand over my heart before downing my drink in one go. Reluctantly, Uriel raises his glass to his lips, taking a small sip before placing it back down in front of us.

"Did you seriously just invite me here to shoot me and then drink?" Uriel asks. and I shrug.

"Don't wars have halftimes?"

"No, they do not," he says, voice clipped. I met his eyes again, and this time they're a tad blurry. I grin, propping my chin in my hand.

"Tell me Uncle, am I pretty?"

"You're exquisite." A horrified expression passes over his features.

"How about, am I valuable?" I smile at him sweetly.

"Even more so than beautiful," he says, his voice shaking slightly as he speaks.

He begins to raise his hands to his mouth, meaning to muffle his future words, but vines sprout from the crack he left in the counter. They tangle his wrists together, cinching tightly up his forearms.

"Babys Breath," I whisper in his face, "is a type of truth serum. Whoever drinks it can do nothing but uncontrollably blubber the truth until it's out of their system." I chuckle. "Now, before you think of it, all I drank was water. So, unless you're willing to bite off your own tongue, which I highly doubt after seeing your reaction to just a rubber bullet, we're going to have a very overdue, honest talk."

"You are all things hellish, all things cursed–"

"Do you want me to return Finnegan to you?" I cut him off, arching a brow.

"The vampire failed us not once but twice. We would soon rather see him reduced to ash." Ouch. He yanks at his bonds, but a snap of my fingers has him hissing as thorns of flame dig into his skin. I blink, shocked, but forge ahead.

"And now for the important questions." I slid to perch myself in his lap just to make him even more uncomfortable. Then I steel myself, voice going flat and expression blank before I ask, "Question number one: where's Mary?"

"The prison above the Silver City." I furrow my brows.

"What do you mean a prison?"

"After your father nearly killed her, she was only graced with a life sentence because you were separated from that Hellcat and did not fall into Lucifers hands." His gaze is full of so much hate as he speaks, it's hard to not look away.

"I saw her body in a pool of golden blood. I heard her heartbeat stop," I said, willing my voice to ice over the way my sisters could. "Mary was dead long before that church burned."

"But did you see her disappear as you saw Lucifer?" Uriel barked a laugh, "Mary lives, Raven. And she wears onyx chains, because of you."

"You must truly believe that," I say, standing from his lap, "otherwise, you wouldn't be able to say it right now. Let's get one thing straight though."

I snap my fingers again and his sports coat dissolves, along with his shirt underneath it. I step behind him, and with a brush of my fingers my sword is in my hand. As I angle the point to be level with a wing slit in Uriel's back, a look of pure panic crosses his face. He struggles against his bonds with renewed vigor as he realizes what I mean to do.

"I was a child, Uncle." My taunts and teases are gone, replaced by a cold emptiness which I have buried down for far too long. I poise my blade, catching his eyes as I finish, "And I don't remember my hands being the ones to chain hers."

Not one person flinches when he screams, his back bowing in agony. Golden blood stains the floor as I plunge my sword in deep, and twist into whatever magical pocket of space holds our wings. When I pull it out, my blade is covered with delicate white feathers ripped from their perches.

Uriel has six wing slits, and I give each the same destructive treatment. When I'm done, and he is thoroughly sobbing against the bar, I sit beside him again and pluck the torn feathers off my blade.

"Question two," I say, accepting the damp rag Jefferson extends my way to wipe off my sword. "What can you tell me about the scrolls you have in your library? Any containing information on forbidden and forgotten magic?"

"Our library vanished a fortnight after our last battle." Uriel's voice was weak and wet with pain. I paused, fist closing tightly around the rag which was the only thing keeping me from cutting myself.

"What do you mean your library vanished?" I growled. Was the Baby's Breath out of his system already?

"Gabriel locked himself in." Uriel gasps for a breath, and I begin thinking he might actually puke. "He took no food, no water or rest. He emerged a fortnight after our battle, claiming the library had vanished. All that was left in its place was a single black feather. A feather like yours!" Those last two words came out in a snarl.

Well, that was interesting. I finished cleaning my blade before securing it back to my earlobe.

"Jefferson."

"Yes, my lady?" He materializes again in an instant, and momentarily I feel sick. I have to remind myself he's not a Hound, so not bound to my order. He's helping me of his own will, in the small ways that he could. I allow him to take the bloodied rag from me, before pressing a pouch of coins into his hands as well with an adamant squeeze.

"See to it that he's fed, and that the guests don't kill him. If he can ever fly again, let him leave."

"Yes, my lady," Jefferson repeats, bowing at the waist.

"How is everyone here just letting this happen?" Uriel wheezes, frantic eyes now searching the room for an ally. I sigh, kind of feeling bad for the guy, and hoping I didn't ask questions like that back when I was ignorant.

"In summary," I say, gripping his chin, "you wanted me to be a chess piece in this war, and now I am. My sister killed me so I may rise, becoming a full-fledged Angel. Afterwards, I killed my father, and took his place on the throne of Hell." My grip on his chin tightens and I yank him closer, forcing him to look me in the eye.

"I am the Devil, this is my territory, and these are my people. So unless you too are a Light Walker, I'm

fairly confident you'll find yourself stuck
here for an extended stay."

I dropped his chin and turned for
the exit. The music below still raged on,
the party goers either oblivious or
uncaring toward what just took place.

"It is reckless to let me live!" Uriel
hurls the threat after me. I turn, unable
to keep the smug smile off my lips.

"It is," I agree. "But I know of a
certain orphan Goddess who deserves the
pleasure of killing you herself."

CHAPTER 18

Rebecca knew better than most what her sister looked like when she schemed. Her rage was easier to provoke. Her words, more formal. Her attention, more easily distracted.

That's why she was less surprised than the others when Raven made her move. The thing that shocked her though, was not being taken along.

An emergency meeting was called midday, as no one had seen her since the night prior and currently no one could catch her scent. Silas revealed the entrance to a network of hidden passageways running through the walls of the castle, but after spending the afternoon searching there was still no sign of the Queen.

Every Hound was called to the dining hall, the only space large enough to house the entire army and adolescents at once. Even the Night Howlers were demanded to join, and surprisingly

Jesibelle showed up with a large number of her ladies.

It was at this meeting where Akashi finally snapped, quite literally. His jaws barely missed Rebeccas' shoulder, moving at the last second. It took all of her self-control not to counterstrike, but instinctively she still transformed into the fierce Hellcat that had most of the other Hounds instantly backing away.

"Where the fuck is she?" Akashi all but roared, lunging for her again.

"I've been searching for her all day." Rebecca dodged his next bite, but not his claws. She hissed as a line of her fur was torn open, blood dripping to the stone floor.

"Every time she's disappeared it's been because of you," he growled, whipping around to come at her again. "When she was abducted, she wound up living with you. When you were abducted, she left us to go get you. Then the two of you went rogue and charged down here with a stupid ass plan to—"

"To what?!" Rebecca yelled, finally losing her patience and unsheathing her silver claws. She swiped, catching him in the rump as he twisted away at the last second.

"You fucking *killed* her!" Other than the soft drips of their blood hitting the floor, the room was deathly silent.

"Yes," Rebecca said, the Hellcat shrinking back into her human form. Naked and bleeding, she crossed the room to Akashi unafraid, walking straight up to his bared teeth.

"I slit my sister's throat. And if I had to, I would do it again if I knew she would come back." Akashi bit the air in front of her, the clack of his jaws louder than some of the guns they had been shooting. Rebecca didn't flinch.

"That's enough, now." Luna's voice pierced the air and the white Hound weaved her way out of the crowd. "This quarrel will not find her now. Akashi, I suggest you cast your spell, and we track your mate."

"It didn't work." Blood roared in Rebecca's ears. She was distantly aware of Silas appearing beside her, of his long dress coat being wrapped around her shoulders.

"What?" Luna asked, her normally dark eyes flashing blue. "You have searched her soul successfully before. You should be able to do it again."

"Yea, well now she's blocking me. And I'd bet she knows something about it." Akashi's eyes narrowed on Rebecca again.

Slowly, Rebecca turned away from him, ignoring the pressure of a hundred stares. She didn't want to think of the night before their raid on Hell. She only wanted to remember the laughing, the drinking, the dancing.

Not the flash of Ravens dagger as she showed her where to cut, how to twist the blade so that both edges would sever their own respective artery. Not the desperate type of glee flickering in her sister's eyes as she described the prophecy Mary had her memorize as a child.

"I still don't have all my memories." Rebecca's voice was quieter than normal, absent of its usual iciness. "My brain was wiped. Twice. I left enough clues in my art, and have been filled in a lot by Silas and my sister, but that's different than actually knowing."

She stepped away from Silas, sinking onto the closest bench at one of the long cedar tables. For the first time to the Hounds, she appeared small and afraid. Enough so that Akashi controlled his rage and kept his mouth shut.

"Raven has always starved for power and control. The first time Mary gave her that dagger, she cut herself with it. The silver side only burned her, and the obsidian made her bleed even if she applied no pressure. I think it was then that she realized the bigger picture. What her parents were, and how she was different."

"She was consumed with avenging her mother by killing Lucifer since I've met her," Luna said, beginning to pace. "But I don't see what that childish obsession has to do with why her mate can't track her now."

"Because she is one body, cleaved in two," Rebecca mumbled. "Most of the powers she's been using up to this point were angelic, but frankly, many of them are mixed even if she doesn't realize it. For example, her vines are growth, but her thorns are destruction. And then there's the fire she already possessed before falling into that lake." She took a breath, her voice cracking on her next words.

"When I… did what I did, I completed the shift her body was going through. She had always acknowledged and utilized the half of her which was angelic, so she was able to rise. That half of her soul Reformed. That half is what Akashi's tracked before. Not the demonic pieces, that even though were slipping through since the beginning, she's denied and suppressed up till now."

"I don't understand," Luna said. She sounded weary, absent-mindedly placing herself between Rebecca and her son as if trying to shield him from her next words.

"Her angelic half is not in command of her right now. It's been muted, in a way. Take me for example." Rebecca stood and held her palms upward. Small balls of light began to form, swelling and pulsing like baseball sized suns.

"My entire life I believed myself a daughter of a demon and magic, and that was all I could wield. After learning of my heritage, new magic of mine surfaced and I've been experiencing some... changes." A look of discomfort passed over her features as she closed her fists, extinguishing the lights.

"Ravens tail hasn't been appearing for show, or from stress. Her whole life she believed herself righteous, on the path of killing the evilest thing in her mind: our father. But while on that path she dabbled... I encouraged her to dabble in his power. And now, well, the demonic half of her soul has fully awakened. And it seems she doesn't trust a single one of us with it."

Akashi staggered, sitting with a heavy thump. Luna was standing stock still, not a single piece of fur shifting.

"So, what does this mean?" Aengus stepped forward. The man, usually appearing formidable, seemed drained. His fighting leathers were rumpled from their earlier search, fire bright hair torn from its braid in several places.

Rebecca tasted acid on her tongue. She wanted to scream. Pound the table. Find her sister and drag her back here by her hair, kicking and screaming if she must.

"From what I understand, she was born with the ability to have either power at full force, but she's been using both. They're so at odds, and there's so many of them… they're likely too overwhelming to hold at once. That's what happened to Lucifer, he was both for a very short time. And he only had a fraction of what she does before it drove him to this," she said, angrily sweeping her arm at the room, the castle, the pit of sand and fog they lived in. "I think my sister is convinced that unlike our father, she's strong enough to wield it all."

There was a sudden commotion at the far end of the room. Jesibelle had collapsed, head in her hands, a thick mist swirling around her in a funnel of light.

"Jesibelle?" Luna stepped towards her sister, but the Night Howler leader snarled in her direction, her eyes now glowing as bright as Ravens purple flames. She staggered to her feet, hands outstretched.

"Someone give me a paper and pen, quickly!"

There was some scuffling, but in a few moments Jesibelle had what she requested. Stumbling to seat herself beside Rebecca, she began scribbling across the pages a mix of images and phrases which she passed to her in quick succession. Jesibelles hands slowed as the mist began to fade, finally coming to a halt when her eyes were once again blue as the sky.

Kuma and Hikari had pushed forward to peer over Rebeccas shoulders at the pages. Silas, seated beside her, was studying them just as intensely. The pad of Luna's paw steps came up behind them, the Hound sucking in a heavy breath as her eyes landed on a drawing at the top of the pile.

"How did she get that?" Whispered Aengus, his voice a mix of awe and fear. He reached over Jesibelles shoulder, picking the image up.

The woman in the photo was covered in scales, and had horns protruding from her short cut hair, but it was clearly Raven. She was flying, her wings a blur behind her back, power exploding from her in all directions, but that's not what drew the Hounds focus. Raised over her head she held a sword of rippling flames, her veins glowing with its power.

"What is that?" Rebecca asked, not recognizing her own voice.

"It's the Flaming Sword of Eden." Luna's voice trembled. "It's been missing since Lucifer fell. Some say he stole it. Others say Gabriel lost it. Whatever truth, that sword played a major role in their rivalry, and sparked many of the battles in this war."

"I'm more concerned about this one," Hikari muttered. Jesibelle held her breath as he reached past her, lifting a paper with a few scrawled lines of text on it.

I am the Devil.

This is my territory.

These are my people.

Rebecca's skin crawled from the first sentence. A rush of cold went through her as she tore her gaze away from the papers on the table. If her sister was in fact turning, she was the one to blame.

"These are my people..." Silas mumbled, before suddenly realeasing a laugh. He stood from the table at a speed only a vampire was capable of, and tossed an arm around Akashi's shoulders.

"I know where she went again."

CHAPTER 19

Akashi didn't know what to expect as he and twenty of his Hounds marched up the steps of the underground nightclub in Atlantis. The last time he was here, Raven was a drunken mess, and that was his only impression of the place. As much as he wanted to find her, part of him was praying she wouldn't be here.

Rebecca, despite his clear aggravation with her, walked directly beside him. If he sped up so did she. If he fell back, she adjusted her pace to tiptoe along beside him. She didn't look at him or speak, but her message was clear. She wasn't going anywhere, and he didn't scare her. She was more like Raven in that aspect than she knew.

Each Hound wore an identical black, cotton mask, while Silas and Rebecca wore a matching pair of silver ones. After everyone was permitted entry without a hitch, the pair disappeared down the staircase. Akashi had ordered his men to search the crowd, his brothers leading them down the spiral stairs. He didn't trust his reaction if he found her among the writhing bodies, so decided to stay at the bar level for now. Curiosity, if not desperation, had him glancing over the railing as he waited.

Out of all the things he was bracing himself for, a shirtless Angel tied to a crudely cut dartboard was not one of them. The Angel looked utterly helpless, and completely wasted. The rope holding him to the board was made of average fiber, but he did nothing to fight his bonds.

Silas alone materialized at the top of the stairs again, hopefully a positive sign since a disoriented Raven was not in tow. He met Akashi's eyes briefly before weaving through the crowd making a beeline for the barkeep at the far end of the floor. Akashi followed hot on his heels.

"Jefferson," Silas called, raising an arm in greeting. The barkeep turned with a smile.

"Master Hagan, it's been a while."
The two clasped hands, Akashi looking on
impatiently.

"I'm afraid I have to cut right to
the chase my friend," Silas said, taking a
seat on one of the highchairs. Akashi
frowned, but sat beside him anyways, not
risking missing a word in the cramped
space with techno music blasting in his
ears.

"Where is our lovely Queen?
Obviously, she dropped off quite the prize
for you." Silas bobbed his chin in the
Angels direction.

"Ah, she left a few hours ago, a
storm brewing in her wake. I'm not sure
what they talked about, but Uriel's wings
weren't exactly left in 'flying condition'."

Akashi bristled, recognizing the
name. He turned to look at the Angel,
Uriel, who had attacked them here the
last time Raven had ventured over the
veil. A golden sheen was on his skin, and
he seemed to be talking to himself. What
in the world was she thinking, meeting
him here alone?

"Do you think he would tell us
where she was headed if we asked?"
Kuma spoke over Akashi's shoulder. He
hadn't even noticed his brother approach,
too preoccupied imaging every way he
would gut Uriel if he hurt her.

"Boys full of Babys Breath,"
Jefferson said, a wicked smile gracing his
lips. "He'd tell you all you like."

"Keep Rebecca away from him."
Akashi turned to Silas, "That's the one
who killed Bastet, right?"

Silas clenched his jaw, nodding
stiffly in agreement. With a quick
farewell to Jefferson, he melted back into
the crowd to find her.

Akashi met Kumas eye, motioning
for him to follow the vampire. Rebecca
had held back with him earlier, and
everyone knew it. It would take more
than Silas to stop her if she decided to lay
Uriel in an early grave.

He slid off his chair, focused on
measuring his breaths as he descended
the stairs and approached the dartboard.
The lesser fey crammed around it were

inebriated, slurring their words, and aimlessly tossing an assortment of darts and fruits toward Uriel. A pair of purple skinned faeries noticed Akashi's approach, chattering something to their friends before abandoning their drinks and flying away over the crowd.

Akashi placed his palm against the dartboard beside Uriel's head, claws digging in. He took note of the many bites and bruises on the male's skin, of the stack of empty glasses and syringes at his feet. Full of Babys Breath indeed. Uriel blinked rapidly as he registered the new company, before grinning up at him.

"My, my, your mate is as supple as she is vicious." He slurred his words, voice thick with drink and hate.

"I can only wish I was here to see how your conversation went." Akashi smirked, but didn't let himself be distracted from the matter at hand. "So, tell me about your wings. What'd she do?"

"She pierced the rift is what she did." Uriel's eyes bugged out of his head, as if in pain, and he lurched forwards. Akashi side stepped as the male heaved up the contents of his stomach, mostly liquid, and got a good look at his back.

He was familiar enough with Raven's wing slits to know that they were very sensitive. Even the lightest touch would draw a large reaction. Uriel's had been shredded, the lowest two connecting in a sickening smile on his lower back. Paths of blood, both old and fresh, were dripping down his spin and hips.

"How long is that gonna take to heal?" Akashi's voice came out hoarse and he quickly averted his gaze.

"Months at minimum. A year if it's not properly treated. Never if it's not treated at all. The obsidian in her blade is poisonous to us." Then Uriel clamped his mouth shut, hard enough that his teeth clacked. Narrowing his eyes, Akashi yanked him back upright.

"Poisonous how? Describe exactly what it does," he demands.

"The obsidian taints our pure blood, slowly turning our souls black. We either die, or become demons." Akashi arched a brow. Now that was information he would definitely tuck away for later.

"She's turning, you know?" Drool hung off the Angels lower lip. "You should have seen her. Black eyes, black hair. She's turning into a Devil."

"She was always a Devil," Akashi said, voice low. "She just never made the world deal with it until now." Uriel openly gaped at him, before releasing a rough laugh.

"What did she ask you when she was here?" Akashi pressed his claws to the Angels throat, running out of patience.

"She asked about her mother." Despite Akashi's grip, Uriel laughed, the sound hallow. "And forbidden magic. She wanted scrolls."

"Her mother?" Akashi yanked Uriel forward so hard the dartboard snapped off the wall. "I swear if you sent her on some wild goose chase for Mary when we both know she's dead—"

"Ugh you *children* don't listen nearly as much as you speak," Uriel interrupts, eyes rolling. "Mary lives, though I'm sure by now she would have preferred death."

Akashi went slack, not knowing what to say. If Mary was alive, then why hadn't she come for her daughter in all these years? Obviously, Raven had gotten the answer and headed down that road, so now he only needed to catch up with her.

"You said something about scrolls?" He forced out, not wanting to leave any stone unturned.

"She was blubbering things about lost and hidden magic. She wanted access to our library, but alas, it was stolen, so that's a barren voyage." Uriel began humming lightly, as if the racket around them was a lullaby.

Akashi dropped his grip on him, turning to search for his brothers in the crowd. Hikari was a few feet away, dancing against a female gargoyle but his focus was wholly on this exchange. Akashi motioned him over.

"Has Raven mentioned anything to you about forgotten magic recently?" He asked, raising his voice over the now roaring bass.

"After keeping the bombshell of my *Mother* a secret, Raven hasn't spoken to me much at all recently." Akashi hardened his gaze and Hikari scoffed. "If it's not abundantly clear, I'm on her side. But I'm allowed to be pissed at my little sister for being a jackass."

"You can be pissed at her later. For now, go find Kuma." Hikari muttered something about the mating bond making him go soft, but turned to find their brother without argument.

In the meantime, Uriel's head had lulled to the side, crude lyrics leaving his mouth matching that of the song. In another lifetime, Akashi would have videotaped that for a laugh later. For now, he just unbound the thin rope holding the Angel, not bothering to be gentle with him as he dragged his weakened body to a nearby sofa and dumped him on it.

"She thinks Vallen is a forgotten magic," Kuma announced upon arrival. Shocked, Akashi whirled on him.

"Vallen? The Hound?" Kuma gave him a screwy look.

"No. The Hellfire she absorbed. Apparently, the damn thing is sentient and has been nonstop yapping in her head."

Akashi's mind was spinning as he thought back to the previous morning. The Hound at the end of their bed seemed to flicker, as if he wasn't really here nor there. It addressed Raven with familiarity, and she shot back with a fearful sense of annoyance that Akashi had at first thought was embarrassment. Or betrayal.

It's not what you think, she'd said. He cursed, turning back to Uriel who was staring at his wrists as if he expected something to grow out of them.

"What do you know about Hellfire?" He demanded, kicking the Angels foot to get him to pay attention.

"Hellfire," Uriel snickered. "Lucifer took the fire with him. Then locked it away out of fear of losing it. And then couldn't use it himself. It hasn't been wielded in centuries."

"And when it can be wielded what does it do?"

"Anything." Uriel smiled, a look of wonder in his eyes. "It becomes what its bearer wishes it to be. Gabriel had brandished it as the Sword of Eden, before our brother stole it."

Whatever its bearer wishes it to be. Akashi thought back to the sword in Jesibelles drawing, of Ravens affinity for wielding fire.

Yesterday morning, she seemed to despise Vallen. Was she unaware of what he was? Or was her awareness what made her revolt against him so thoroughly? Based on that picture, it seemed he would win her over in the near future. Akashi didn't know if that was good or bad.

He turned on his heel, intending to go find Silas and inquire if he also knew about Vallen, but came up short. Rebecca was standing at the edge of the crowd, staring at Uriel with a calculated threat in her cat-like eyes. He had completely forgotten he asked Kuma to stay with her, and it seems his diligent brother brought her along with him.

Silas was a shadow behind her, making no move to interfere as she stepped around Akashi with purpose. She cupped Uriel's chin, claws extending from her fingers as she pulled the Angels gaze to hers.

"Do you know who I am?" She asked, so low they could barely hear her over the music.

"Spawn of Bastet," Uriel said, a cold glee in his eyes. "Her only spawn. I saw to that, kitten."

Rebecca tilted her head back and laughed. The sound ricocheted in Akashi's ears like shattering glass, cold and cruel. She did not look at anyone as she said,

"Bring him."

CHAPTER 20

Rebecca couldn't stop the sob that tore through her when they reached the dungeon. The bars of Finns cage were warped, still melting from the flames clinging to the walls, burning out. Or just melting because her sister wanted them to.

Clearly, there had been a struggle. Tendrils of nightshade and stinging nettle hung from the ceiling, the green stems souring to a grey as they reached the floor. The bed was overturned, the cream sheets tainted red. Gold stained the walls and floor, dripping to gather in small puddles. And then there was black, like the blood Raven had been using to make those bullets.

"Be careful not to touch the thorns," someone said, maybe Hikari, maybe her.

The vibrant orange thorns blossoming from the growth in the cell were over a foot long and sharp like a needle. Rebecca didn't want to find out what their poison did.

Silas stood in the center of the cell, a statue. She could hear his heartbeat ticking, such a rare and terrifying thing. In his fist he clenched a lock of Finns golden hair.

That's all that remained of the vampire who had once been in this cell.

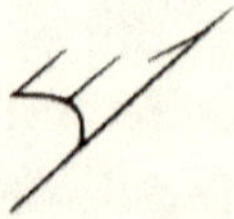

It had been easier to get Finn out of the dungeon than anticipated. When I crossed back through the veil to Hell, I was shocked to find it so empty.

The majority of my guards had left the castle, the remaining Hounds tucked somewhere deep within the walls, so the place was all but defenseless. I was pissed, but I guessed my disappearance was the cause. The scents of my family were still fading, proof they had followed me as soon as they realized I was gone.

A few Betas had guarded the dungeons, but it took little effort to knock them out. In fact, the hardest thing about breaking Finn out was Finn himself.

The vampire had limped as we left, the stab wound in his calf healing slowly. He got me good a few times, teeth tearing into my shoulder, and making me shout when the sharpened point of his toothbrush punctured my ribcage.

"Black blood now, eh? How many secrets are you keeping Angel?" He'd hissed.

I answered by wrapping my tail around his throat, strangling him into silence. Then I made the golden halo on his head grow thorns straight into his skull. It was this which finally made him yield.

"I can't believe you stabbed me with a fucking shiv," I said, breaking the silence which had settled over us. In the human world, it was Sunday morning. Together we sat in the polished pews of a church, watching the sermon take place.

"I thought you were into violence?" He mused, the look on his face betraying his anger. I feel myself smirk.

"I meant the shiv. Getting desperate in there were you?"

"Bored would be a more accurate description," he said, not taking his eyes off the priest behind the alter. I leaned closer to him, pressing against his side lightly.

"Should I have sent a she-wolf to your bed to keep you occupied?"

"There's only one wolf I'd want in my bed," he said, gaze finally sliding to me. His eyes were glowing a savage crimson, a heavy combination of disgust and desire there.

"I'll be sure to pass along your admiration to Akashi." He scoffed, and I turned back to face the altar. I could feel his gaze lingering on me, hot and demanding. I checked an imaginary watch on my wrist, untangling myself from his side as I stood.

"So, what's the grand plan Angel?" I heard the squeak of Finn's shiny shoes on the floor as he stood to follow me. He didn't really have a choice but to, I made him aware of his plight with the Angels on the way here. He had nowhere he could run.

I exited the chapel as silently as the old oak doors allowed. To anyone here, we looked like a young couple, strife with worry, stress, perhaps just needing a moment to speak without interrupting the service. The corridor was narrow and dimly lit. I tread my fingers along the peeling, lilac wallpaper, ears straining for any sounds of churchgoers around the bend. I made a right, down an old concrete staircase, and then a left into what appeared to be a rec room.

"Angel?" Finn's whisper bounced off the tile floor. We passed through the rec room, and then a kitchen, before quickly ascending another staircase. This one was made of metal and spiraled straight up.

"Raven!" He hissed my name, hand latching onto my wrist. I paused, turning to look at him over my shoulder.

"What's the matter?"

"Where are we going?" He asked, voice gruff.

"The bell tower." Finns' lips pursed, trying to piece together this series of events. I rolled my eyes. "How else do you expect me to Light Walk without something blessed involved?"

"You mean to take me there?" Horror laced his every word, his hand relinquishing its grip on me.

"Well, I don't intend to leave you to your own devices," I said, beginning to climb again.

"But you said they wanted to kill me!" I rolled my eyes.

"I said they would *rather* kill you than put their faith into you once more. I can use that." He scoffed, angry steps following me up.

The door to the tower was locked. Rather than destroying it, I grabbed his hand, dragging him through the veil with me to step directly through the door. A shiver went through me, a sigh of caution toward the ease of shadow jumping now. I ignored it.

"Raven I really, *really,* don't wish to die." Silent tears had escaped him, but I refused to allow my empathy to rise to the surface. I studied the male before me, beautiful and intelligent, and wondered for the first time what had urged him towards the steps he took in his life. Instead of asking that I just lightly inclined my head, voice monotone as I stated,

"Anzen didn't want to die either."

And then my power struck the bell.

Finn was in agony, but surprisingly, I was not. I remembered the pain clear as day, the feeling of my skin burning from my body, like my bones were about to shatter. But this time, I was just sweating, and squinting against the harsh light. Unfortunately, I had no better control over how fast or what direction we travelled in than I did last time.

Finn wound up clinging to me, crying out in the pain I knew he felt. I sinched my arms around his waist, half afraid I would lose him as we moved. Half wondering how he didn't burn up completely. He was undoubtedly receiving a supernatural sunburn.

Finally, we blasted through the veil, this side of it glittering like a quartz wall, and slammed into the ground. Finn groaned beneath me, laying spread eagle on his back. The water on the ground was so clear it reflected like a mirror, and I paused as I caught a glimpse of myself.

My eyes were glittering, iridescent pits. But two coal-colored horns protruded from my hair, long enough to have tiny curls at their tips. My stomach flipped and I didn't analyze myself further.

"We're here," I said, hauling myself off him and slowly turned to peer through the thick mist surrounding us.

"Terrific." His painful reply was heavy with sarcasm.

This was unwise.

Vallen sidled up next to us and I resisted the urge to punch him in the snout. In this light, his Hound form was clearly made of flame, the texture of his coat rippling between shades of silvery white to ashen grey. Like the hellfire in my veins.

"Did you have a better idea?" I asked, miraculously keeping my voice even.

I did not say it was wrong. His amber eyes revealed nothing.

Frustrated I turned away. Finn had sat up and was gawking at the towering mists around us, fresh tears shining in his eyes.

"Is this real? How is it... how am I...?" Disbelief and something like sorrow filled his voice.

"You've been drinking my blood for months; that's the only reason you're not dead." I frowned at him. "Also, I didn't bring you here for eternal peace, or to be killed. You're here to atone, if you even can."

Finn paled as his gaze drifted to Vallen for the first time. He opened his mouth, but nothing came out. Smugly, Vallen sat at my side, curling his tail around my legs.

"I've been doing some research," I said, allowing my hand to rest atop the Hound's head. His fur was freezing to the touch, more like ice than fire. He didn't react, though I swear I felt a pleased shiver reverberate from his body through mine. "Lucifer's library is useless, but there's one here that I think holds the answers I need."

"That's too dangerous." Finn was on his feet in a millisecond but a low growl from Vallen made him halt. He grit his teeth. "Believe me or not Angel, but I don't want you getting yourself killed for something so trivial."

"Mary's alive," I said, power thrumming beneath my fingertips. "And you're going to help me get her back."

CHAPTER 21

"Well. I didn't see this coming," Akashi mumbled, gently taking a seat beside Silas at the meeting table. He didn't acknowledge the Hound's arrival. His gaze was locked on the body shaped crater in the stone wall where Raven had left his brother to hang when Heaven invaded.

The stained-glass window painted the room in a constant kaleidoscope of sky blues and berry pinks, leafy greens and sunset oranges. Her shimmering magic clung to the glass, making the air itself reflect rainbow tinted light as if an evening sun was constantly shining.

The vampires pale face intersected with a beam of navy blue, casting his clenched jaw into stark relief. A raised patch of stubble was the only sign of the usually impeccable male's fatigue. Akashi nudged him with his knee.

"No comment?"

"I was wondering when she would finally kill him." Silas' voice came out guttural.

"He's not dead." Akashi averted his gaze as the vampire pulled out a black, silken kerchief and dabbed at his eyes. "To me, it seems she pulled a reverse card and kidnapped her once upon a time ago kidnapper."

"Maybe she should have killed him. I'm honestly not sure what would be more beneficial," Silas said. Akashi was quiet for a minute, before saying under his breath,

"He doesn't deserve that."

"Doesn't he?" Silas met Akashi's gaze, and the Hound pretended to not see the tears clinging to the vampires long lashes. "My brother is a main factor in your brother's death. Frankly, I don't know how you could stand Finnegan remaining alive all this time."

"As far as I'm concerned, even though Finn lead him here, Gabriel shot that arrow." Akashi was trying to be gentle, but he couldn't fully contain his snarl. Silas narrowed his eyes.

"It'd be stupid, trying to hide your bloodlust from a vampire. I know you want to kill him, and would be proud of her if Raven actually did."

"Well, don't you?" Akashi snapped, a bit harsher than he intended and threw up his hands. "For fucks sake, if she hadn't woken up, he would have torn your throat out!"

"He was crying." Silas moved so fast that Akashi could barely track it as he raised his body to hover over him, fangs bared inches from his face. "I could taste his tears while he was killing me."

"I don't understand why that matters." Akashi kept his own teeth clenched together, kept his breathing even. He fought the urge to stand and shove him back, the Alpha in him roaring at the clear challenge.

"Vampires do not cry. Not unless we are in agony." Akashi pointedly stared at the tears still clinging to his skin, and Silas clucked his tongue in annoyance before easing back to sit beside him again. He propped his head in one hand, and began counting off with his fingers.

"My mate was kidnapped. My brother betrayed us. My best friend was killed by my mate. And then I was almost killed, had the gamble not paid off and she not risen. Agony does not begin to describe what I feel."

Something in the air shifted, a missing piece of understanding clicking into place as Silas and Akashi eyed one another. Akashi was aware they shared one another's anguish to a degree, but realized that through Raven they shared a bond even deeper. One he didn't think a vampire was capable of. Loyalty.

A bolt of shame went through him as once more he recognized another relationship in which he had misplaced jealousy. The Hound took a breath, and lowered his hackles.

"So, Raven's your best friend?" He arched a brow slightly, trying to ease the tension in the room.

"Out of everything, that's what stuck out to you?" Silas let loose a rough laugh. "I guess it makes sense. After imprinting on her, everything must be extra heightened." A tiny, teasing smirk flit across his lips.

"It's intense," Akashi conceded with a grunt. Silas snickered.

"Which part? The bond or the bed?"

"I'm glad this is amusing enough to battle your depression," Akashi grumbled, and Silas laughed louder, dropping a good-natured slap on the Hounds shoulder.

"I sometimes forget how young you actually are. Don't take my teasing too seriously." After a beat he added, "But seriously which one?"

Akashi snorted, lightly shoving the vampire off him. He stood, feet taking him across the room of their own accord, fingers reaching out to trace the panes of colored glass. It was warm, like her skin. He couldn't decide if that was comforting or creepy.

"The last thing Anzen said, begged really, was to trust her." Silas hadn't moved, but he could practically hear his focus, feel his attention. "I thought that through everything, I've been able to prove to her that I do. But here she goes again, taking all the weight. Lying to me now, too."

"What did she lie about?"

"Her blood," Akashi groaned, rubbing a hand over his face as he recalled his earlier conversation with Rebecca that day.

After a thorough screaming match, the two put their heads together trying to figure out what Ravens next move was, and how they would follow. During the conversation, Rebecca let it slip that Raven was dabbling in demon blood, and she was unsure if she was drinking it or not. That led to a comparison in appearance and scent to the black puddles in Finns cell, and Akashi revealed the tourniquet and syringe Raven had been hiding. Silas rolled his eyes when he began explaining their theory about the bullets.

"Well, I could have told you that. You think she's producing everything she's given us out of thing air? Her magic needs something natural, something tangible, to grow from."

"Super glad you knew but decided not to share with the rest of us. Had I known–"

"You would have stopped her, and that's why she didn't tell you."

Akashi leveled a glare on Silas, but the vampire would not be subdued. "You obsess with helping her, but you refuse to acknowledge what she wants or needs. You have your own definitions of what's safe and necessary, and they don't overlap with hers."

"She knows I would never intentionally hold her back. I'd be an idiot if I even tried to cap that power," Akashi argued but Silas just smiled, albeit a little sadly.

"She knows we need an upper hand over their ariel attacks, and she found a solution. Obviously, she didn't trust that you'd let her bring that plan to fruition.

You'd rather take months of time we don't have to hunt down every demon in existence, or even drain yourself dry, before letting her put herself in any discomfort. You need to take your brothers advice, and trust that she knows what she's doing."

Despite the growls reverberating in Akashi's chest, Silas crossed the room to him. He placed his hands on the Hounds shoulders, smoothing the bristling muscles of his arms.

"I understand your position better than anyone." He was no longer teasing him. If anything, he seemed vulnerable.

"Rebecca and I were our own twisted mess for a long time. When I'd taken her in, she was an angry adolescent, brimming with power and loss. Yet I sensed what she was immediately, just as you had when you first met Raven. Similarly, I said and did nothing until she acknowledged the bond several decades later, and even then refused to act on it until she had Reformed."

Akashi didn't say a word, the revelation striking deep. It had been pure torture, having her within reach but staying at an arm's length. Somehow, he felt relieved knowing that Silas had made the same decision.

Silas leaned back then, and ran a hand through his hair leaving it bedraggled. Through everything, the man remained impeccable and poised. It was rare to see him ruffled, let alone get a real glimpse of how much time he actually had endured. It was easy to forget.

"Since then, we've had almost seven years to establish the boundaries and expectations of one another. And though I can acknowledge your boundaries are far more restrictive than mine, I assure you that you and Raven will be fine. Once we all get through this, and you get some privacy to sort it out. *Real* privacy." Silas leveled a gaze on him which seemed to say, 'more than just time to fuck'.

"Fine." Akashi relented, and shook off Silas' grip. Privacy? Who was he kidding. He hadn't even been able to fully explain the effect imprinting had on him to her, and based on her recent behavior, he was fairly certain she'd begun piecing it together on her own. He grit his teeth, trying to focus on the problem at hand.

"For entertainment purposes, let's say Raven knows exactly what she's doing. I don't see how kidnapping Finn is step two of a plan."

"I think she's far past step two." Silas heaved a sigh, "But I have to admit I don't know what purpose she has for Finn either."

"She's been pouring over books, every night," Akashi said, more to himself than to Silas and began to pace, fingers rubbing his jaw. "All the oldest ones, about ancient magic and the creation of demons. She either found what she was looking for, or Finn knows the answer?" He glanced at Silas quizzically, who was also now deep in thought.

"When Rebecca was taken, she brought a scroll back from Heaven. It was a part of records they keep there."

"Records that could hold information she didn't find here." Akashi bit back a strained whine, the rapid onset of fear making his heart hammer in his chest. "She's breaking into Heaven's fucking library."

"With Finn as her collateral." Silas sounded equally distressed. "He is a prisoner of war after all."

"There's gotta be more to it than that." Akashi was almost panting now, the urge to shift into Hound form becoming close to unbearable.

"Depends on the information she's looking for. You said it was ancient magic right?" Akashi stopped pacing, giving the vampire his full attention. Silas, surprisingly, glanced away. "She's got this... thing in her. She calls it Vallen."

"That fucking wolf again?" Akashi snarled, unable to help himself. Silas' eyes flew to his.

"She finally told you?"

"No. Yesterday the bastard woke us up at the foot of our bed," his annoyance was rolling off every word. "I, of course, wasn't given any details, but

Kuma and you apparently got to know all about him."

"She's not a fan of him, I assure you." Akashi snorted, casting a look of doubt towards Silas. The vampire sighed, "Fine, she is *intrigued*, but he annoys her more than anything."

"Never mind, I'll deal with that bit later." Akashi dragged his hands down his face, exasperated.

"Is there anything I can do for you?" Silas asked, a stroke of empathy lacing his typical haughtiness.

Akashi slid to the floor, back pressed to the glass. He already chased Raven across the world once. This time, he needed to be patient. He leaned his head back, his heart on his sleeve as he said,

"Convince me she's gonna come back in one piece, so I don't kill myself trying to get to her."

CHAPTER 22

Bearing someone else's weight while flying was fucking difficult. My wingbeats were silent against the heavy mists, but my labored breaths were not. Finn wasn't trying to make the trip any harder, he just dangled from where I had him scooped beneath the arms, but this was not a sensation I ever wanted to repeat after today.

The muscles in my back screamed as I touched down. The entrance to the gilded hall was essentially the same, the veins of crystal, copper, and silver running gently like tiny streams. Magic made the air shimmer a bit more heavily since my last visit, most likely with added wards.

Vallen had trotted along beneath us as we flew, and if he was in any way discomforted by the place his posture didn't show it. He strode into the hall confidently, albeit somewhat arrogantly. His amber eyes danced around appearing bored, but I didn't miss the imperceptible huffs of breath he took as he scented the space for any nearby Angels.

I didn't mistake the hall being empty for any kind of luck. At most we had a few minutes before we were no longer alone. I craned my neck, looking up into the blinding rafters toward where the library perched.

"Do you plan to follow?" My eyes darted to Vallen, who was pacing deeper into the glittering corridor.

I would, he mused, voice ping ponging in my skull. *But if the need for a quick escape arises, it would be best to have someone on the ground to catch your vampire.*

"Alright. Hang on then," I mumbled to Finn, his only warning before I launched us into the air once more.

I was panting when we landed this time. Fighting against gravity, the extra weight, and whatever magic clung to the air was almost too much for my still young wings. I shook them out, annoyed at the near creaking down my spine before letting them droop for some relief. And then my annoyance turned to cold, throbbing panic.

Uriel hadn't been lying. The library was as bare as sheetrock. Blank, blaring white walls stared at me from all sides. Not even the shelving units remained. It was as if the whole thing burned, and someone swept out all the ash just leaving the stone.

"Angel," Finn's voice echoed to me off the bare walls. "Perhaps you chose the wrong room. You were distracted with Rebecca's safety the last time you were here."

"This is the right room," I said defensively, stalking to the corner Gabriel had pinned me in. The corner which I used my own shadow to sneak out the truths of my sister's bloodline.

"Okay," Finn conceded. I heard the tap of his dress shoes crossing the marble to me. I turned, my fangs bared with a threat fueled by my anger and confusion, but I froze. Finn just smiled softly, while shrugging his already unbuttoned shirt off one shoulder. "May I suggest you do what you can to replenish your energy before we continue looking?"

From below us, a hollow howl echoed off the rising columns of marble giving me no time to argue. I didn't meet Finn's gaze as I slid a hand up his chest to his neck, tugging him down the few inches I needed before my fangs sank into his bronzed skin. A quick breath released from his lips, and wisely he kept his hands off me.

"I'm tempted to see if Vallen would actually catch you, should I chuck you off that ledge," I muttered as I swiped my mouth with the back of my hand. Finn's cheeks were flushed a warm rose, and the corner of his mouth ticked up as he fixed his shirt.

"A theory we wouldn't have to test if I could teleport."

I held his stare for a long moment, before my eyes rose to his golden halo, debating. Before I could fully consider the option he was alluding to, a second howl rose from below, this one louder and more insistent than the last.

"Come here." Quickly, I dropped us back down to the floor. I had a good guess to what direction Vallen was in, if the flaming pawprints melting into the floor were any indication. I slid my hand into Finns, ignoring the way he laced our fingers together as I followed the trail of Hellfire back the way we'd come. Vallen was growling as we approached, and as we exited the hall I realized why with chilling clarity.

The mist had all but evaporated, the souls of those resting in the afterlife disappearing with it. The bare expanse of the glasslike ground reflected the light, a putrid yellow, which made Finn and I both wince as we stepped outside. Without thinking better of it, I tightened my grip on his hand while leveling the most sever glare I could muster on the legion of Angels before us. There had to be thousands of them, posed in the shallow water and crowding the air above us.

They taunt me without knowing. Vallen's voice invaded my head with a franticness I'd never heard from him before.

He was no longer chilling, banked flames. White hot sparks popped off his fur, and the withering heat rolling off him had even me sweating. The fire in my veins pulsed in answer, and from my peripheral I could see my skin glowing with a mixture of violet and silver light.

"Neither of you panic or we're dead," I kept my voice low, hoping that only the two of them heard me. I raised my free hand as I strode forward into the water, tugging Finn to stand beside me as I called out to the legion before us. "I was wondering where you all were. As you can see, I brought you a gift. Or peace offering, if you'll take it."

With a force Finn wasn't expecting, I sent him toppling to his knees in the water. It was so clear I could see his glare reflecting up at me, so I tilted my lips into a cruel smile. "Also, if you've been wondering where your brother is, he's been enjoying my hospitality."

"I can imagine that." Gabriel's voice flowed across the water, stepping out from behind a cluster of Angels a few layers deep in the lines. He strode to my side, completely at ease with the situation. "Should we expect him to return soon?"

"If his wings regrow, sure." A murmur rolls through the Angels, a few questions sparking from them. Gabriel frowns.

"I'm not even going to entertain what you mean by that."

"Uriel would have," I prodded, hoping to crack his pride a bit, but Gabriel only chuffed a laugh.

"And that's why I'm not the one under your capture." I suppressed a growl, changing tactics.

"Are you interested in Finnegan or not? Because I could just kill him and rid us all of the nuisance."

"Raven?" Finn's voice came out choked, head lifting to look at me beseechingly. I grinned at him.

"What, are you begging me now? I'm not your master." Finn clenched his jaw, but I'd gotten the reaction I'd hoped for. Gabriel turned from me, slowly assessing the vampire at our feet like he was a God deciding a lesser being's fate.

"And why your sudden change of heart? Just a month ago you were sending me corpses in order to convince me he was dead."

"Call it boredom." I shrugged, "Truthfully, I'm new to this Devil thing. I couldn't get him to break and give me any information, but Uriel shared your aggravation with him. So, I figured to use him as a talking piece because we needed to have a chat." I was running out of thread to keep weaving this, but thankfully Gabriel took the bait.

"Indeed," he drawled, eyes returning to me. "Though I'm curious as to what you want to speak with me about."

Vallen, can you speak into Finn's head?

Yes.

Good.

"My mother." I slid my hands into my pockets, keeping my voice even. "I've been hearing that she's not dead. Care to comment?"

"She's not, in a way," Gabriel said, seeming to measure his words. I arched a brow.

"What's that mean? Is she one of the souls resting in the mist?" Gabriel said nothing, but I saw the twitch under his eye and the slight flex of his fingers.

"Yes, she is. She's one of the souls we help rest." Liar.

"Funny," I mused, turning away from him to pace as if deep in thought. "I would have assumed her soul would be somewhere in hell with me, given what she's done."

Gabriels wings flared behind him as he reached out to grab me, but he was stopped short by a wall of fire rising between us. He stumbled back, actually falling into the water as he gaped at the blistering burn on his palm.

"So that's not a rendition of your magic," he said, almost to himself. His enraged gaze slid to Vallen, who was now crouched between us baring his teeth.

Slowly, Gabriel stood, eyes never leaving the Hound as he raised his voice for his army to hear, "She has obtained Edens Flame!"

A series of cries went up as Gabriel finally unsheathed his sword, and my stomach plummeted back to hell as it burst into the same golden flames I'd seen poised against Lucifer's throat. Vallen snarled at the sight of it, but his body shuddered, like the proximity to the weapon alone caused him physical pain.

Before I could clarify any of the rushing thoughts in my mind, I saw movement in my peripheral vision. Finn had stood, slowly rounding the two facing off between us. I risked glancing at him, and his eyes were blood red in the light. *Please*, he mouthed, and I felt all my muscles tighten in hesitation.

We would need to fight our way out of here, of that much I was certain. And I didn't have any more cards left to play.

Wordlessly I raised my hand, a shimmering flash of magic pulsating off my fingertips to encompass the halo around his temple. Gabriel finally reacted, turning to Finn too late.

Finns honey sweet voice reached my ears, but his spell passed around me, immobilizing the swarm of Angels who had begun to dive for us. I didn't linger, not with Gabriel lunging for me with his blade of fire. I launched myself skyward. If Uriel's words had been true, I would not be leaving this place without her a second time.

CHAPTER 23

For a prison, the place was pristine, and void of guards. Whatever spells Finn was spewing kept the Angels just outside the doors from bashing them in to pursue me, and I wasn't going to waste any time I had here.

I jogged down the halls, gun in hand, opening each door I passed to peer into empty rooms. Literally empty, there wasn't even any furniture. I guess Heaven didn't keep prisoners very often, and somehow the fact was comforting. Or maybe I was just a lunatic.

At the end of the hall, there was a door already cracked open, and gentle voices filtered from inside. I slowed my steps, my breaths falling into the low, practiced rhythm Luna had taught me as a child. I approached the door silently, using my elbow to swing it open. The sight inside made me stop in my tracks.

My fingers instantly went slick, the gun slipping from my hands. It clattered against the marble flooring, battling the shrill scream of the child before me. In my shock, I could only stare down at the smallest Angel I had ever seen.

She had dropped her coloring book in her fear, and the edges of the paper were curling against the heat of my flames. Whisps of smoke began to rise, and that yanked me out of my stupor. I quickly waved a hand, dousing them with a damp breeze before the pages could alight. She stood frozen, gaping up at me in absolute terror. I let my eyes drift beyond her, to study the dozen or so other children in the room.

All of them Angel-born. Like me.

Each of them stared back at me, expressions ranging from terror to hate. There was a rustle of wings as one flew forward, dragging the trembling girl out of my reach.

"It's a Devil." The whisper might as well have been a bomb going off. "A Devil has breached the gate."

From their belts they pulled daggers, and the sight of the two-tone blades had my stomach somersaulting in agonizing recognition. Oblivious to my inner meltdown, the children scrambled into a pathetic formation, the eldest at the front and youngest at the rear.

My free hand shot to clasp my ear as suddenly, the dagger within my mutilated sword began to sing in the presence of its sisters. I knew their blades couldn't kill me anymore than mine could kill Lucifer. But my sword...

Gabriel's laughter rose above the pounding thoughts in my head. I cut my gaze over my shoulder to see him standing halfway down the hall behind me.

"There's only two ways to end this war, Raven." Gabriels words sank into me like spikes of ice. "Surrender and repent. Or destroy us completely, like your father had intended."

He's right, Vallen's voice now cooed in my head, and I felt the press of a feverish kiss against my necklace of a scar. *Just how far are you willing to go, Angel-born?*

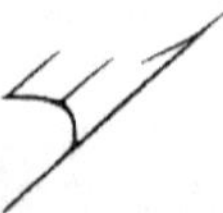

Something was wrong. Akashi's earlier resolve hadn't slowly trickled away, it had been completely yanked out from under him like a rug. His hand slammed down over his hip, like his body was trying to thaw the imprinting mark which had gone cold as ice in his skin.

If Raven had any awareness about the connection it gave them, she never showed it. Akashi, though he felt steadily guiltier each time, used it to his advantage, keeping his end of the bond wide open for any sign or feeling from her. And right now, the only feelings powerful enough to pulse through the barrier of the holy realm, were panic and cold resolve.

"I can't fucking take this anymore," he growled, the veins in his neck bulging as he fought the urge to transform. The Hound in him wanted blood, wanted to do whatever necessary to relieve her of the anguish she was in. But she was in the one damn place he couldn't go without turning to dust.

"Trouble in paradise?" Silas, thoroughly drunk on wine, lounged in Ravens high-backed chair with his legs thrown across the table. Akashi couldn't hold back the snarl that ripped from his lips, making the vampires gaze widen. "Well, I think that was a bit dramatic."

"Somethings wrong."

"And? Is that supposed to shock me?" Another growl rumbled in Akashi's throat as Silas swung his feet to the floor, propping his elbows on the table so he didn't faceplant against the wood. "At this point I think I would be more perturbed if the lot of us were thriving. This is just our average Tuesday."

Before Akashi could entertain the urge of throwing himself over the table to throttle Silas, the doors at the far end of the room swung open. Hikari, flushed from his sprint, slowed his pace as he approached his brother.

"Is there a reason your aura just flooded the valley?" He asked, glancing at Silas sidelong, who had begun humming to himself as he refilled his glass.

"She's... I feel..." Akashi struggled to find the right words. "It feels like she's drowning." Understanding flashed in Hikari's gaze, and he reached to pry Akashi's vicelike grip off his mark to check it. They both gaped at it, the once pale impression on his skin now standing as a proud stamp of dark ink.

"Well... that's not normal," Hikari commented unhelpfully. At Akashi's glare he rushed to add, "But it's not like any of us have imprinted on a demonic Angel before. Though it's different, she could be fine. You can still feel her, right? Then she's alive."

"If I stop feeling her right now I'm gonna tear apart everything I fucking see." Akashi was at his breaking point. His teeth lengthened to fangs, his muscles went taught, warping as he turned away to drag his hands through his hair.

"That's not going to happen." Hikari said with absolute certainty. "Anzen said to trust her, and so far she's done nothing that–"

"So far I watched her fucking *die.*" A wave of veridian power exploded from Akashi, knocking the wine bottles off the table to shatter on the floor, and blasted the door off its hinges. Silas released a squawk of protest, cradling his remaining goblet to his chest as Akashi's Hound lunged against the table, throwing it across the room. He was pacing haphazardly, the sounds of his heavy breaths filling the room as he fought to contain himself.

"Well, I'm surprised he held it in for this long." Kuma's humored voice drifted in. Akashi was blind to his presence, as well as his mother's and Aengus' as they gathered in a small crowd in the doorframe. Luna's eyes shone with concern, but Aengus' gaze was sharper, his own instincts awakening, assessing the potential threat in the room.

"You all transform over the slightest of inconveniences." Silas frowned at the puddles of wasted alcohol as he tip-toed over to join them. Kuma released a laugh, slapping his palm down on the vampire's shoulder.

"Nah, this is what you get after an Alpha imprints on somebody. An out of control, horny lunatic, who obsesses over one person to the point they can't function for more than a few hours without them.

In answer, Akashi clacked his teeth together, leveling a burning gaze on his brother which just made him laugh again. "Well you're proving me right! Look at you, ready to tear our throats out because you're scared and can't control her."

A bark echoed in the hall as Akashi dove for Kuma, the latter cursing under his breath as he shoved Silas out of the way and transformed. Claws met in the air, Kuma deflecting each of the Alphas blows without advancing on him.

"You're fighting lazy!" Akashi snapped, his teeth narrowly missing Kuma's shoulder. "Aren't you supposed to be a fucking brute? Do your job and knock me out!"

"My most humble apologies, but I choose life. The best you're getting from me is being your punching bag until your temper tantrum is over." Kuma retorted, his back legs catching Akashi's jaw to redirect another bite.

"There is a third option." Both Hounds swung their heads towards Aengus, the gravity in the room seeming to shift to center around the Commander. He had silently transformed, his blood red fur glistening in the low light.

"You could fight me." His voice droned in Akashi's head, like a machine on the verge of blowing up. "You won't need to fear injuring your sparring partner then, and I assure you that your rage will be thoroughly spent."

"You wanna risk that?" Akashi's voice was serrated, his ears flat against his head. The other Hounds in the room had fallen deathly silent, enough so that Silas began turning to look between them all before releasing an exasperated groan.

"You dogs and your hierarchies are killing me." He threw back his glass, chugging the remainder of his drink, oblivious to the red lines of it spilling against his porcelain skin.

"It's not a risk if it's deserved," Aengus said, ignoring the vampire. His lips curled to reveal his teeth. "Plus, aren't you wondering if you're strong enough to remain by her side? This is a test that can prove your worth."

Akashi was a blur, and Aengus grinned.

"Move!" Hikari forced Silas out of the room, Kuma joining them at Luna's side as the Hounds in the room battled one another. Luna was frozen, not knowing if she should intervene or cry out for them to stop.

"He won't kill him," Hikari said, trying to reassure her, but Kuma whistled.

"Which one you talking about?"

"Do I even want to know what's happening?" Rebecca's voice bounced off the walls, somehow still shrill above the Hounds fighting just a few meters away.

"Oh, it's fabulous love." Silas whirled to face her, arms looping her against him. "Akashi is all hot and heavy because of your sister, and, unlike me, has little self-control—" Rebecca's small palm raised to clamp over Silas' mouth, effectively cutting him off. He just nuzzled into her, taking the opportunity to sink his teeth into her hand.

"Luna, can you explain why your son looks like he's trying to kill his dad?"

Rebecca asked, blue eyes finally shifting off the scene to study the she-wolf.

Luna was less composed than a few minutes ago. The scent of blood now permeated the air, a mixture of both their scents. A wave of red power just forced Akashi back against the wall, pinning him down as Aengus swung for him again and again.

"When a Hound first imprints, everything is heightened. Taste, scents, emotions. He's been struggling to control himself for her sake, but now that she's gone…" Luna trailed off, eyes actually shining with unshed tears. The sight was enough to make Rebecca gape.

"Wait, he's not actually going to kill him is he?"

"He could," Kuma muttered, earning a slap on the back of the head from Hikari. "What? That's how a new Commander was always chosen. Doesn't have to happen, but if Aengus doesn't knock him out or submit, I'm not gonna stand here and pretend Akashi's in the mental space to be able to stop himself."

"Then I'll fucking stop him. There's been enough death around here lately." Annoyance laced Rebecca's words as she took a step toward the room, but Silas' grip on her tightened. He gave a small shake of his head, a flash of warning in his eyes.

"Forgive me for not wanting to see him use you as a chew toy."

"He's out of control," she argued. "Somebody's gotta step up and do something. What do you think Raven will say if she suddenly waltzes in during this bullshit?"

"Unless that's in the next thirty seconds I don't think we're gonna have to worry about it." Kuma's drawl, tinged with remorse brought Rebecca's attention back to the fight in the room.

"I only instigated this because he looked about ready to go beat a group of Omegas to a pulp. I didn't think it would escalate to this."

"What's happening?" Rebecca was sick of not understanding the functionality of the Hounds lifestyle. She would never understand how Raven grew up in such a strict, yet haphazard community.

To her, the blasts of green and red power filling the room looked of equal size. Each Hound was bleeding, which meant they both were strong enough to get good hits on one another. And Akashi wasn't pinned anymore.

He wasn't exactly advancing on Aengus, but based on the other's reactions, she could guess that once the Commander got someone pinned the way he had Akashi a few minutes ago, they didn't get out of it unless he let them go. And based on the malicious growls echoing from the Aengus, he hadn't let Akashi up. Akashi had somehow gotten up on his own.

"This was just supposed to help him take the edge off." Kuma was still talking, jaw slack with his shock as they all watched Akashi continue to bite and pounce and eventually, throw Aengus across the room to roll into the table which somehow still managed to not break.

"Akashi!" Luna's voice was pitched with panic as the male Hounds lunged for one another again. Akashi's teeth tore enough of Aengus' flesh, making the Hound yelp out loud. "Stop! That's enough!"

"Nah, dad's the one who shot his mouth off, but now the old man can't keep up?" Akashi stalked towards him as the Aengus fought to stand, teeth bared in defiance.

"Do you hate me that much?" Aengus' voice rolled against the walls, a touch of pain behind the anger. Akashi cocked his head, his gaze threatening to burn him on the spot.

"I can't stand my mate being in a dangerous situation. You let yours, and your child, go be in one for almost a century, and because of what? Lucifer?"

"He would have killed all the other Hounds," Aengus protested. Akashi laughed, turning his back on the Commander.

"No, he wouldn't have. He would have had no one to use otherwise. He was a coward, and so were you."

Aengus just stared at him, before a flash of ebony power blurred him as he shifted, leaving him standing there as just a man. Luna broke from the door then, rushing between her son and mate as Akashi turned around, all but pulsing with power. Power that just kept growing.

"Akashi please," she murmured, but Aengus' fingers reached forward, lacing with hers.

Rebecca blinked, surprised. He had never looked so old before, so worn down. So... tired. Hikari and Kuma had gone stiff beside her, and she didn't dare move.

"For fucks sake." Silas, still drunk, rolled his eyes and gestured towards Akashi sloppily. "Just get the dramatics over with so I can open a fresh bottle in peace."

Slowly, Aengus lowered his head. Luna sighed with relief. And Akashi transformed with a flash of green fire.

"Damn," Kuma muttered. "I shoulda bet money on this."

CHAPTER 24

I banished the faces of those children from my mind as I ran. I may be a monster, but I wasn't evil. Killing them wasn't an option I was willing to even entertain. Gabriel though, somehow had the audacity to be shocked when I whipped around and shot at him. I didn't wait to see if the bullet struck true, just flung myself around the corner in a full sprint.

A glance behind me confirmed he was following, the same swirling funnel of light he unleashed against Lucifer bearing down on me. I swung my arm, sending a gust of shadow-tinted wind ahead of me to fling open the doors lining the hall. I ducked into one of the rooms, waiting for the fiery light to thunder past before springing out and shooting blindly twice more.

"Cadere in tenebris!" Streams of shadows burst from my arms, writhing like my vines as they wrapped around the funnel of light like a serpent, choking it out.

"Mary?" I screamed, running again
as Gabriel rounded the corner behind me,
sending another bolt of light at my back. I
flared my wings, gasping in pain at the
impact, but kept moving. He was cursing
behind me now, and I heard the singing
of the arrow before it flew past my head
to embed in the door I just sprinted past.

"Mary!?" I screamed again; this
time more frantic than before as I skidded
around another corner at random. This
place was like a labyrinth, all blank white
walls and twisting hallways intersecting
at random.

The scent of blood reached my nose
seconds before two more Angels burst into
the hallway ahead of me. I twisted, barely
missing the swing of one of their swords.
Gold splattered the pristine floors as I
shot the first in the thigh, before shooting
the other through both his wings. Once
both hit the floor, I darted through the
door they exited and slammed it shut
against the insults they hurled at my
back.

Before they recovered themselves,
or Gabriel caught up, I dug my fingers
into the metal, twisting with a scream
until the door melted away. I braced my
back on the wall, heaving for breath as I

took in the room. There was sparse furniture, but clearly it was an occupants cell. The majority of the space was dominated by a hospital bed, and various potted plants lined the blank walls surrounding it. And the scent of blood in the room was nearly overwhelming.

"Hello?" I whipped my head to the left, eyes locking on a human woman. She was perched in a worn leather armchair beneath the rooms single window. Her brown eyes were unremarkable, other than the slight golden tint encircling the irises. Near-black hair was pulled back from her face in a knot against the nape of her neck, making her pallid skin stand out even more. It was like she hadn't seen sunlight in years, her cheeks appearing hollowed from malnourishment. My eyes zeroed in on the drip she was connected to, a blood bag filled with glittering gold pumping straight into her veins.

This could be a massive error. I had no idea if this was even her. She certainly didn't match the visions of my mother that I remembered, strong and unyielding. Regardless, I wasn't about to leave her there in that state.

"It's time to go." She didn't flinch as I approached, allowing me to carefully remove the needle from her arm. Then I hauled myself up onto the windows ledge, relieved to see Finns spell was keeping up this long, and no Angels were waiting outside to kill us both.

It took little effort to melt the glass against my touch, and then I was lowering to the floor and lifting her into my arms. She was far lighter than a woman her size should be. I reached for the cuff which held my shield, swirling into place on my forearm to block her as I cradled her against me. As I climbed back up on the ledge I carefully kept my gaze off hers, which was burning into me with an overwhelming sense of curiosity. And then I stepped off, falling into the open air.

I was a black comet across the sky, the marble prison above us rattling so hard I thought it would actually come crashing down. To her credit, she didn't scream as the Angels swarmed us. I didn't bother aiming as I fired off the remaining bullets into the mob of them, before calling my sword to hand.

Forget my bitching about carrying Finn earlier. Holding someone while flying *and* fighting was agonizing.

The fire in my veins pulsed and tugged, like a leash between myself and Vallen, who I could now hear howling far below. Blinded by the never-ending flurry of wings and flash of swords, I let it drag me through the air, focusing on not dropping the woman perched in my arms.

The Hound knew his way around here. His behavior in the hall and our magics current tug-of-war were clear indicators. And that exclamation about Edens Flame did not go missed. I vowed not to have Becca freeze him on the spot, but he *would* answer me clearly as soon as we got a chance to speak.

As if he could sense my thoughts about him, his voice echoed in my skull, the tether between us going taut.

I have the vampire. We will meet you at the gate.

There was a break in the ever-moving cloud of wings surrounding me, and I caught sight of him and Finn below us. They ran side by side in a dead sprint, matching each other's strides and speed almost perfectly. Finn was shouting in foreign tongue, releasing the chants and spells which froze most of the Angels diving for them. The ones who did reach them were swiftly handled by Vallen's flaming jaws.

Ahead of us rose the gate, a dark and twisting thing that I wasn't expecting. It rose higher than I could see, the marred silver and pearl forming branchlike patterns across the horizon in a seemingly never-ending stretch.

"You'll need to sheath that. To transport us." It took me a second to realize the woman in my arms spoke. I risked a glance at her after parrying another volley of arrows.

"If I put the shield away, you'll die," I answered, not recognizing my voice. A smile pursed her lips.

"If you don't, we both will." I ignored her, slicing through another Angel with my blade. "I'm not the one that the two of you need anyway." She was morbidly calm as I turned the mechanism on the hilt, replacing the blade with a concentrated burst of violet and white flame.

The Angels on our tail began flying faster, some of them even shrieking at the sight of it. Glancing down I noticed Vallen had disappeared, but Finn was still running, his gaze straight up and locked on me.

Vallen?

You called me to be wielded Angel-born. I'm with you.

The white flames mixing with my natural violet seemed to blaze in affirmation. Hellfire. Edens Flame. I grit my teeth, tucking my wings into a dive.

"Remarkable," the woman murmured, fingers trailing down the inside of my arm, tracing the glowing veins beneath my skin.

"Please stop distracting me," I snapped at her. "I only have one shot at this working."

"It'll work." She said it simply, but stopped touching me as I requested.

The waters parted beneath the beat of my wings, spreading outward into cresting waves. I was a force this place was not built to withstand, and it wouldn't. A cruel flash of glee ricocheted through my body as I heard the gilded hall behind us crack against the sheer pressure of my growing power.

Finn was drawing closer at unprecedented speed. His brows were knit together, his focus solely on keeping up with me so he wasn't left behind. A wounded piece of me considered it, after all he's done. But I forced the thought from my mind, and reached out my hand.

Inches from him, I flared open my wings, casting the dimmest shadow onto the water beneath us. His hand clasped mine in a viselike grip, and together the three of us tumbled into the dark.

CHAPTER 25

To everyone's shock, Rebecca calmly volunteered to go to the dining hall and retrieve their meals. With the new hierarchies established, dealing with any more questions regarding Ravens location or when she would return were not topics the pack could currently endure.

More than ever, Hikari and Kuma were glued to their brothers side. The aura now radiating from him was enough to make them buckle a few times as the trio righted the table and moved it back to its place in the center of the room. Akashi parked himself in a seat at the far end, refusing to comment on what had just been done. Aengus also seemed content with remaining silent.

Luna though was unable to contain her thoughts on the affair. How wrong all of this could have gone. How rare it was for it to not end in bloodshed. Her nervous chatter, something none of them had seen from her before, only fell quiet when Rebecca slammed her plate down in front of her and hissed at her to eat.

Akashi ignored the food in front of him. Ignored Hikari's insistent comments to not starve himself. Ignored Kuma's idiotic comments about bulking up his body now to match his power. Power that still couldn't hold a candle to Hers, but maybe, just maybe, could close the distance between them a little.

Dinner was so quiet, he wound up dozing at his end of the table. But when the scent of Ravens blood flooded his nose, he snapped awake in an instant and scrambled to his feet. Kuma had stood with him, a question on his lips that he didn't get to ask as Raven, Finn, and a third person appeared, falling from the shadows clinging to the domed ceiling.

Luna was a millisecond faster than him, shifting into her Hound and catching the trio before they crashed into the stone floor. Aengus immediately rushed to her side, yanking Finn up by the collar of his shirt. Finn, who had a very empty forehead.

Hikari's grip on his arm was the only thing which kept Akashi from ending the vampires life right there. Instead, he allowed his brother to guide him to his mates side, the they helped her to her feet.

Raven sagged against his chest, clearly exhausted. After a quick sweep of his hands to confirm she wasn't wounded, he finally dropped his head to hers, calming down at last. Her wings had disappeared before she even hit the floor, and Akashi noted her tail was absent too. In fact, there was no sign of her magic at all, other than the slight glow to her skin.

"Let's get this off you so you can breathe," he murmured, working at the buckles on her breastplate. Hikari had already gotten the armored leg pads off her and was working on unlacing her boots.

"You're not mad at me?" Her voice came out breathless; confused. Akashi paused long enough to cup her face, and tilt her to meet his mouth for a devastatingly short kiss before lifting the metal armor off her.

"I'm not," he said, and was shocked to find it true. He smoothed her hair, pulling her to rest all her weight against his side. "Though in the future I would appreciate being allowed to know about these things before they happened."

Raven, too tired to argue, just nodded as he pulled her in. If she noticed the new power radiating from him, she didn't react to it like everyone else had. He pushed down the flairs of annoyance and anxiety that triggered. They would make time for it later. They had to.

"My word..." His mothers voice drew Akashi's attention back toward the woman on the floor. The very human woman, who was wide awake and peering around the room curiously. With a flash of blue magic Luna transformed again, catching the woman's thin wrists in her hands. Aengus immediately threw his jacket around her bare shoulders.

"Are you all in there?" Luna asked the newcomer, eyes still glowing intensely. The woman drew her gaze to Luna's, and a trembling smile curved her lips.

"As far as I'm aware."

With a small cry of thanks, Luna pulled her into a tight embrace. Raven had stiffened against Akashi's side once more and he followed her weary gaze to Finn who was now kneeling on the floor between their brothers. Was seriously no one else worried about his lack of halo?

The vampires eyes were blazing and locked on his mate in a way he hated. As if he could feel the Hound's attention, he shifted his gaze upward, and flashed Akashi a brazen smile.

"She's been forcing me to my knees quite a bit lately. You get the same treatment?" The temperature in the room plummeted, making the smug smile drop from his face almost immediately.

"*Finnegan Esmeraldas Hagan.*" A sound between a whisper and a hiss left Silas as he strode from the shadows. Any sense of drunkenness had evaporated, his voice now laced thickly with magic. Even the air around him seemed to ripple as he stalked towards his brother.

Raven took a step toward them, but Akashi cinched an arm around her waist. At her glare he just shook his head once. This was not their business to interfere in.

Silas loomed over his brother, a flurry of emotions in his eyes, but the rest of his face was stone cold. Finally, with an extra snap of exasperation, he said, "Shut the fuck up!"

Like a cartoon, Finn's slack jaw snapped shut like it had been kicked. Akashi couldn't suppress the short bark of laughter at the sight.

"Your daughter has done well." Luna said, once again drawing the attention back toward their mystery guest.

"Wait." Akashi's face was a mask of horrified confusion as he asked, "What did you say?"

"Yes." The woman was staring at him now. No, at Raven still wrapped protectively in his arms. "Yes, she has. Thank you, for staying true to our bargain."

If he wasn't holding her, he wouldn't know she was trembling, and the fact that she was made the imprinting mark once again flame to life on his hip. Before he could move though, Raven turned wholly towards the woman, her face unnervingly blank as she held her assessing stare. There was nothing unkind in it. Just... way too much joy, considering the state everyone was in.

"Raven, do you remember me?" The woman asked, standing with Luna's help.

"I do." Ravens voice was all wrong. Soft and airy. Scared, like a child. She rested a hand on his forearm, squeezing in silent request, but he refused to budge.

"That's okay." The woman just smiled again, before her eyes flickered beyond them. "And you, Rebecca. Have you regained your memories? You must have, since you're still by your sisters side."

Akashi turned to see the Hellcat leaning against the wall, examining the deadly sharp claws protruding from her fingertips as if she were bored. Her voice was flat as she answered.

"I know enough."

"So, everything went according to plan then?" The woman turned back to Luna, and his mother flinched.

"Almost." Her answer was soft, anguish cutting the word in two.

"Mom," Raven ventured, still with that not right voice. Mom. Akashi felt like a bomb went off in his chest and he looked at the woman anew as he finally realized who they were talking to.

"If I messed up, I'm sorry." Raven was still talking but he was barely listening anymore as he raked his gaze over the woman. Mary.

Not much was similar to his mate. Her hair, maybe her complexion if she wasn't so languid. Raven continued speaking in that not right voice, finally slipping free of his grasp, "I had to do some things... some which you probably wouldn't have liked."

"I trust your choices," Mary said, but her eyes searched the room anxiously. "Though, I must ask: where is my son?"

Raven froze, a wounded look of uncertainty crossing her face. This time Akashi couldn't hold back his growl. Mother or no, he didn't care for anyone who made a look like that cross his mates face. Rebecca, seeming to share his feelings, materialized at Ravens opposite side looking about ready to remove Mary's head from her shoulders.

"What do you mean where is your son?" She seethed, ice weaving a trail across the floor between her and Mary. "Your daughter is right in front of you. She literally died to fulfill your plan, but you'd rather know where your precious baby boy is, even though he's done nothing to help?"

Mary shook her head, taking a step back, "That's not what I meant. I just…" She trailed off, wringing her hands. Luna stepped up beside her again, taking her by the shoulders to steady her.

"Now is not the best time." Her voice came out pained.

"I don't care!" Mary's voice rose, tears brimming in her eyes.

Akashi was about ready to knock Mary out himself, but before he or Rebecca could take another step towards her, she asked a question that damn near made his heart stop.

"Where is Anzen!?"

CHAPTER 26

I had passed out. That much was evident since I was suddenly on my back on the floor.

My mothers were in the same spot, neither of them rushing to my side when I fell. Most likely because Akashi had transformed and placed himself squarely between me and them. No, me and Mary.

Becca had transformed too, the sleek black fur of her Hellcat glinting with icy power as she stood head-to-head with him to keep him back. Whatever conversation they were having, I couldn't hear it.

To my left, Kuma and Hikari looked horrible. Each had a hand firmly pressed to Finns shoulders where he kneeled on the floor. His eyes were bulging, jaw clenched shut so hard it looked like it hurt.

Anzen. Mary had mentioned Anzen. Her son.

A rush of clarity, and then I was rolling to my side, upheaving the sparse contents of my stomach right there on the floor.

A whine sounded from above my head and I felt Akashi step closer to me, his worry throbbing through my chest. It didn't keep me from puking a second time. I curled on my side, coughing more than breathing.

"This is good, My Lady. Finally letting something out of you." Fingers that sparked with electricity threaded through my hair, pulling it back from my face. I glanced up at the man who was gently shifting my head to rest on his lap.

At first, I thought it was Aengus, or at least a younger brother of his. Fiery orange hair with platinum highlights framed his face in waves. He wore no clothes, which would have been off putting had I not locked eyes with his familiar amber gaze.

"Vallen," I forced out, before another mouthful of bile came up. "You have a lot of explaining to do."

Akashi nosed me gently, and I turned my face toward him expecting anger. Instead, his gaze was warm, and reassuring. Vallen clucked his tongue,

"I identified myself while you were napping down there so that he wouldn't attempt to tear out my throat."

"This was not a nap," I groaned, anything but humored. He grinned at me, but when he looked up at Mary all the niceties vanished from his demeanor.

"I remember you. How long has it been since you fled?"

My head was swimming, but I followed everyone's gaze to Mary. Luna held the smaller woman in her arms, a protective air about the gesture. That in and of itself was enough to make me nauseous again.

"I'm not quite sure." Mary's eyes flicked to mine, questioning. I realized she was inferring my age.

"I'm supposed to know?" I whispered, but the rage was back in my voice. Good. I needed that right now to not fall apart. I cleared my throat, allowing Vallen to help me sit up.

"You have about thirty seconds to explain what you said about Anzen before I allow his brothers to tear you limb from limb."

Beside me I felt Kuma and Hikari reflexively tense. I could taste their confusion in the air, but no anger. In fact, the only one who seemed angry was Akashi, but now that I was somewhat functioning again, he was subdued.

"Raven." Luna let go of my birth mother and stepped towards me. I felt Vallen flex under me, about to shift, but I halted him with a hand on his wrist. Luna paused a few feet away glancing from me to each of my brothers in turn.

"I'm sorry." It's all she said before turning away, hand reaching for Aengus who was by her side in an instant.

Without Luna beside her, Mary looked incredibly tiny. And weak. Something my sister noticed as the feline twisted to face her.

"If they don't kill you, I sure will for what you made us do." Her voice rolled around the room now, the threat weighing heavily. Mary though, didn't even take a step back. She slid her irritatingly calm gaze back to me.

"I will explain myself as you've asked. After arriving here of my own free will to plead with Lucifer for aid against Gabriel, he took me hostage. I was not able to escape until several centuries later. During that time, I was not the only one sharing your fathers bed. Bastet found herself in similar circumstances as I, especially after you were born. It was too large a risk to flee with three children. Two was risk enough."

"So, you chose your pick of the litter and left the runt to die?" Becca dragged her claws across the floor, leaving deep gouges in the marble.

"We took the ones he would be most tempted to kill to maintain his own level of power." Mary squared her shoulders.

For a brief moment, she resembled the faint memory I had of the Angel fighting Lucifer in the church. That moment was shattered by the more vivid vision of her body in a puddle of golden blood. She continued on, as if that never happened. "Anzen was not born with powers that could rival his. He wasn't under an immediate threat."

"And yet he's the one that's dead." It took me a minute to realize I had said it out loud. My voice wobbled as I added, "And he wasn't a powerless runt. He was an Alpha, who suppressed what he was in order to protect me."

Mary's eyes widened in surprise, and Becca's flashed apologetically. Akashi was beside me now, thankfully with jeans pulled on from some hidden corner.

"Get Mary out of here," he ordered, lacing our fingers. "Give her access to a shower, and proper food. But don't let her out of her room." Hikari and Kuma simultaneously jerked, every single one of their muscles straining, but they didn't budge.

"I'm not touching her," Hikari said, the veins in his neck bulging with the effort to resist Akashi's command.

I had never a day in my life seen him be defiant to anyone, let alone his Alpha. Similarly, Kuma was poised like a statue, fists trembling by his sides. Tension threaded through Akashi's body, his eyes simmering with held back power. I swore I felt a literal pulse of it wash through the room, but then he conceded with a relaxed nod, and it disappeared like I had imagined it.

"Fine." His eyes lowered to Finn, and he outright smirked at him. "Then get that leech out of my sight."

276

"You'll need me close by, until he gets a new halo," Silas crooned. He too was smirking, but his glittering gaze was trained on my mate. I didn't like that look, or the sense of being on the outside of something important.

"If you want a new halo on him, put it on yourself. His chains will be enough to keep him from teleporting." Silas and Akashi both snapped their heads to look at me, but neither of them argued.

"I shall assist the vampire." Vallen rose to his feet, fingers brushing my cheek before transforming into his Hound with a flash of white flame. I didn't bother to ask which vampire he intended to assist as the group made their exit.

"I guess that means you're with me," Rebecca purred to Mary, anything but sweetly. Mary turned to me once more, but I faced my back to her. With Akashi's hand firmly in mine, we slipped into a shadow without looking back.

CHAPTER 27

"You really want to risk letting Finn paralyze people?" Akashi asked the question shortly after we appeared in my rooms. He hadn't said a word while I stripped off my bloody leathers and made my way towards the bathroom.

It was smaller than the one at the vampire's mansion, but had a similar charm. The triangle shaped room had flickering candles clustered in the corners, and each wall boasted a floor to ceiling mirror flecked with diamond. Or stardust. At this point who knew? The tub was in the center of the room, carved from a massive chunk of smokey quartz. Above it was a square showerhead, where the water would fall like summer rain.

As I sank into the steaming water he shucked off his jeans to join me. I was too surprised by the sight of our imprint marks, now resembling genuine tattoos, to protest. The tub was large enough so that even with us fully seated our ankles were just brushing.

"I'm not particularly worried about it," I said quietly, sinking so that my mouth hovered just above the water line. "He would have done it already."

"He may just be biding his time." Akashi stretched his arms out along the rim of the tub, water sloshing with the movement. "I don't understand how you can trust him."

"He's in love with me." Silence struck the room, ripe with Akashi's tension.

There wasn't a doubt in my mind about Finn's feelings. Even through his schemes and rage, he had pursued me relentlessly. He never bothered hiding that my wellbeing was a priority, juggling that with his own agenda.

"I know you're going to say not to believe a word he says to me," I murmured. "But he would say the same about you. Unfortunately, the two of you are on the same side when it comes to me. You just take very different routes towards what you think is best."

"If I didn't love you, I would kind of hate you for comparing me to him."

"Exactly," I said, glancing at him sidelong. "You both want to tear each other to bits because I'm what you want."

Akashi opened his mouth but immediately clamped it shut, unable to find an argument. Slowly, I made my way to his side, the water rippling around me as I traced the bare patch of skin through his left brow where I'd cut him with holy metal the first time we met.

"I'm terrified I'm going to hurt you again. In a way we can't fix." I whispered the admission, trying not to let my voice shake. "I'm not doubting your strength, I know you can handle yourself. But look at everyone who gets close to me. Rebecca's memories are permanently fucked up. Mary's human. And Anzen—" I stopped talking as his hand circled my wrist, yanking me into his lap.

"You can't keep everyone out, and you won't." He brought my hand to his mouth, mumbling against the wet skin. "Us getting hurt has nothing to do with your actions, just the environment we're all in."

"I bit Finn. More than once." His shoulders tense slightly, but other than that he remained composed.

"Why?" Such a simple question.

"Because I wanted to. And he's not afraid of that half of me bring in control." Akashi opened his mouth to protest, but I silenced him with a finger against his lips. "I know you're not afraid of me, but sometimes you fear too much *for* me, and it's just another weight on my shoulders."

Understanding flashed in his eyes, and he gave a shallow nod. Slowly, he shifted, releasing my wrist to grip my legs and settle us into the curve of the tub. I curled forward, resting my cheek on his warm skin.

"Then give me the rest of the weight," he murmured, almost like a prayer. His hands slowly traced the length of my spine and again, I felt that strange new sense of power settle in the room. In the mark resting over my heart. He tipped my chin to meet his gaze, eyes damn near sparking as he said, "The only time I'm afraid is when you force me to watch you bear it all yourself."

I felt a shiver of power, a tamped down echo of Vallen in my veins, and sighed. He'd been urging me to give in for months, as had Silas. After the day I just had, I had no more energy to fight it. As soon as I stared talking, upheaving the storm inside my mind, I couldn't stop.

Mary and Bastet were formidable teachers, and yet somehow, loving mothers. The contradiction of expectations vs emotions still shook me to my core.

Rebecca and I were given ample time to be children, but made aware enough of the reality surrounding us that if we had any innocence, it was gone before we had left hell. Our training began early, before I was large enough to hold a sword properly. But our magic was potent enough to begin to coax out.

Perfecting our powers was a relentless task. If we weren't focused at all times, including in our sleep, it would burst from us in uncontrollable waves. More than once our mothers had to physically overpower us, or even knock us out, just to get our unintended onslaught to stop. I think this was why my body automatically knew what to do when I took myself off my leash a few months ago. It was unnerving at first, how easy it was to draw on this power, but after the decades of practice I didn't know I had, muscle memory kicked in.

Mary was absolutely certain I would rise just as her first born did. Though her confidence in me made me feel on top of the world, I had also felt continuous underlying senses of fear and, as I got older, disgust. She bet her aspirations on my actual life and though it paid off, it sickened me.

But what really threw me off was Anzen being connected to this. As far as I could remember his name was never uttered in front of me until he introduced himself. As a Hound, he would have been taken from Mary as soon as he was done nursing. Before putting the plan into action, Mary must have confided in Luna. She in turn, must have passed along at least some of the information to her final child, and given her track record, urged him not to tell me.

How often Luna and Mary communicated, and what was shared, I was unsure of. I felt like if Luna knew the severity demanded of me, she wouldn't have become a part of this. At the same time though, it would explain why she was so determined to keep me hidden, and the restrictions she gave me when it came to my powers.

And that's what it all came down to. My powers, my lineage, my ever-wavering fate. To Lucifer, my birth gave him a route to Heavens destruction, but under my mother's guidance I wound up destroying the devil and claiming hell for myself.

If Anzen was aware of my role, it would explain many of his behaviors towards me over the years. He was always the gentlest with me, and the most forgiving. I killed his mate for fucks sake, and he still remained by my side till the end.

But it would also explain how he suspected and planned ahead for Rebecca and I to sneak to hell alone. Out of all my brothers, he hadn't appeared the least bit surprised by the appearance of her, and wisely stayed quiet while Luna prodded the subject all those months ago. He'd already been prepared with his own agenda, his own powers, to ensure my part in this was a success no matter the cost.

"Is there anything else you want to know?" The water around us had long since cooled, and I picked at the dead skin around my fingernails anxiously. Other than the shift of the water as he worked the million little braids out of my hair, he'd been utterly silent.

"Do you not have the urge to bite me?" I froze, shocked by the question, and quickly glanced up at his face. He wore that neutral expression Luna trained into us, but was holding his breath. Like he was nervous.

Averting my gaze, I focused on that steady pulse of connection within my imprinting bond. It was fluttering rapidly, like it was his racing heartbeat in my chest. Feeling myself blush, I whispered the admission.

"I fight the urge to bite you, daily." My fangs had already elongated, my instincts reacting to the prospect before I could control it. I dipped my head, fighting the shame, and tried to hide them as I spoke. "After getting a taste in the garden, I'm scared that if I give into it I won't be able to stop."

His hand cupped my cheek, swiveling me back to face him. His forest green eyes held curiosity and a restrained, flickering heat as his thumb slid against the seam of my mouth.

"You'd stop," he murmured, and his faith in me made something deeply buried and broken gasp in relief and agony all at once, the serrated shards of myself snapping back into place violently.

"So I'm not allowed to protect you?" I asked, trying to sound annoyed. "I'm not allowed to be scared of hurting you?" He grunted an affirmation, still not releasing his hold on me. I lifted my chin a bit higher, just enough so that his thumb couldn't continue to caress my mouth, tempting me to bite, and his eyes gleamed with amusement.

"What would you be protecting me from, exactly? Your needs? Your desires?" With a surge of movement we were out of the tub, and he was settling me on the vanity, caging me against the mirror. My heart raced in my chest, heat instantly blooming low in my belly as my body recalled the first time he had me in this very position.

"The more I drink, the more intense, my magic becomes," I whisper, feeling my teeth begin to chatter as I pushed against his chest, still trying to fight it.

"Like growing a tail and your blood turning black?" He leaned closer, his breath rolling over my pulse. "If it wasn't abundantly clear, your devil side has never scared me. It shocks me occasionally sure, but for fucks sake Raven," his forehead presses to mine, his scent like a pine forest after a summer thunderstorm. "One day you're going to have to accept that I love you. That with or without imprinting on you, you're my *mate*. And I'm all in."

My emotions were threatening to overwhelm me. The imprinting mark on my chest thrummed between us, relief, and compassion and love coursing through my whole body in waves. Slowly, my fingers drifted down his ribcage, my palm pressing against his matching mark. His was beating in rhythm with mine, sending a fresh wave of emotion crashing through me at the contact.

"I can feel you," I murmured against his wet skin. His lips ghosted across mine.

"Then believe me." He kissed me again, deeper this time. It took all the self-control I had left to tangle my hands into his hair and pull him back, to look him in the eye and say what I'd been feeling but avoiding for so long.

"I love you, too."

After a few more kisses, Akashi untangled himself from me to fetch us towels, and I turned to the mirror trying not to wince at myself. To accept what I was becoming.

Steam still clung to the glass, but it was clear enough to see the faint gleam of scales clinging to my skin in the flickering candlelight, like an iridescent snakeskin. Both my eyes were glowing slightly, like little pockets of starlight against my dark hair.

Akashi's hand slid up my back reassuringly as I raised a finger, touching one of my own fangs before grabbing the towel from him and wrapping it around myself. Without a word he scooped me into his arms, carrying me out of the room bridal style to our bed.

A version of my past self would have made some sarcastic comment about it or faked a gag. Now, I just nuzzled into his arms as he settled us onto the plush mattress. With his steady heartbeat beneath my ear, rest found me for the first time in weeks.

CHAPTER 28

I woke long after the sun rose. At least I think it was a sun, I wasn't about to begin trying to figure out what made it lighter and darker down here. Akashi was already gone, but there was a notecard left on the bedside table, right next to a tray piled generously high with food.

Stomach roaring, I pulled myself across the mattress and grabbed the closest thing to me, some type of jam filled tart thing, and stuffed it in my mouth. An appreciative moan vibrated deep in my throat as the bright notes of creamsicle ice cream coated my tongue. Like a starved goblin, I grabbed four more.

Once I'd finished them, I picked up a bowl of fruit and the notecard before flopping back against the pillows. I popped a swollen purple grape in my mouth and scanned Akashi's familiar scratchy handwriting, snorting at the 'you're sleeping like the dead' comment before pausing on his final line.

'Drink it.'

My eyes cut back to the bedside table, locking on a small aluminum water bottle. I picked it up, and the second I began to unscrew the lid the scent of his blood hit me. I debated for a second, looking at the note, closing my eyes, breathing. And then I chugged it like a woman stuck in the desert for a month.

Quickly, I tossed the covers back, trying not to think about the lingering taste on my tongue as I walked across the room to my neglected closet full of clothes. Rather than conjuring a new outfit, I sifted through items my sister must have brought from the mansion. My favorite leather jacket was hanging in the front, so I grabbed that with a low-backed tank. Then I snatched a pair of dark cargo pants, adjusting them only slightly to include a Velcro sticker in the back to accommodate my tail. Today would be the first time I didn't try to hide it from the Hounds, and I ignored the tiny flair of anxiety in my chest as I glanced at myself in the mirror.

The dark swirls of my imprinting mark peeked out from beneath the collar of my tank. Akashi had said nothing about the change, so I tried to relax and not overthink it. Besides, I was glad it was visible anyway. I didn't want to hide that anymore either.

After dragging out my most trusted pair of combat boots, I slipped into the shadows. As per usual, my brain was going a million miles a minute, but for once the asymmetrical ramblings flowed together, and I was able to place a sense of direction.

Vallen. Anzen. Mary.

The three of them were without a doubt interconnected. With one unwilling to talk, another dead, and the last already making me feel nauseous just to think about, I hadn't a clue how I was about to start following that tangled ball of yarn.

A flash of light in my peripheral made me pause. Out of the dark, a small orb of blue floated towards me. My stomach rolled once more, but I weaved through the shadows anyway until I emerged atop that grassy plane beside my mother.

It was dusk in the human realm. A waning crescent moon hung low in the sky, casting Anzens gravestone in a pale haze. Fireflies bobbed through the air, sometimes getting swept up in the breeze to streak through the night like mini shooting stars.

"I shouldn't have kept it from you." Luna sounded broken, and immediately vines swirled to life inside my wrists. I groaned, not letting them surface as the familiar onslaught of emotions already threatened to ruin my body. She whipped towards me, eyes glowing blue and brimming with tears.

"After being forsaken by my pack, Mary became my family. We vowed that we would get out. That we would stop him. All of them." In all my years I had never seen Luna so undone, and the raw vulnerability of her state had any lingering sense of anger or betrayal being snuffed out.

"The plan changed when she got pregnant. At the time, Bastet had not yet arrived. Lucifer hadn't realized until conceiving you that he could have children, and we believe he captured Bastet as well as others with the intention of spreading his lineage and his powers. With you, he could overthrow Heaven. He never assumed his own blood would work against him." A chill that had nothing to do with the night had my hair standing on end, and something deep inside me began wailing as Luna continued, barely taking time to breathe.

"But when her belly began to swell a second time she swore it wasn't another of Lucifers. I didn't fully believe her, thinking her trauma may have altered her recollection. But when that child was born it was undeniable he would become a strong Hound, and I swore that when I ran I would take him with me. That I would keep all of her children safe." Her voice broke off as a strangled sound left her throat.

I took a measured breath, wave after wave of exhaustion and loss slowly crashing over me. And then it eventually drifted away into a more bearable weight.

"You knew he would be an Alpha?" I spoke barley above a whisper. There was nothing accusatory in my tone, but Luna winced all the same.

"How could he not be? You saw your mother in her full power. You wield it, and more. Despite my efforts to delay it, there was only ever going to be one path for Anzen. Just like there was only ever one for you."

I felt the dark, twisted thing inside me threatening to creep up, and reflexively wrapped my mental chains around it. Immediately, the thorns poking at my skin receded, and the night wind lulled to a stop.

"Thank you for raising us the way you did," I said. Luna blinked, a look of surprise crossing her face.

"You're not enraged that I kept so many secrets?" I hated the look of doubt on her face. The way she searched me from head to toe with her eyes as if I were trying to trap her. I cocked my head, averted my gaze, and continued to measure each breath, remaining in control.

"Would you rather I cause a tempest like the last time we discussed the random appearance of one of my siblings?" It was a poor attempt at humor, but it got a corner of Lunas mouth to tick up.

My brain however, launched past the moment. The continuous stream of thoughts began to overflow again, branching out and converging as memories and thoughts and coincidences piled atop one another. I let my eyes drift back to Anzen's headstone, and considered the question for only half a second before blurting it out.

"Did you see him? In his coffin?"

The night breeze flowed once more, the shiver of grasses dancing against one another the only sound for several minutes.

"Why do you ask?" Luna's words were not as strained as they were earlier, but they were far from relaxed. I knelt slowly, fingers curling into the dirt above where my brother's body should be.

"Mary was shocked that he wasn't with us," I murmured, heat resonating from my fingers. Roots and rock and soil began to twist and shift beneath me, slow enough for Luna to notice my intention and demand me to stop. She didn't, so I went on.

"She was upset, but not devastated. Not in the way you would expect a mother to be if they learned their child was dead." Not the way that Luna was, and still is, since his death.

She stepped closer to me as the earth began to groan and shudder below us, folding away from my brother's grave.

She pressed a hand to my shoulder, but I didn't stop.

"Raven before you do something drastic, might I remind you that Mary isn't quite in her right mind? Numerous outside sources may be impacting how she reacted to your presence, and his lack of."

"But that's the thing that was off, isn't it?" I asked, mostly to myself, as I sat on the edge of the hole I just made. It was a short drop, only six feet down to stand beside my brother's coffin. I inhaled sharply, but the only scent was damp cedar, not decay.

The wood was stained and polished, shining like a penny in the dull light. This was the first time I'd seen it; he and the rest of our dead were already buried by the time I was stable enough to make my first visit up here.

"You know Mary far better than anyone else here." I slowly drifted my fingers across the lid. "But from what I remember of her, she functioned in two different ways.

"One, she felt deeply. My magic functions just as hers did. Our emotions are so powerful they affect everything.

And two, she was devoted to the plan more than anything. She wasn't distraught by his death, and literally planned mine as a key factor to our success." I grit my teeth, feeling my anger rekindle.

"I know that makes you feel as if she values the plan more than your life," Luna interjected, trying to be a voice of reason when it wasn't needed. "But Raven, you were going to come back. It was a certainty that even God bothered to confirm despite his lack of intervention." I brushed off that bombshell of an admission, sliding my gaze to hers.

"Exactly."

We stood there for a moment, just staring at each other. Then her eyes flared with blue power as she finally caught on to what I'd already figured out.

"Oh my God," she whispered, shock making her legs give out. I curled my fingers under the lip of the coffin, ignoring her cry as I threw it off.

The heady scent of Alpha clung to the cream-colored bed and silk pillow, but that wasn't what made my blood run cold.

My brother's body was missing.

CHAPTER 29

My hands were shaking with the effort to keep my panic and fury from obliterating everyone and everything in the room. It took all of ten seconds for Akashi to reach us after I screamed. After noting my dirt-stained hands and gaping at the empty coffin, he helped Luna and I carry it down from the hills, and through a shadow to the meeting hall. I sent for everyone in our circle: Aengus, Hikari, Kuma, Silas, Jesibelle, Rebecca, and, despite all protests, Finn.

Upon seeing the empty coffin, my panic was shared by each of them. My rage, however, was all my own. I flicked my gaze back and forth between our two guests seated opposite of each other, Mary and Uriel.

My mother had entered with Jesibelle. She'd been given proper clothes since we parted yesterday, but the fine silk dress dwarfed her thin frame. I also caught a glimpse of bandages on her wrists and forearms beneath the emerald shawl she had wrapped tightly around herself like a security blanket.

Like yesterday, and much to her sister's visible displeasure, Luna had positioned herself by Mary's side. The silence between the trio was palpable, so much so that even Aengus gave them a wide berth.

To avoid staring a hole through Mary's skull, I locked my gaze on Uriel. The Angel's wings still hadn't reappeared, and he looked deathly pale. It caused a sick current of satisfaction to course through me. His wrists and ankles were manacled in onyx shackles, with a long chain connecting the sets together.

Becca had brought him in with her, offering few words as to why he was here. It didn't matter to me where he was, I reasoned with myself. He was her revenge after all, not mine.

Uriel didn't return my look though. Unlike me, he showed no restraint as he stared down Mary like he wanted her to crumble before him. I tried not to be humored by her pretending he didn't exist.

Her eyes were studying the stained-glass window on the far side of the room, hints of wonder and approval clear on her face. My wings flared with agitation. I didn't want her pride.

"Rav... the table." Becca was the first to speak, gently, as if I was a cornered predator.

"I'm aware," I said, voice void of any emotion as I uncurled my fists. Smoke was rising from my fingertips, flames flickering beneath my skin. "What I'm unaware of, is where my brother's body is. And I have about two minutes of patience left before I start burning things to the ground."

"Limbo." We all turned to look at Uriel, who was grinning smugly.

"Limbo?" Akashi prodded, green eyes narrowing on the Angel. "And what exactly is that?"

"The first layer of hell. Baby stuff, really. Heathens who tried to do good float in an endless blank abyss, occasionally harassed by monsters or lesser demons." He cocked a brow, smirking like the self-righteous prick he was as he faced me and asked, "Sound familiar, wench?"

So that's what that place was. It was like an acid trip, high and terrifying and absolutely empty. Something was crawling around in there. I'd felt it purring, reaching for me. I'd been able to rise out of it, but I have the blood of two Angels in my veins. Anzen doesn't. Suppressing a shiver, I gave a subtle nod of acknowledgment.

"So, he's stuck in Limbo." I drummed my fingers on the table, wrestling with the flames inside me to remain banked. "When I was there, it was hard to find the will to leave. I remember nothing mattered anymore, and the relief was enticing." I felt the weight of my family staring at me, so quickly got to the point. "But with Mary's blood, he can rise out of there too, can't he?"

Uriel downright sneered at me, refusing to answer, but a smile flickered on Mary's face. She still seemed so undeterred by the situation, like it was a little hiccup to weekend plans. Her calmness just served to piss me off more.

"How do we get him out?" Hikari spoke first, his eyes still glued to the coffin. Uriel didn't bother suppressing his laugh, and Kuma didn't pull the punch he sent into his gut.

"You don't," Uriel gasped, barely able to gather himself enough to speak. "The beast either uses the shred of angelic blood he possesses and rises, or he remains there for eternity." Before he could laugh again, there was a blast of cold and Uriel was encased in a block of ice.

"I'll deal with him properly later." Becca's tone matched her magic. Sharp, cold, and unforgiving.

"How did you get out of there?" Akashi's focus had shifted to me. There was a flurry of emotions on his face as he struggled through a war I recognized all too well. What role should he play right now. Brother? Alpha? Mate?

"I don't know," I admitted. The stress bearing down on me was like a planet's gravity, but I didn't entertain it. Instead I slid my hand into his, feeling my imprint mark pulsed once before I steadied, and I could tell it did the same for him.

"You had a reminder." Jesibelles voice sounded serene and far away. Glancing to her, I noted the lilac hue which now coated her skin. Similar to Luna, her power also sparked in her eyes, her magic showing her something that the rest of us were blind to. Like a marionette, she raised a hand to her earlobe. "Your earrings. Hers." She pointed to Mary.

I jolted. That's right.

After Rebecca had dragged that blade across my throat, all I had and all I was began fading. And I liked it. And yet, floating away in that darkness, there had been a flicker of gold. My mother's ear cuffs. The heart-stopping reminder of what I had left, and what I still needed to do, launching me back towards life.

My blood roared in my ears like a freight train as I drew the sword from its perch. If I could barely find the will to rise when I still had shit to do, how was Anzen, after scheming his own sacrifice, going to be able to?

"Tell me more," I all but hissed. The world grew hazy at the edges, and then I was behind Mary, lining her own blade up against her throat.

Despite Lunas growl, Mary remained perfectly poised, folding her hands on the table in front of her. My skin prickled with the awareness of Akashi's slow approach just as a bite of ice began stinging my palm. I growled low, my grip on the blade not wavering until Mary whispered with a voice full of sorrow.

"Our bloodline is just as cursed, as it is blessed. Only we may come and go from that place. And you've already returned."

"Stop speaking in riddles!" I nearly shrieked. The blade was vibrating wildly against her skin now, the bite of ice turning into a full-on burn as my sister's power crawled up my arm.

"What she means to say is," Vallen's voice curled into my ear now, a sweet caress I wasn't prepared for. "Only she, or you, can go to that place and have any hope of finding him. But each time you fall, you risk not coming back."

Mary was crying now; I could smell the salt of her tears even though her shoulders didn't shake. One of her tiny hands rose to also circle the handle of the blade, fingers brushing mine.

A sickening feeling churned my gut as I realized she wouldn't fight me. She would let me kill her right here, and she would fall to find Anzen. She was a human. She probably wouldn't survive it. Why did that matter?

"No," I growled in her ear, knocking her grip off the blade and stepping back. She twisted in her seat to give me a pleading look and I glared back at her.

"Raven, I need to do this," she said. "All of this is because of my choices. I need to take responsibility for it, and stop watching my children pay the price."

"No," I repeated, voice going dark. "You don't get to control the outcome any longer. I do." She didn't get to be a hero. She didn't get to be a martyr and kill herself to save her son.

An eerie calmness had settled over me and with a twist of my wrist, I had flipped the sword to lay against my own neck. It barely took half a glide to shred the elastic choker I wore, and for the first time in months, I bore the silver necklace my scar to the world. My blade wasn't shaking anymore, grip so tight on the hilt my knuckles were white.

I was supposed to be the strongest one here. I've defied every odd I came up against so far. I already rose. I could do it again. I *had* to do it again. My brother needed me. But before I could move another millimeter, a pair of teeth I knew intimately pressed against the other side of my neck.

"Angel, don't."

Finn distracted me long enough for my sister to yank the sword from my grasp, sending it flying across the room. My scream was bordering on a howl as I punched Finn in the face, blood spurting from his broken lip. Arms wrapped around my waist as Akashi all but tackled me to the floor.

"No, no, no!" I pleaded, my fists pounding down against his spine. I didn't know if I wanted him to get away so I wouldn't hurt him, or get out of the way so I could do what I needed to.

"Anzen said to trust you," he snarled in my face, his hands slamming my wrists into the stone floor above my head. The imprinting bond was thrumming wildly with his panic, the dominance of his Alpha blood taking over. "Don't you dare make me watch you die again!"

Tears were streaming down my face, and electrified shadows were pouring off my skin, turning the room into a field of crackling energy. I was vaguely aware of someone kneeling by my head, of Akashi growling again as a cool palm rested on my forehead.

"How long has she been wielding both sides?" Mary's voice filtered through my internal collapse, and another sob tore from my throat.

"Nearly half a year." Vallen's voice now, laced with bitterness as he added, "Ever since she joined with me."

"I knew she could do it." A flash of light between my eyes, and then a sudden calm, like the eye of a storm. Instantly, my shadows fell to the floor, dissipating into nothing. The static electricity hanging in the air faded into an early spring breeze.

Mary's fingers threaded through my hair and a sensation like warm sunlight on bare skin filled me, making the tension in my body release. That was the last thing I remembered as I once again drifted into the promised quiet of sleep.

Blood was not enough for Rebecca, not now. Even after feasting on Uriel, and giving him several new ice-induced piercings, her rage would not quell. Her claws itched to shred something; her fangs screamed to kill. But she couldn't. Not when her sister just tried to kill herself for a second time.

She vomited up all the blood she drank, and even after rotting in her stomach it still glittered up at her. A mockery of her sisters, or was her sisters the mockery? After all, wasn't she bleeding black now?

She very well might have killed Uriel in that cell if Silas didn't drag her out when he did. The Angel was giving up nothing, and did nothing but continue to smile that smug, asshole smile at her between his screams.

After a brief physical fit of protest she relented, and Silas rewarded her with his hands. And his tongue. The adrenaline in her blood shifted from bloodlust, to plain, basic, good old-fashioned lust, and offered a kind of release far more rewarding than a killing blow would.

With a gasp, she arched as he thrust up to meet her, his steady hands on her hips guiding her back down to sink onto him fully. Her blood stained his lips, just as surely his stained her own, and it made her feel absolutely feral.

The room spun around her as he flipped them with ease, able to sense the shift in her even if she couldn't. A few deep, long strokes had her shaking and him cursing, and finally she was once again able to breathe.

"I don't like solving rage with sex," she grumbled, turning to lay facing away from him.

"Oh?" Silas grazed his fingers down her bare spine. "You seemed just fine with it a couple minutes ago."

"Shut up." She moved to bury herself deeper into the pillows, but he snaked his arms around her, pulling her back to him.

"You can't control your sister," he murmured into her hair. "None of us can. Especially when she believes what choice she makes is the best for everyone."

"Sounds like someone else I know." There was an underlying bite to her tone.

"I know you think what you're doing is the best fallback plan, but you're running out of time. Everything is falling apart."

"I don't think our situation is quite that dire yet my dear," he said, voice forcefully upbeat. She frowned at him over her shoulder.

"Your brother doesn't even know the extent of it." Silas stiffened.

"And thank God for it. Look at what he's already done. Imagine what worse he could have done if he knew the full truth of what was buried in his blood."

Rebecca didn't have a response to that. Nothing stubborn. Nothing witty. Nothing, she realized, but the faint echo of fear in her chest.

CHAPTER 30

My sister did not return my sword. And Mary... I didn't even want to think about her, but I couldn't stop.

The last thing I remember was her looking at me like she was begging me to forgive her. Out of all the things my mother put me through, the expectations, the loss, the guilt, the *weight* of it all. That look was the most unforgivable.

I could justify everything else, I honest to God could. There were good motives, sound reasons, desirable outcomes that could benefit all. But that look made me wish I never found her. That she'd stayed the dead, idolized version of herself in my dreams.

Once I came to, I realized Akashi had locked us away in our rooms. He was quiet as I dissociated, utterly calm when I screamed verbal responses at Vallen whenever he dared speak in my head. Periodically, knocks would sound at the door, but Akashi intercepted them with a finesse I'd never have. Food was brought and taken away, and I could smell that blood was delivered but he must have refused it.

I felt like I was a ghost, watching this happen around me, not having any part in it other than the voice in my head and the emotions in my blood. I had no sense of time but could feel the minutes ticking into hours, and as we approached a second day of solitude, I began to itch. He could keep everyone else out, sure. But he couldn't keep me in.

I was a flash at the next knock, my body more scales than skin, my growl more monster than person. I was in the hallway before Akashi could protest, and instantly everyone present froze.

Halfway down the corridor, Finn was on his knees. Though he wasn't putting up a fight, four large Hounds were holding him down. Everyone's head was turned in my direction, unable to hide their shock or wariness of my appearance.

"Let him up," I said, voice echoing against the stone.

"Always so considerate, Angel." Warmth circled my body, threatening to plunge beneath my skin, and Finn grinned at me. We assessed each other, aware of the others power and unwilling to submit to it.

"I simply stopped by to coax you out. It seems Lady Jesibelle is under the impression that any male within a mile of her is willing to be an errand boy." He chuckled, but I could hear the underlay of annoyance in his tone.

"And yet here you are, all but running an errand." I didn't bother masking my humor, and flashed him a mocking smirk.

Akashi's shadow clung to me as I paced down the hall towards the vampire. As I approached, the Hounds holding him backed up a few paces, but to my shock Finn remained on his knees. I narrowed my eyes at him and asked, "What does she want?"

"It seems Mary has requested your presence in her chambers." I blinked.

Truthfully, I was unaware of her whereabouts during her stay here. I never bothered to seek her out. Finn smoothed his hair back, rocking back onto his heels. "She also mentioned something about glowing snakeskin? Oh, and of course your two-toned blood. Her chatter about it is making all the ladies squeamish." Yea, that tracks.

"Very well." I sighed. Without further comment I reached backwards. Akashi's hand met mine halfway, and I dropped us into the shadows at our feet.

"My urge to kill him has been renewed," he muttered as we waded through the dark.

"Would you rather he not intervene?" My question dropped like a nuke in the silence of the shadow realm, and Akashi's answer was its instant shockwave.

"No." He swung me around in the dark, but the only thing I could see was that flickering cauldron of green fire in his eyes.

"Perhaps, you appreciate his actions then?" I said, gently raising my free hand to smooth against his cheek. Despite the scales on my skin, he melted into my touch.

"Tch." He didn't respond further, and I didn't push.

"I promise I'm going to find out what's going on, and get out brother back," I said, voice softening. "And that I won't hurt myself anymore to do it."

"Shut up," he hissed, his grip moving to my upper arm and yanking me closer. "I trust you, but if you *ever* do something like that again I won't hesitate to throw your ass into one of your homemade cage's downstairs. Got it?"

"You know I can just make the cage disappear, right?" I hedged, trying to be funny, but he didn't play along. He just turned his face against my palm, and bit.

I flinched, not in pain but surprised. His teeth felt sharper than I thought they would, like just his mouth was transformed into a Hound. The move was downright possessive, and I felt the imprinting mark on my chest flare with heat in response.

"W-we really shouldn't linger in here."

"Mhm." Then he licked my skin, and this time the mark literally vibrated to life.

"Seriously?" I tried to yank my hand away, but he held fast, pressing something small and cool into my palm.

"I risked Rebecca skinning me alive, getting this back for you," he murmured, and I was surprised to see my golden ear cuff glittering up at me through the dark. I opened my mouth, but he silenced me with a chaste kiss.

"Don't make me regret it." I wouldn't.

We stepped out of the shadow realm and into the Night Howlers luxurious seating room, shocking a few of the Hounds who were present. One even screamed, but Jesibelle just finished taking a sip of tea, her sky-blue eyes meeting mine.

Akashi had gone tense beside me as the ever present floral scent of a Hound in heat slowly wafted towards us. I growled, and two of them immediately saw themselves out, the scent fading with them.

"My Lady. Akashi." Jesibelle greeted us, rising from her seat. "I wasn't prepared for you to visit this quickly. Would you like for me to have some refreshments prepared?"

"Cut the crap." Akashi stepped forward before I could even open my mouth. "You sent Finn with the request, so you know why we're here." My mark once again hums, this time with appreciation and the foreign notion of feeling safe. My grip in his hand tightens subtly, and his thumb answers by tracing affectionate circles across my skin. Jesibelle glances between the two of us, already appearing exasperated.

"Your mate always seems exceptionally tense when he's here, even though my girls can't lay a finger on him," she comments, with an uncharacteristic roll of her eyes. With a quick gesture for us to follow, she rises. The folds of her sunset gown billow behind her as she leads us down one of the corridors.

I feel the tension creeping up my spine as we begin passing doors to personal chambers, and chastise myself mentally. I could walk into a battle just fine, or train for hours and be unbothered. But being face to face with my Mother was making my stomach curl in apprehension.

It was easy to be mad, but somehow empathy still clawed its way into my chest. As for her, I didn't know what to expect going in. More apologies? More pleas for forgiveness? Or would it be the version of her I knew best: focused on achieving her end goals, which I now understood fully. If that were the case I think I would actually punch her.

At the end of the hall Jesibelle raised a silver door knocker, and let it fall against the pearl washed wood. A second went by before we heard the lock click, and the door swept open.

"Hello." That voice reached my ears again, melodic and low. Mary was positively beaming at me, and it made my skin crawl. "I didn't think you would accept my request to see you."

"Well, killing myself to avoid you doesn't seem like an option." I stepped over the threshold, watching the verbal blow hit her and the smile on her face wavered. Akashi moved to follow me, but I quickly shook my head.

"Jesibelle, can you please take him with you so he doesn't press against the door to eavesdrop?" I asked, squeezing his hand again before dropping it.

"With pleasure." She rested a guiding, if not adamant hand between his shoulder blades, and nudged him ahead of her. His eyes ricocheted between the three of us, before he shoved his hands in his pockets, relenting.

"I'll be right down the hall when you're ready." I offered only him a smile as he let himself be led away.

As their footsteps faded down the hall, I slowly shut the door, the resounding click echoing dully. I could feel her eyes on me, but I couldn't bring myself to look at her yet, so I studied the room.

The floorboards were almost completely overgrown with moss and ferns. Dangling sprouts of Asian lilacs swayed above us, dotted with the occasional butterfly or woodland critter running about between the twisting boughs. Though the scent in the room was positively human, it seemed not all of Mary's magic had been fully stripped from her.

"There are many things I wish to ask you," she finally said, taking a few steps away as if she could sense I needed the space. I couldn't help but watch her once her back was turned.

Even in less than a week, her complexion had grown healthier, and the way she held herself was less feeble. The woman she once was, beginning to slowly reappear.

She settled herself on the windowsill, the blue fabric of her skirt shimmering in the low light. "I want to know what's on your mind first though. I'm sure there's many things going on inside that beautiful head of yours."

I let the compliment pass me by, and instead searched her face for a hidden motive. In the past, her praise had always been downpayment for a request. But other than the slight flickering of gold close to her irises, she just continued to look at me warmly. Gently. As if I needed comfort from her.

I grit my teeth, narrowing my eyes at her. If she was giving me the floor to speak my mind, I was going to tear the wound open, instead of letting it simmer with infection.

"Since I got my memories back, I've been reanalyzing everything. I can empathize with how out-of-control most of this was. Lucifer's choices. My existence. Gabriels fucking crusade." I balled my hands into fists as I felt them begin to shake.

"But I can't justify your expectations of me. Every area which you could control, you grasped so damn tightly, that you wound up putting me in a similar position. You controlled the trajectory of my life to the point where I literally killed myself to meet your expectations." Tears were burning against my cheeks, but if I stopped here I would never finish.

"Instead of protecting me, you trained me so I could protect not only myself but everyone else. Instead of working together, you manipulated the cards at play so that I would have all the aces to throw at your say so. You made me strong enough to bear it alone, but I was just a kid. I never should have had to."

Mary's expression hadn't changed while I ranted at her, she hadn't so much as moved. Anyone passing by could mistake her for a statue. Finally, she released a heavy sigh, raising her gaze to the florals above us.

"Ever since I was a girl, control has been foreign to me. I was told my position one day, and just had to accept it. No time for fear, no time for bargaining." She pushed off the windowsill to lower herself to the floor, laying back against the greenery.

"You were the first thing in my life which I was able to choose. Lucifer did not know that even with his demonic blood, we were capable of bearing an offspring together. So, in truth," her voice grew somber, "I never intended to protect you. At least not in the ways you needed me to. This world needed a savior again. So, I created another one."

My veins began screaming at me, a violent, burning wave of power rushing through me, before numbing to icy coldness. My entire life I'd believed I was the product of sin. Of force. Of cruelty. That I was an accident everyone scrambled to utilize in their favor. I never thought I was a plan from the beginning. A scheme to trick everyone involved. And somehow that was worse.

"You can't even muster up a single apology? All you can do is pile on more?" I choked the words out, my legs buckling under me so roughly I had to lean against the wall for support. Mary gave me that same sad, pleading look, like I was the one breaking her heart.

"I gave up on finding a way for you to forgive me long ago. I'm just glad I have the privilege of seeing you alive, and for the most part happy."

"Happy? You think I'm happy?" I was fully yelling now, loud enough for petals to shake free and begin falling around us like snow.

"I have a mate that I don't know how to accept, a sister I'm constantly butting heads with, two vampires stalking my every move, an entire army counting on me for their survival and oh yea, so much magic in my body I'm pretty sure I'm going to implode on myself!" Mary sat up, eyes flashing to mine as she spoke with new conviction.

"Yet even now, you're in control. The angelic and demonic halves of you exist at perfect equilibrium. You're the only being in history capable of this control between chaos and peace."

I turn from her, throwing the door open. I didn't want to hear this. I couldn't hear this, I couldn't handle it. Whatever I expected when I walked into the den was just blown to smithereens.

"Raven." She entered the hallway behind me, but wasn't chasing me. I knew I needed to leave, now, before I lit this place up, but something in her tone made me pause.

I cut my eyes over my shoulder to glare at her, and found something flickering on the edge of warning in her gaze. Nothing would have prepared me for her next words, obliterating what little was left of me for her to hurt.

"Beyond your powers, I do hope you learn how to accept your mate. For just like your magic, your womb is ripe.

CHAPTER 31

I didn't want to talk about Mary or her words which left my ears burning like someone had poured acid in them. Wordlessly I took Akashi's hand and walked out the front door without so much as a glance at Jesibelle.

Mary had left me with more questions than answers. More rage than sense. So, I figured it was high time to interrogate the other withholder in my life.

I paused halfway across the lakebed, sending Akashi ahead of me in case I couldn't wrangle Vallen as well as I'd planned to. He took my request, and my warnings as to what he might see, at face value without flinching. After asking a few questions about when and if he should intervene, or if my sister would be a better option, he placed a quick kiss on my cheek and hiked up to watch from the edge of the pit above.

I thought back to the first time I unleashed my full power in purgatory. It only felt like minutes, but an entire day had gone by. I had no way of knowing how long it would take now, as that was before my Reformation. And, more importantly, before Vallen.

The air around me began to shimmer and pulse, an invisible dome rising to contain my magic within the pit. Fire, water, earth, air, light, and darkness bled from my skin, with the crackling of static humming between each atom. I was a kaleidoscope of power, a pulsing river of creation and decay. A reaper and creator sewn into one body.

"This feels amazing, doesn't it?" Vallen purred in my ear. His bare skin was made of flickering white flame, so bright I could barely make out his face. It was like every time he manifested, he was evolving from that distant voice in my head into an individual being.

"Hellfire," I muttered by a way of greeting. "Or Edens Flame?" I arched a brow, and he smiled wider.

"And what else?"

"The source of both Holy and Hellish magic," I growled. "Mine. My parent's. My sister's. Gabriel's. Akashi's, Luna's, Finn's—" He cut me off mid-shout.

"Yes, yes, I've been sprinkled in many places throughout the centuries, haven't I?" He began to circle me slowly, appraisingly. "But somehow, you've managed to absorb me undiluted. And not only that, but you manage to keep me at bay as well. That has never been done before."

"Well, yippie for me." Sarcasm made my words thick, but I quickly forced my annoyance down. "I want to know why you never told me anything."

"Because you'd figure it out when you were supposed to," he mused, completely unbothered.

My rage flared, and I focused it on that chain in my head. The one usually reserved for me, to keep me back, to keep my urges and reactions buried.

Vallen's eyes widened in shock as that chain physically manifested now. I felt the cool shackle close around my wrist as a matching one appeared on his. The links binding us shifted in the air, like silent, glittering shadows.

"You took my wings as payment," I said, the storm around us doubling in size as I recalled our first conversation in this very spot. "I never realized what else you

tried to take, or that it failed
spectacularly, until speaking with Mary."
For the first time, he frowned, and the
sight of it made me grin.

"*My magic is ripe,*" I quoted her,
leveling a glare on him. "All this time I
thought I absorbed you, but you actually
tried to possess me. And now we're
connected by this twisted, two-way
leash."

He didn't even try to deny it,
standing there holding my gaze in silence.
In a way, I could understand it. Lucifer
locked him in a literal frozen prison, and I
didn't want to imagine what Gabriel had
done to him before that. But that didn't
mean I was going to cut him any slack for
it. When he finally spoke, his voice
dripped with disdain.

"Your father had me on a leash. As
did Gabriel, and for a short time, your
mother as well. In fact, she had me when
I was first bound."

"I don't care about those details."
My wings flared to life behind me, four
black shadows laced with purple fire and
crackling with raw energy.

"Well, you should," he countered.
"Mary is the one who planted me here,

giving your father access to my power. She wasn't a very righteous Angel."

"What do you mean she planted you here?" I felt my brows knit, confused, but he just stared at me.

"Figure it out."

I fell quiet, and Vallen seemed content to watch me think this through. History suggested Eden's Flame and Hellfire were two separate things, but now I wasn't quite so sure. The Angels reacted vividly enough to the silver fire I now wielded, proving it was something different than my own flames. But beyond that, the research that Silas, Kuma and I had been doing finally began to make sense.

Although we found nothing specifically about Vallen or the Ashen Hound he could appear as, Lucifer did have a few records on the Hellfire buried deep in the back of the library. Kuma's hunch about the fire had been true, as before it was sealed away the Hellhounds were often born with or granted magical abilities; take Luna and Jesibelle for example. I imagine the process of gaining those powers was similar to how Luna described Gabriel's blessing on Akashi last year.

"So Gabriel had you first, followed by Mary," I finally spoke, my words slow as I continued to piece it together. "Did they both wield you as Eden's Flaming sword?"

"Yes," Vallen growled the confirmation. I bristled, understanding flashing through me. So all this time, the Angels had been pretending to have remnants of Edens Flame. To trick Lucifer into submission? Or to trick the others they sought to destroy?

"Then, if you're no longer in their possession, how do they still have flaming swords?" I asked, and a slow smile crept across his face.

"Flaming swords? Or just swords on fire?" His words were heavy, and dripping with a restrained malice as he added, "I told you. They mocked me."

"Mocked..." I pondered the word, head tilting. "Because you've transformed into Hellfire, and are no longer a power they view as pure?" He leaned forwards, eyes blazing.

"Are you not more than one thing yourself?"

"So you are both," I murmured, so low I could barely hear my own voice.

"Yes." The relief on his face was palpable. With a wave of my hand, the chain on our wrists dissolved into nothing, sinking back into the invisible bond between us.

"You're not just a sentient piece of magic I picked up, so what are you?" His smile faltered.

"I can't *tell* you," he emphasized, and I suppressed an annoyed huff.

"Okay, but why the hell not?" I asked. He was literally living magic. What could possibly have enough influence over him to make him measure his words like this? As if reading my mind, he grinned apologetically.

"God."

Well. That was that then.

With a snap of my fingers, I called my power back to me. Just like last time, there was stained-glass left in its wake, but instead of a rose garden we stood beneath a glowing domed ceiling.

Tendrils of flowering vines and branches made from blown glass swept down towards us, reflecting the dim light from above like an upside-down botanical garden.

Vallen, whose skin had lost the luster of flames, now sat cross legged in the sand before me. With the absence of his fire, I could study him clearly for the first time. His only clothing was a pair of simple tan trousers a shade darker than his skin. A mole dotted his left cheek just under his eye, the amber iris shimmering with faint specks of silver. And his hair was it's own type of fire, with layers of burnt orange braids twisting away from his face to fall down his back to his waist.

"Were you given to Mary or stolen?" I asked, slowly lowering myself to mirror him.

"Given." Relief coursed through me, but I didn't revel in it.

"Did she mix her magic with yours? Or are you evolving a different way."

"We did not mix, though you could say I was altered to fit her benefit." Okay, I could work with that.

"Then is it safe to assume that there was another change for you when you came in contact with my Father?"

"Yes."

"Were you sentient with my mother? Or with him?"

"Him."

If he was only sentient with Lucifer, that would explain why he went mad. He couldn't handle all that warped, mixing, growing power. And to add a voice in his head on top of it? I grimaced, thinking back to my first few weeks of it. And even now.

"I have reason to believe that Lucifer was able to use you to give powers to the Hellhounds. Is this true?" Vallen nodded, but the movement was tense. I continued speculating aloud. "Since you were sentient, you probably had control over the bond. Which meant he couldn't use it to puppeteer his army."

"As you can imagine, that didn't go over well with him." No, I can't imagine it did, since the result was Vallen being casually frozen in a lake for a few centuries while the Hound's power was nearly depleted.

"You don't happen to have any amazing advice on how to end this shit show, do you?" I asked grimly, and he barked a short laugh.

"You truly don't know that you are one of many, still believing that you're the one and only." He flashed me a crooked smile. "Look for the answer from a different angle, with the help of a friend."

"I'm really getting tired of everyones riddles," I grumble, pinching the bridge of my nose. "But you do mean a friend, specifically?"

"Yes." He nodded, pushing to his feet. "They know the answers you seek, and can tell you what I cannot."

I ended it there, before we crossed whatever magical line was drawn. I knew more than enough to at least narrow down my next moves. Before climbing out of the pit I called him back to me. I felt the familiar, quick rush of power as our magicks entwined before he lay settled somewhere deep inside. He deserved a rest. We all did.

I slid between worlds, shadows morphing to glass before morphing to air as I emerged above the dome forged in the sand. I shielded my eyes against the sudden light, scanning the shoreline for Akashi. I was surprised he'd disappeared from where I'd last seen him, but that's not what sent my nerves skyrocketing.

He was a few hundred yards away now, Becca in front of him. Her hands flew around, frantic as she spoke, and a single glistening tear rolled down her cheek. They both turned, seeing me emerge, and she broke into a sprint straight for me.

"It's Atlantis!" She screamed before I could get a word out. "Gabriel is burning it down!"

CHAPTER 32

We moved as one. It was as if the Hellhounds could feel my will and immediately reacted to it.

Whatever was going on with Akashi was even more apparent now that we were surrounded by our entire army. Hounds were flocking him, sometimes not even exchanging a verbal word before running off with determined looks on their faces. Hikari and Kuma flanked him on either side, the three of them a flawless unit of order amidst the chaos on the ground and growing in my chest.

His eyes rose briefly, instantly finding mine. A spark of reassurance echoed from the mark on my chest, dampening my panic into a manageable wave. His gaze was flickering with power, surely as mine was, before he turned to continue directing the Hounds around him. All without Aengus I finally realized.

In no time, all the guns I'd manifested, and all the bullets I'd drained myself to make, found their way into the hands of the army who had been training for weeks. I still wish we'd had more time.

Becca slid her hand into mine, anchoring me back to the swell of magic emanating between us. A vortex of our merging powers rose before us, a looming black hole descending on the sand. The effort was making her pant, and even I broke into a sweat. We were about to shadow jump an entire army. I didn't even know if we could.

"Do not break the chain," I ordered, feeling the words roll off my tongue like second nature.

"Do not release the person's hand in front of you or behind until every single Hound is through, or they will be lost. We will provide cover with our shadows. Only when this gate closes do you drop each other's hands."

And then, we moved. Becca first. Me after. Akashi gripping my other hand, and the rest of the Hounds following.

The vampires had already gone, teleporting back to the city before my sister found me. My grip tightened in hers. I could feel her vibrating with the instinct to shift and run to their sides. To defend her home.

But even after we stepped out into the vivid wilds of Purgatory, she stood and waited. The Hounds spilled out behind us like a growling sea, the guns strapped across their backs reflecting the light of the fuchsia sun. And high above, hovering against that harsh light: Angels.

There were only a few hovering above us, but I still doused the ground with shadows pouring from my skin. We were submerged in inky night before the Angels could start to shoot or dive. As soon as the last Hound was out I dropped my sisters hand, and the portal collapsed.

"Go."

"We know the city," she said, already beginning to shift into the massive Hellcat she usually kept hidden away. "We'll fight from within and drive them out."

We took off, her running on all fours, and me flying above her toward the massive crater which had been blown in the stone. Whatever had struck the rock made it molten, forced so hot it was literally dripping at the edges.

The sharp pop of gunfire came from behind us as the Hounds narrowed in on the enemy above. I sent one final blast of shadows out from the cracks in the earth to billow up and around them like a sandstorm, giving them a place to hide as the Angels began to dive. And fall.

Becca hadn't overstated: Atlantis was being burned down. The walls of the cave rippled with hissing golden fire, matching the flames coating a few of the Angels swords. A rage that wasn't my own flared to life inside me as Vallen stirred, my fingertips flickering with his silver fire. Not yet.

I landed on the third tier, in an explosion of color and power. To my left, Angels were serrated by neon blue cracks of electricity. To my right, they imploded on themselves as beams of red flame graced their pure skin. I kept my focus off the bodies in the dirt, jumping to meet the next Angel midair.

My tail sank into their gut, impaling them. I hadn't even realized it had hardened from leathery membrane to scales, sharpened to a point like an arrow. Behind me, vines exploded from the wall, snaking out to yank a few more Angels from the air as they dove for me, and the earth swallowed them alive.

A glowing black and blue storm that was raining hail and sleet was taking place two tiers down on the opposite side of the cave. Judging by the way the Angels were locking up midflight and dropping to the ground like stones, or turning to begin fighting one another, I assumed Silas and Finn were fighting at my sister's side.

Despite our strength, there were far too many Angels inside this damn cave, and not enough of us to drive them out for at least a few hours. I felt Vallen curling up my spine, his purr rumbling deep in my chest.

Angel-born.

He didn't need to make the request, because I was already moving. A foreign power fizzled and crackled over my skin as I dove forward into the open air with my bribe, and the weight of a million eyes shifted to me as I raised the sword of glittering white flame.

The Angels who were still diving for Rebecca suddenly stopped. As if possessed, they all turned in synch, like moths drawn to the flaming sword held high in her sister's grip. It was different than the Angels flames. Brighter, with chords of power spiderwebbing out into the air. It sputtered and hissed like a live wire, like it too was enraged.

With a beat of her wings– her fucking SCALED wings– Raven was catapulting back the way they'd come. The Angels followed her like a hoard of locusts, colliding with one another in their desperation to reach the sword.

Where was Silas? She could smell him a moment ago, but now in the sudden quiet he was gone. She could hear Finns ragged breathing somewhere ahead of her. The painful moans of her neighbors and friends who had yet to succumb to their wounds, and the broken-hearted wails of their loved ones.

Where was Silas?

The club's front porch was all but gone, so she didn't hesitate to break in the rest of the way. The glittering pool beside the dance floor was now stained with mixing shades of blood.

"Silas!?" She screamed, catching his scent at last, and her carefully controlled panic began to swell into a blizzard between her paws.

"Rebecca." He sounded like he was choking. She transformed, launching herself over the bar to find her mate hunched over on his side.

But he wasn't cradling himself. No, in his lap lay a body. Silas had sliced his wrist open with a piece of shattered glass, but the blood just spilled out of Jeffersons mouth.

Jefferson. The man, no, the *friend* who was Finn's anchor during his Reformation. The friend who taught Rebecca how to control her shifting– he was a Gorgon after all. The friend who saved Silas from the very witches he once burned.

He was gone. His warm skin was placid. Bright eyes, dead. Jefferson was dead.

"Silas." Her voice burned in her throat, ice melting as something ancient in her blood awoke and she whispered, "Don't follow me. I don't want you to see."

Fuck, that had done the trick. Akashi almost threw up when Raven burst from the hole in the cliff and saw how close the entirety of Heavens legion was following behind her. He didn't even bother to aim, there were so many of them. And damn her, but these guns were a good idea.

Soon, the Hounds weren't dodging swords or arrows, but bodies falling from the sky. He lost sight of Raven, but he didn't panic. If things kept going like this, it would only take a few minutes for them all to either die, or retreat.

But something was wrong. The Angels didn't acknowledge the Hounds presence at all. They didn't even glance at their comrades who were shot, and collided into one another as the fell. They moved as a singular unit, each of their turns and dives identical. All of them chasing after the bright blur of fire clutched in his mates hands.

Another wave of shadows erupted from the sky, so thick and dark that he couldn't even see above him anymore. There was no more clear shot.

"Close your eyes!" Raven's scream came from somewhere above him. Then he suddenly felt weightless, like the ground gave way to water. He blinked against the dark, looking for the Hounds who were to his left and right. He didn't see his brothers, or his mother for that matter, but they all heard their Queen loud and clear just before a bomb went off above them.

Silas followed at a distance. She didn't want him to see... what? What he had been waiting for all these centuries?

He was the monster hiding in plain sight, a wolf in sheep's clothing. And there she went, running away, once again afraid she would be too much. So much like her sister without even knowing it. He sighed, exasperated at the notion.

Everything was too much right now. And it all zeroed in to the steady drip of power he drew. Subtle enough to not draw attention from above. Weak enough to not make a difference anyways. He was done not making a difference.

He had left Jeffersons body covered in his jacket, two silver coins laid over his eyes for the boatman. Jefferson. *Jephson.* Honest. Benevolent. Brilliant. He lived up to his namesake. He was the opposite of everything Silas was. And he was gone.

Now Silas stood in his shattered doorway, his home a warzone all over again. His mate stood in the window, a pulsing beam of raw energy. Finally, she realized what she was. When would she realize they were both equal and opposite? When would she finally draw on her full potential, so that he could draw on his without fear?

It took half a thought to utter the words, to feel the snap of control against his spine. He didn't know what was happening to his brother as he drew his true power back, and in his current state of mind, he honestly couldn't bring himself to care.

His focus remained solely on folding an invisible barrier of space over their home, one Rebecca's power couldn't destroy because she was not too much for him to handle. She was exactly what he had craved, satiating his centuries of patience. He didn't dare blink as she lit up the world.

Holy Light. The Angels were shifting into their true form, all eyes and wings and light and heat. And pain.

The pain was greater this time, now that I was a true Devil, but I could take it. I had to take it, because if I didn't everyone would die.

Gabriel had broken from the swarm of them moments after the transformations began. He alone held his human form, his eyes rabid with rage as they glanced between my face and the sword in my hand. I smirked at him, feeling a rush of adrenaline from Vallen as I spun the blade tauntingly.

"Is this your toy Uncle Gabriel? Am I playing with it right?" With a hiss of fire, the blade sank into one of the Angels dumb enough to attack me, and they burned from the inside out, turning to charcoal as they dropped from the sky.

"Witch!" He all but screamed, sending a flurry of arrows for my heart. Vallen flares in front of me, turning them each to molten ash. And then with a twist of my hands, his fire vanished inside me once again.

"You'll have to pry each millimeter of his essence from my veins when I'm dead," I hissed, now drawing my mother's sword from my ear. I didn't bother with the shield. With the number of scales on my body, I doubt I would need it anyway.

The Angels, no longer drugged by the call of Edens Flame, began attacking the Hounds once more. And Gabriel moved in on me.

"You kidnapped and tortured my brother!" He screamed again, completely lost in his own emotional battle as he swung his blade for my head. I wonder if this is what I looked like at times growing up, if this was what Luna was warning me of. I parried his attack, lashing him in the ribs with my tail.

"Are you kidding me right now?" I snarled out the words, "You *killed* mine."

I swung the edge of my blade for his neck, but he turned at the last moment causing the flat of it to slap against his chest instead. It sent him somersaulting through the air, end over end, and I dove after him. I jabbed the point of my blade for his back as he went down, but again he twisted faster than I anticipated, and this time I was the one screaming.

My hair went taunt against my scalp as he caught it, using it like a leash to snap me to a stop. Each flap of our wings had me gasping in pain as he dragged me higher into the air, yanking me closer. I slammed the hilt of my sword against his fist, breaking the bones but he didn't let go.

His sword flashed as he deflected my blade and then my tail, which had started striking at him like a viper. With both his hands occupied I lunged forward, digging the sharpened nails of my free hand into his throat until I drew blood. He choked out a laugh as we hovered there, not loosening his grip on my hair, but let his sword go limp as the point of my tail lined up against his spine.

"I don't know what will be more satisfying to watch." His voice came out strained with pain, but there was a malicious humor in it which made every nerve in my body go on high alert. "Your dying breath, or your face as you watch hers."

"What?" I barely got the word out before Gabriel jammed his knee into my gut. I doubled over in pain; he had on serrated amour under his robes, sharp enough to puncture my scales. And now I could see what he meant.

Most of the Hounds had listened to me, keeping to my shadows out of sight, out of the holy lights reach. A few milled around the edges, calling toward each other with their eyes closed or heads bowed as they helped each other seek refuge.

But there were far too many outside my shadows. Far too many bathing in holy light. Far too many blinking milk-stained eyes with their arms held out in front of them. But what had my grip on Gabriel loosen, was the sight of one Hound in particular.

In their desperation they had transformed, inadvertently making themselves a bigger target. I choked on a sob as I watched them stumble and trip over fallen bodies, yelping as their paw sank down onto an upturned arrow. They knew they were in danger, but could only snap blindly at the air, and continue hobbling forward in hopes it was the right direction.

Gabriel laughed cruelly, gleefully, as she wandered further from my wall of shadows. And another Angel had already dove, sword raised to kill the Hound with moon-white fur.

CHAPTER 33

I heard rather than felt the tear of my hair as I swung my blade, eliminating Gabriels hold on me.

And then I dove.

I was screaming. I was crying. I was too slow, too far behind.

I could only watch in horror as the Angel closed in on Luna, unable to defend herself as they came in for the killing blow.

But before I could scream again, there was a flash of honey gold. Luna bit down on her assailant with a savage growl and they tumbled across the dirt. The Angel diving for her slammed into the space she just occupied, making a crater with the impact, and its holy light went out.

I released another sob, this time in relief as Finn rolled with my mother, prying at her jaws with bloodied hands. His mouth was moving a mile a minute, trying to communicate with or control her I didn't know. But her ears perked, and she released him with a whine as she finally identified his scent from all the others. He regained his feet, all but dragging her towards the wall of shadows now only a few feet away.

Gabriel let out an enraged cry above me, clearly displeased by his once allies' intervention. I turned in the air, ready to launch myself back at him. But then the temperature rose about a hundred degrees in half a second, and a sun peeked over the horizon.

My sister stood above the gaping hole in the cliff, her silhouette gleaming in the frame of the mansions shattered window. She was radiating beams of light, and even from here, I could see her eyes had shifted from their icy blue to a burning gold. As she continued to glow brighter, the air continued to grow hotter, and a new sense of awareness and urgency had me diving for the Hounds again.

The Angels had also changed course, diving for her, for the ancient magic they once tried and failed to fully destroy. They wouldn't be able to stop her. I could tell at this point she couldn't even stop herself.

With the world beginning to burn at my back, I seized control of the two-way shackles in my mind. After a moment of terrifying numbness, Vallen's power flooded me. Edens Flame reappeared in my hands, and with a single sweep of it the world rippled, tearing a hole through the veil between us and the shadow realm.

I summoned everything at once. Waves of water to push, vines to drag, shadowy hands to grab and lead. My magic forced my Hounds through the gap, and kept them connected to me so they would not be lost.

I fisted the torn edges of the veil in my hands, lining up the seams and wrapping their loose ends around my wrists. Sinching them close to my body, I effectively trapped the Hounds on the other side to protect them from what was about to happen. I crouched to the ground then, my wings flaring behind me, the last of my feathers hardening into scales as the final boom of a collapsing star came.

Rebecca exploded like a supernova, obliterating all sense of sound or light or taste beyond herself. I'm pretty sure I was screaming again as I fought to keep her power from destroying us all, but the sound was lost in the vacuum she had created. The aftershock left my ears bleeding, but *finally,* the heat started to bank.

As the weight of her power receded, I felt myself crumbling, the edges of the world in my hands slipping. In a free fall I tipped forward, shifting through the shadows with no control.

"You did so well, Angel-born." Vallen appeared from nowhere to cradle me in his arms. I was limp, barely grasping the now fading tendrils of my magic.

"I'm going to lose them." Unrestrained terror was pulsing through my veins, but I was so tired. Vallen hummed against my skin, unbothered.

"I trusted you to control my end of the shackles," he said, hand cupping my cheek. "Allow me that same grace. I can get them for you if you let me." It wasn't something I even needed to consider. I felt his smile against my cheek, before he invaded me completely.

My magic responded to him even as my body shut down. Everything was staticky and in slow motion, like I was sucked underwater. I could pinpoint the individual moves, knew what parts of my body and power he was using even though I had no control of it. For a moment I wondered if he would possess me permanently, as he intended to do when we met, but then I was back on shore, hurling up black water as my body became mine again and Vallen retreated into my dark corners.

"Raven!" The heavy footfalls of someone running approached me, and through tears I made out Akashi bolting towards me. He had a fresh cut on his arm and his shirt was torn, but otherwise he was untouched. I'm certain if I wasn't already on my knees I would have collapsed against him.

"Luna..." I couldn't do much more than breathe but he was there, catching me, filling me. Shit, my teeth were in his neck. Basic senses recovered I yanked myself away, heaving air into my lungs and held him an arm's length away.

"I won't stop. I can't stop," I said through chattering teeth, pushing him back forcefully as he tried to close the distance I created.

"Hikari," he demanded, eyes flashing over my shoulder. Instantly I felt Hikari's palm pressing against my mouth, and I bit down like I was starving.

Akashi gingerly took hold of my hand, before twisting it sharply to set my broken wrist. The flare of pain made me release my bite with an angry cry. "Kuma," he murmured, not missing a beat. My chin was lifted until my mouth found purchase against Kumas shoulder.

Another bite, another gentle touch, this one to my shoulder before Hikari and Akashi worked together to pop it back into its socket. This time I pulled back with a yell, but it was working. The blood was helping me heal faster. I could feel some of my cuts even closing on their own.

"Finn." I blinked, unsure I heard correctly. Akashi's face was carefully blank as the vampire materialized by my side, making a show of pulling down his collar to offer me his neck.

"Your wing is broken, Angel," he said softly. Akashi released the quietest of growls as Finn brazenly looped an arm around my waist, tugging me close. "I have a feeling it won't be pleasant at all while its set, so don't hold back."

I hesitated before sinking my fangs in, a wild mix of emotions racing through me. Akashi's hands were on me in an instant, probably wanting to get this over with as soon as possible. But I curled into Finns side and wrapped my arms tightly around his waist.

My brother died because of him. But my mother lived. I didn't know what to do or feel. A loud snap of cartilage and bone had my vision going black. I felt myself digging my fangs in deeper, muffling my scream against his skin. Then Akashi's hands steadied me, fingers resting on my hips, lips pressing gentle kisses against my sore scalp.

"That was the last one. I promise that was the last one," he murmured, breath hitting my bare neck and making me shiver.

I felt like a noodle as I untangled myself from Finn. I was sore, but fine. Aching, but okay. Tight, but loose. Slowly, I rolled my muscles, working out the final kinks, the fresh blood flowing through me working wonders.

"Where's Luna?" I asked, unable to keep the franticness from my voice as I searched my brothers' eyes. They all held the same mixture of concern and confusion, which made my heart drop in my chest like a stone.

They didn't know. Of course they didn't know. It was chaos. They shut their eyes, they hid, they didn't–

"Come with me." Finn's gentle voice interrupted my panicked thoughts, and he slid his hand in mine, entwining our fingers. In a daze, I let him.

Akashi was on my other side, now more concerned about our mother than the vampire clinging to me. Kuma and Hikari pressed in behind us as the crowd of Hounds grew thicker the farther we walked. I felt Akashi stiffen beside me as he realized why.

Hounds who were blinded by the Angels' true forms had been grouped together, brothers seeking one another out, friends trying to help in any way they could.

"No, no no..." He, Hikari and Kuma pushed past us, breaking into a run as they realized what Finn and I already knew.

Ahead of us, Luna's Hound was curled on her side, mourning a loss none of us could relieve. Aengus had found her already and had also shifted, his massive bulk cradling her against his ribcage.

Her ears flicked forward, hearing her sons' shouts and she raised her head in their direction releasing a gentle, hollow howl. I wanted to scream at the sight of her eyes. Vacant. Gray. Blind.

But alive. I clenched Finn's hand tighter.

"Thank you," I whispered. He said nothing, just rolled his thumb across the back of my bloodied knuckles. Behind us, a commotion was beginning to stir. Unable to bear the weight of Lunas current state, I locked down my sorrows and called on my rage.

Dropping Finn's hand, I forced my way through the crowd. A few of the Hounds began shoving their comrades back as they saw me making my way through, making a path toward a ring of angry voices.

"Bastards!" My eyes scanned the crowd, locking on my sister as she spat at the feet of a group of Hounds being pushed forwards.

Someone had given her a shirt which hung off her like a loose dress, but it did nothing to hide her severely sunburnt skin. If she was in pain, she didn't show it as she shoved all of her tiny body weight into one of them. Her voice broke as she screamed into his face, "You were supposed to protect them!"

I didn't even realize I was growling until everyone turned towards me. My sister's eyes were blue again, and burning with the desire for blood. I knew why.

"I let you go." My voice boomed like distant thunder in the space around us, low and full of danger. I stalked closer to the Hellhounds that had chosen to leave at the beginning of my reign, my eyes taking them in one by one.

"After years of forced obedience, I gave you free will. I gave you a choice. I gave you a home, here." My voice was shaking now, my emotions barely contained. "All for the simple exchange of defending the defenseless."

The group had the good sense to lower their chins, not daring to provoke me further. A wind was kicking up around me, spraying dust and ash up into the blackening sky. Beyond the crowd, a full moon was crawling north from the horizon, a spotlight within my storm clouds.

"I know you did *nothing* to help them." I lowered my voice to a hiss as I replaced my sister in front of them. "Because I genuinely forgot you were here until now. There was no sign of you. No scent. No existence of a Hellhound in this place until one of us smelled you out."

Becca had stepped away from me, curling into Silas' chest as she finally let her tears begin to fall.

"People are dead. Families. Children!" That darkness in me began to spiral, and for once I let it. Fed it. It drowned out the rest of me until nothing, but numb savagery remained.

The Hound closest to me cried out as the ground exploded beneath him, a spike of raw mineral impaling his chest. As he fell limp, his pack started to back up, blubbering frantic excuses that fell on deaf ears. One even dropped to his knees to beg. I didn't know if it was tears on my cheeks or rain as I snapped my fingers, stealing the oxygen from their lungs.

I took a long, shaky breath. The power in me ebbed and flowed like a drug, more potent than anything I'd felt before. And I loved it. I zeroed in my gaze on the group of Hounds, feeling my head tilt and a smile spread across my lips.

"You were selfish, and cowardly, and abused my kindness, which resulted in innocents dying. You thought I would make a weak Devil." Real thunder boomed now as purple flames lit on my skin. "You thought wrong."

CHAPTER 34

"How did she control it?" Finn flinched ever so slightly at the sound of my voice echoing off the cracked marble around us. We stood in the ruins of our cliffside mansion. It was burnt, and dilapidated, just a shell of its former gothic glory, but it was in one piece. Not gone, like the landscape beneath us.

I didn't know how Rebecca called on that buried power, or how she managed to control such a large blast for the first time. I also didn't know if she'd cooked the Angels alive, or if they'd had the good sense to flee when she appeared on the horizon. What I did know, was nothing that her light touched was left. She was too close to it all; too strong. Everything outside of that little pocket space I somehow managed to hold together had just dissolved, and was gone.

Like the Hounds I had just killed. It was a foreign feeling, emotions off, powers on. Discounting my attack on Lucifer, I'd never fought another being with the pure desire to kill them. It was always just to win. To stay alive.

But I just tore them to shreds for fun. For relief. I pulled their bodies apart piece by piece like it was nothing, while my family and army watched on. There was nothing left of them to bury when I was finally done.

Akashi had reached for me of course, somehow not horrified by my actions. I didn't understand as to how he could manage to look at me in that state, let alone want to comfort me. Even my sister hadn't been able to meet my gaze when I was done, instead disappearing into one of the few shadows left.

I realized in that moment I probably looked more like my father than myself. After giving a brief order to split into two teams, one to help our wounded and another to aid the residents of Atlantis, I'd come back here expecting no more than a little hole in the rock. Apparently, Finn had sought the solace of home as well.

"Hell, if I know," he finally mumbled, fingers drifting aimlessly against one of the remaining silver bars of the staircase. "I learned years ago to stop asking questions. She and Silas make a mighty pair, and guard their secrets closely." Something like resentment soured his tone.

"What would he have to do with anything?" I asked, confused by why he brought up his brother. Finn paused, going unnaturally still for a minute, before finally giving an uncommitted shrug.

"I wouldn't be surprised if he was present, to ground her in some way while she unleashed herself. Just as Akashi strives to be present for you." The weight of his ruby gaze slid to meet mine, and it was my turn to flinch.

"It's different," I say, toeing a piece of rubble by my foot. "We both are powerful, but... it's different." I repeat, feeling stuck in a conversation that doesn't need to be happening.

"Bullshit." Finn's tone takes me by surprise, a sense of annoyed gruffness making the word serrate in my ears as he closes the space between us. Instinctively, I slam my hands against his chest as he backs me into the wall. He just scoffs, catching my wrists and pinning them above my head. We both know I could get out of his grip, but for some reason I feel frozen.

"Finn. Stop." I fight to keep my voice even, which is difficult with my heart slamming against my ribcage.

"Oh no, we're far past that Angel." His eyes harden as he stares down at me. "Akashi may be fine with giving you your space and exercising patience, but my dear we both know I am quite the opposite."

"This has nothing to do with Akashi!" I hiss, baring my teeth. He laughs in my face.

"Of course it does. You don't trust him."

"I don't trust *me*!" The room around us vibrates with the intensity of my voice, making Finn fall silent. My breaths are coming all sloppy, and I feel tears brimming at my eyes as the truth threatens to shatter me. Finn's eyes flicker with concealed sympathy, his free hand raising to gently wipe at the tears that escape.

"There's nothing wrong with you, Raven." His voice is a warm cocoon around me, comforting me instantly.

There's no sign of that sticky, sweet honey of his spell, but the air between us shifts all the same.

As I regain my breath, the hold he has on my wrist's shifts from a sharp squeeze to the distinct press of his weight. His eyes had noticeably darkened, his own breaths coming deeper. Before I can react, his lips are brushing mine, slow and curious.

I freeze, not knowing what to do. His schemes got Anzen killed, but he single handedly saved Luna. He tried to drain his own brother, but offered himself to me enthusiastically. His actions constantly contradict themselves, but always revolve around what he views as my best interest. I hate not knowing what's going on in his head, and not being able to predict his next move. But most of all I hate how easy it was to kiss him back.

His tongue slides into my mouth, obliterating my rushing thoughts. His hand descends from my wrists to my neck, curling around the back of my head to grip my short locks in his fist. And my traitorous hands drop to his shoulders, pulling him closer.

I don't know how long we stood there, tongue and teeth and bodies tangling. Our broken pieces seeking each other's out and hoping to become whole again. When I finally pushed him away for air, we were both flushed, and my lips felt swollen from the pressure. His own were tinted gold as he stood there wide eyed, panting slightly as he stared down at me.

"I don't trust all of me," I repeat, needing to fill the silence and all I have is the truth. "I can't. Not until I know all of me. If I accidentally hurt Akashi before that, because I just give in and let myself go like out there..." I trail off, hands fisting his shirt as I begin to shake at the thought of my rage even trying to tear into Akashi. It felt so good, so relieving. Like I was finally in balance, and that was a major problem.

"But accidentally hurting me, isn't something you fear." Finn looked like he was in a daze, shaking his head as he stepped back from me. When he spoke again, his voice was hoarse with pained realization.

"Your attention was never because I was able to provide something for you that he couldn't. It's because you don't fear harming me, in the way you fear for him. In the way you care for him."

"Finn I'm sorry." I didn't know what to say, and seeing him burying himself before me felt like a knife to my gut. "I do care for you, for your safety. But look at us. Look at what you've done." I didn't need to verbalize his actions to see the blow strike home.

He instantly went rigid, face blanking. His hands snapped to straighten his jacket, before tossing his mussed golden locks over his shoulder, and when his gaze finally met mine it was cold and empty. I could feel my anger rising to defend my heartache, or maybe attack it. My heart shouldn't ache for him at all.

"I've longed for you since the first time I met you." Though it was spoken harshly, his admission still rocks through me, anchoring me to the spot.

"Watching Silas fight off Rebeccas advances for decades was torturous for me. Because I didn't know where you were. I didn't know how to find you. I didn't know how to get you out of that god damn house once we did finally track you down." He was pacing the floor now, his attempts at feigning composure coming undone before me.

"When I finally did get my hands on you, you seemed to reciprocate my feelings. I knew your body reacted to my touch, but I was watching your eyes every time. You've wanted this since I cornered you in that coffee shop, but you've fought it. You've fought me.

"And then, you let a damn Hellhound imprint on you even though you will never give yourself wholly to him. Instead, you ping-pong back and forth between the two of us, refusing to allow yourself to care for me, and use your care for him as an excuse to deny yourself."

His hands smack the wall on either side of my head, desperation in his voice as he shouts, "When do the games end Raven? How many times do I have to watch you walk away?"

"Well fuck, she was actually right. We have something in common after all."

A look of annoyance crosses Finn's face as he glances over his shoulder, but a cool wash of fear is spearing through me. As he leans his body away again, I shrink further back into the wall, praying more than I'd ever prayed before to disappear.

"I overstepped," I heard Finn say, sounding anything but apologetic. "I'll leave her–"

"Yea, no." Akashi treads across the floor, replacing Finn in front of me. His fingers dip under my chin, but I shut my eyes, unable to handle whatever hurt or anger I was certain I'd find in his gaze.

The mark on my chest tingles, but I shut it out, and after a few moments of silence he releases a heavy sigh. His voice is a velvet pit as he asks, "How long are you gonna keep running, Raven?"

CHAPTER 35

At least one more time.

I didn't utter a word as I slid straight through the marble. People maneuvered out of my way as I stumbled out of the shadows, jaws dropping at the sight of me. I tried not to fear why.

I knew I had two horns on my head now. I could feel their weight just as I could feel where my skin morphed into scales, the bite of them harsh enough to make me bleed. And my tail, the serpent-like thing, was whipping around as if we were still in battle.

A door fell open in front of me and a tiny, feathered creature came barreling out. Quickly its mother followed, eyes widening at the sight of me as she picked up her child. Incoherent apologies fumbled from her lips as she retreated, causing the familiar build of my self disgust. I didn't even bother acknowledging her, knowing it would change nothing. And there were more important things than a single mothers fear of me.

A harsh light now filtered through the settling dust where the hole in the mountainside was blasted. I expanded my wings, silently drifting over to perch on the level beneath it which took the most damage. Entire segments of the catwalk had caved in, burying most the buildings on the levels below. The ones still standing were little more than rubble.

But my eyes had already drifted away from the damage, the boiling of my blood chilling to ice as I surveyed the real carnage. Beneath a crumbling brick wall, a single leg was visible. Above it, laying in scattered pieces atop what was left of someone's marble floor, was the shredded body of a chimera. A few inches from my left foot lay a single iridescent wing, much like the fey women's from the club. The bodies, more accurately the body parts of my people, stained every corner of what was left of my home.

"Raven..." Becca's voice echoed cautiously from behind me. The temperature was continuing to plummet, her heartache quickly matching pace with my fury.

"How many?" I asked, my voice sounding foreign to my own ears.

"A lot." Was her voice trembling?

"I asked how many," I growled, the sound reverberating through the stone and shaking loose pieces free.

"Half. At least." A winter wind whipped through the city, so cold it made my vision blur. "I really think you should step away," she added quietly, her warm hand closing around my icy fingers.

I blinked hard, gaze snapping down to the point of contact. Silently, I took in the splintering veins of ice traveling up my arm, following the jagged valley between my scales. Her fingers squeezed mine once again, this time more adamantly.

"What are you doing?" I whispered, yanking my hand out of hers. Bolts of red flames shot upwards from my wrists to my shoulders, hissing as they sputtered out against the icy shield covering me like a second skin.

"That's not my power." She said, and the weight of accusation in her gaze sank me like a stone in water. I turned away from her, blinking against blackened snow. No, it had to be ash, so something must still be burning.

"We need to put that out." I felt like I was in a daze, searching the space around us for fresh flames. The ash was melting against my cheeks, dripping like tears to fall boiling against the dirt at my feet. Becca grit her teeth, patience waning.

"You *really* need to step away, before you plunge what's left of this place into an artic freeze." She grabbed me by the shoulders, shaking me as her voice rose. "I've already lost enough here today. If you can't control yourself, get the fuck out of my city before you destroy what's left of it!"

"I'm not! I can't do that." But even as I said it through chattering teeth, I could feel the power building beneath my skin. Ice was slowly taking over my fire, and my fingertips elongated into blackened claws. My tail had also transformed, now a spike of permafrost; pure white and lethal.

"You've been lying to me for months, and now my friends are dead." Rebecca unsheathed her own claws, pupils narrowing to feline slits. Teardrops dribbled down her cheeks, hardening into shards of ice as she continued to lash me with her words.

"They would have been fine if you hadn't led Gabriel here!" Her voice was breaking off into something guttural and enraged. Deep down I think my heart was shattering as well, but I was too iced over to feel anything.

"I was trying to protect them." My voice was hallowed, not nearly carrying half the venom or pain she currently possessed. "I never wanted this to happen. I never wanted to become like Him, either." Her eyes shuttered, face suddenly void of everything she had been hurling at me, and I wanted to scream.

"None of us have ever looked at you and seen Lucifer. You did that to yourself, and now they paid the price for it."

She shoves me backwards into one of the many piles of rubble and bodies. This time I do scream, scrambling on all fours to get away from the still wet blood, the still warm skin. Rebecca though just turns her back on me, her voice colder than the day I met her as she repeats, "Get out of my city."

CHAPTER 36

"What the hell did you just do?"

Silas didn't know what he walked into. He arrived just in time to see Raven all but float through the crater in the cliffside like a ghost. At first he didn't even know it was her. She now had two horns curving from her temple, and her skin and wings were covered by argent, burgundy scales.

The scene before him was a frozen horror-scape. Ice covered limbs littered the ground, ashen foundations half burying them before blowing away on a winter's breeze. Whether this was his mates magic or his queens, he didn't know.

"She made her choice." Rebecca sounded almost as feral as the day of her Reformation. Cold, and hungry for blood.

"I'm afraid I'll need more of an explanation than that." He did well to mind his tone, but Rebecca threw her head back and cackled anyway. At the very least, she sheathed her claws.

"I tried to warn you all before. Her body is at war with itself. It can only endure one side of her magic, and apparently she's just as weak as our father, and is gonna let it destroy her."

A shiver wracked Silas' spine, but he offered his mate a sympathetic smile as she turned to face him. Her true feelings were reflected in the icy tears staining her skin and the tremble in her whisper.

"Her blood is black."

"I know."

"She's covered in scales."

"I know."

"She's losing."

"Or winning." Rebecca jerked as if he slapped her.

"What?"

Silas released a sigh, voice serene despite their circumstances.

"She's finally not holding herself back." The statement was blunt, pleased even, and he brushed at the ring of snowflakes collecting on his collar. "She's too angry to minimize her power. Too numb to control it. For once, we are receiving all of her at full force."

"And look at the cost." The sorrow in her voice made him realize his error, and he dropped his head, ashamed.

"Everyone is dead, because of her. Because I *killed* her and made her into this."

"No." Silas closed the distance then, cupping her cheek to pull her gaze back to him. He was unwilling to watch her blame herself more than she already had.

"This is war, and not one that you or your sister caused. Whether or not you drew that blade across her throat, she would have become this eventually. She needed to." Rebecca's eyes drifted shut, leaning into his touch as she calmed.

"I don't think she can handle it," she admitted guilty. "You just saw her. She's on the brink of becoming–"

"She won't. I won't let her." Silas' tone was inarguable, his grip on her tightening the slightest degree. "I believe you were right my dear. It's high time that I play my ace."

CHAPTER 37

Akashi wondered how many more times he would be tempted to kill these people. He and Finn hadn't exchanged any words as they left the destroyed mansion, mainly because he didn't know what to say without making himself look like an inferior male. That thought in and of itself, made him feel like a raging idiot.

He had imprinted on her, and somehow secretly believed it would keep her from craving the vampire. Luna warned him that the bond would probably affect her less intensely than it would a Hound, but sometimes he believed she didn't feel it at all.

For him it was an instant change, something deep within himself rewiring to only react to her. *Always* react to her. And yet she just had another males tongue down her fucking throat, and there was nothing he could do about it without feeling like a jackass. He didn't imprint on her to control her, and didn't expect her to go a literal eternity without exploring other pleasantries, but he still thought he would have more time to prepare for it. More time to talk with Silas about how he endured it with Rebecca.

After walking in on them, he didn't deny himself the satisfaction as he watched their conversation swiftly plummet. Whatever she felt for Finn, it clearly wasn't as potent as what they had. That gave him some reassurance, until the conversation shifted in his direction and confirmed his worst fear.

She didn't trust him. It wasn't like she trusted Finn either, but she didn't hesitate, hold back, or hide with him. In Finn's arms, confidence and control radiated off of her in waves. Akashi had to bite back a snarl when he first saw her, all glittering scales and iridescent skin. He wanted that version of her for himself.

Before he could tear the two apart, both he and Finn realized that her confidence wasn't out of trust or care. It was the power dynamic between the two. She wasn't giving herself to Finn, she was wielding dominance over him like an Alpha Hound, and he always submitted not her.

That fact seemed to finally hit the head over heels vampire square in the face. Akashi wanted to laugh, maybe even taunt him, but instead he found himself feeling bad for the guy. The guy whose schemes got his little brother killed. Yea, back to hating him.

"She's gone again," Silas said by way of greeting. "She and Rebecca got into it. Pretty bad."

"Seems like it," Finn said, voice still hoarse from yelling as he observed the wreckage before them. Or perhaps he was on the verge of tears. Akashi muttered a curse under his breath.

"I'm done fucking chasing her." His statement seemed to take both vampires by surprise, and he shrugged. "I'm done fighting her. We can't convince her, and literally can't force her to allow us to help. We can only be here if she decides to come back, right?" Silas averts his gaze.

"Yea, about that." He pinched the bridge of his nose, sounding utterly exasperated. "Rebecca pretty much banned her from the city."

"She what?" Akashi's voice lowered, eyes flashing with barely restrained power. Silas held up his hands.

"Hey, if you want to go fistfight a demonic demi-god, be my guest. However, I suggest you let her calm down first. This was the only home she ever knew, and as you can see, there's not much of it left."

Immediately Akashi lowered his hackles, not allowing himself to lose his cool and make this whole damned situation worse. After a few moments of silence Finn cleared his throat, but Akashi refused to look at him.

"Do you seriously have nothing to say to me?" Finn asked, a hint of cool judgment buried in the words.

"I would prefer not to," Akashi admitted. "Wouldn't you?"

"On the contrary, I want to tie her to a chair and force her to explain herself." Akashi's head whipped to look at him, a shocked glare on his face, but Finn's gaze was deadly serious.

"I don't expect anything." Pain tainted every word. "I wouldn't, even if I deserved it. But she keeps coming back to me. I was in a cell for over three months for hell's sake. I couldn't have pursued her even though I wanted to."

Hearing him say it out loud made Akashi descend a slide of jealousy he never experienced before as his gut feeling proved true. He'd misjudged at the first appearance of Vallen, but wasn't wrong thinking there was another male all this time. He exhaled a pained laugh.

"Look. The imprinting bond affects me differently than her. I knew that going into this. I just didn't think I would have to get used to the idea of... competition. At least not right away."

Silas burst out into laughter, getting so carried away that he actually doubled over, smacking his knees. Finn and Akashi stood there, eyeing him with withering, incredulous stares.

"I'm sorry. But this is like bad television." Silas elegantly wiped a tear from the corner of his eye as he straightened. "From the outside looking in, this situation is very simple. Finn, you hurt her so badly that she's not afraid of hurting you. Akashi, you love her, so she's terrified of making you hate her. Powerful as she is, she's still a person like the rest of us."

"What's your point?" Akashi grounds out between grit teeth, but was unable to keep the embarrassment from showing on his face. Silas grinned wider.

"Well, your acceptance knows no bounds. You've been smitten for so long, I dare say you couldn't hate her if you tried." Akashi covers his mouth with the back of his hand, turning to hide his blush, but Silas is already shifting his gaze back to Finn.

"And you, despite your idiocy, force her beyond her comfort zones. She needs that. Someone who's not bonded to her but still willing to push her for more. It's the only way she'll continue to grow." As an afterthought he added, "And I'm ninety percent certain you'll survive, should she actually attack you."

"As enlightening as that is," Finn murmured, now almost as embarrassed as Akashi, "that fails to solve the problem we're in." Silas rolls his eyes.

"You're hopeless. Truly. If this is a problem, gentleman, then you're both the solution."

"Easy for you to say, when you don't have your soul tethered to your girls," Akashi grumbles under his breath. Silas narrows his eyes slightly.

"Rebecca will always be mine, but I don't I own her. I'm her mate, not her keeper." His voice softens slightly. "Though I can acknowledge my connection to her is not as restraining for me as your imprinting bond is. That's something that you, brother, will have to be considerate of." He once again leveled his gaze on Finn.

Finn, unable to help himself, smirked as he asked, "How intense can the bond be if she's still reacting to me just as feverishly as before?"

"Didn't you just get done crying about her not giving a shit about you?" Akashi snapped, his annoyance spiking. This entire conversation was ridiculous and petty and uncomfortable. He opened his mouth again to end it, but Silas beat him to it.

"*Finnegan Esmeraldas Hagan.*" The air seemed to grow staticky as the vampire strode towards his brother. All the beauty in Silas' face seemed to flicker, morphing into something beastly and chilling as he whispered, "Yield."

Finn's body balked violently, before his legs folded under him and he was on his knees. Akashi just watched, slack jawed, as Silas took hold of his brother's blond locks and yanked his head back at a severe angle to glare down at him.

"I did not save you all those years ago for you to lose sight of the goal." His tone was as dark as the shadows their mates possessed as he leaned down into his brother's face, growling in a way that had even Akashi bristling. "Pursue this respectfully, if you must. Otherwise, I will not hesitate this time to take back what I so generously gave."

Finn didn't need Silas' spell controlling him to make him freeze, the threat was heavy enough to make him wither even lower in the dirt. The weight of the words, and intensity of the scene, gave away that this was no longer just about Raven. There was something going on between these brothers, something dark. Akashi resisted the urge to ask questions as Silas finally released his hold on Finn, but he just stayed on the ground.

"Now, where is *my* mate?" Silas, mood soured, scanned the cave with his eyes like a serpent. With a sudden curse he vanished, the veil snapping in his wake as he teleported across the space.

Akashi shifted into Hound form, sprinting as he followed the scent of the vampire to one of the lowest levels. He came to a screeching halt when he finally saw what Silas had somehow realized.

A warning growl rumbled low in the back of his throat as Rebecca jumped down from the rocky outcropping above him. She had transformed, the massive bulk of her Hellcat nearly the same size as his Hound. And her manic type of rage was directed toward one of the males who started all of this.

Uriel stood in the center of the walkway, broken shackles adorning his wrists and ankles like oversized bracelets. He was covered in blood and wielded no weapon, but his eyes were locked on the Hellcat with an unbridled, savage hate.

"Finally." Rebecca's voice curled into Akashi's head. Beside him, Silas' expression was the picture of serene calmness, but his eyes were alive as she sauntered up to the Angel. She circled him tauntingly. "I don't know why I waited so long for this."

"Spare me the monologue, demon." Uriel spat, his phlegm already tinted with blood. "You want your revenge, I'm right here. But let me remind you that revenge has not served your sister well."

Rebecca was a blur. Silas' smile was earth shuddering. And as Akashi turned away and tried to block out the Angels screams, he realized the vampire was right. When it came to Raven, absolutely nothing deterred him. He just needed to find a way to prove it.

CHAPTER 38

Hikari was exhausted. The past few hours had been a blur. The war. Luna. His sister emerging from the rock with black waves of power rippling off her to drift across the desolate landscape. She had been speaking Latin, Greek, Sanskrit, and many other languages he failed to recognize. But the message was clear: get out.

Whatever portal she and Rebecca had created earlier had vanished, but the torn fabric of reality which led to the shadow realm still stood open. He hadn't thought before he moved, grabbing her hand as she stepped directly into it, and they emerged on the other side at the edge of the pit.

When she just stood there frozen, literally with ice dripping off of her skin, he looked back into the dark and released a howl. Kuma's answering call echoed from the other side, and a moment later his brothers hand gripped his. Slowly, the Hounds rebuilt the chain of connection through the dark, and led one another home.

Raven had dropped his hand long ago, and he became the tether. He didn't know when, but Akashi had appeared by his side. He didn't take over the task, but didn't abandon him to it either, and for the first time in months Hikari felt useful.

It was a longer process than before, taking extra effort from everyone to guide their blind comrades back across the veil. When Luna stepped through his instinct was to rush to her side, but he held fast to his position, unwilling to risk the safety of everyone else. Aengus was with her, but of course, she walked unassisted. The only source of support she'd allowed herself to have was a black, wooden staff. Akashi was also tense as she passed, her head high, but a sharp look from Aengus kept both brothers from intervening.

After what felt like an eternity, the last Hound finally emerged from the dark, and Hikari collapsed in a sweaty heap. Akashi finally broke from his side to check on their comrades, but before he left he clasped his brothers shoulder. Though he said nothing, the evident praise and appreciation in the touch gave Hikari the relief he needed.

Since there had been no violent assault, most of the Hounds were uninjured. It was the mental blow to their ranks which stripped them of their security, and their pride. Twenty-seven Hounds, including Luna, had lost their sight. If not for Raven and Rebecca's shadows, they all would have suffered the same fate.

Hikari forced himself to sit up, bile rising in the back of his throat as he made an unwelcome realization. The Hounds often wondered why Lucifer never engaged in a battle outside of Hell. There were a few small operations of course. To pillage, or to catch a small group of Angels off guard. But if he had marched the Hounds against Heavens full legion like they had today, this would have happened sooner. There had always been too much power working against them.

Hikari couldn't bring himself to enter the castle yet, relishing in the silence and solidarity he so rarely got. In front of him, the tear in the veil rippled gently on an unseen breeze, and he found himself staring into its inky darkness unsure of what to do.

Even if he had the mental energy, Akashi wouldn't have the patience to deal with him right now. He would be focused solely on whatever was going on with Raven. Likewise, as worried as he was, he didn't want to seek out his mother right now. There was nothing he could do for her, and he was quite certain Aengus would rip the head off of the next person who approached her with condolences that would further shatter her dignity.

He finally stood, eyes searching the few groups of Hounds still milling about outside, and suddenly became aware of Kuma's lack of presence. After a brief moment of stunned numbness, he launched into motion, flinging himself into the empty belly of the lake. He hit the ground on all fours in a dead sprint. Contradictory flares of disgust and protectiveness rose within him as he followed his brothers tracks and scent to the Night Howlers front door.

He was unsure of what his unwelcome emotions were preparing him to do, but luckily didn't need to find out. Voices filtered to him through the door, which was left slightly ajar. He worked to get his breathing under control as he approached, nosing it open an inch or two further just as he heard something hit the wall and shatter.

"I said to leave!" The voice was sharp, feminine, and made a snarl form on his lips. A booming laugh echoed after it, seconds before another object hit the wall and broke.

"I just wanted to check on you." In all his years, he never heard Kuma speak so gently. And knowing that this side of him was reserved for the Hound who birthed him just reignited the flames of anger in his chest.

He pushed the door fully open, forcing his bulk through, and instantly wrinkled his nose against the overwhelming floral stench. Chaos had unfolded in the entry hall. The floor lay littered with shattered vases and mirrors. A ceramic pot was raised in Jesibelle's hands, poised to throw at Kuma's head. Kuma had gone pale, unable to meet Hikari's glare which just triggered another growl deep in his chest.

"I told you to stay away from her."

"I just wanted to check on her." His brother repeats, this time with the usual snarky edge he was used to.

"Well you have checked on me. Now you may go." Jesibelle placed the pot back on the ground, leaning against the wall seemingly unbothered. Hikari found himself staring at her. At her arms clenched around her belly, the rosy glow to her cheeks, the buried desperation in her eyes.

"Unbelievable," he growled, beginning to pace. "You're in heat."

"Preposterous." She scoffed, but the blush crept down her neck. "I haven't been bred in over a century."

"So I was your last?" Hikari growled, turning on her and snapping his teeth.

"Hey." Kuma's voice held a warning growl, but Hikari ignored it.

"Did you get bored of pushing out pups and sending them off to war? Or just get too old for it?"

Kuma punched Hikari straight in the jaw, sending stars across his vision.

He groaned, shaking his head roughly, before lifting his glare to his brother.

"Don't act like it doesn't bother you. Your birth mother is probably cowering in here as well."

"She's not," Jesibelle snapped, interrupting what was sure to be an all-out brawl. It surprised them both to see her trembling slightly. A hoarse whine came from Kuma, but he resisted the instinct to reach out to comfort her.

Hikari stopped breathing as she pushed off the wall, crossing to him. He didn't know what to expect, but her arms looping around his neck wasn't it. And the sob she buried against his fur made the feelings twisting in his chest even more vile. Kuma stared at the two of them wide-eyed, undoubtedly reflecting the shock on Hikari's own face as she spoke through her tears.

"I had to send you. To send all of you. More than once I had to tear pups away from their mothers, each screaming and thrashing as they lost you. It was hand you over, or watch my girls be killed for not upholding our end of the bargain." She pushed back from Hikari, eyes finding Kuma this time. "Lin did not hand you over. I didn't even know she had you, until she was taken from us."

"You're saying you fought?" Hikari felt like he was going to pass out, his anger and his shock and his longing mounting into a beast that was becoming too much to bear.

"I'm saying we died, trying to protect you. Trying to resist." The elegant façade she wore had disappeared, her irritatingly relentless confidence withering away as she crumpled to the floor.

"I cannot, and I will not, sully Lin's memory by imprinting the child she died to protect," she whispered. Kuma's face remained impassive, but Hikari could damn near hear his brothers heart break.

"I wasn't asking you to," Kuma said, taking the first step away from Jesibelle since he arrived. "I just feel like lately, we're always on the verge of dying. And I just wanted to get to know you."

His hands curled into fists as he brushed passed them to leave. Jesibelle was still on her knees weeping softly, and Hikari, unable to bear the sight, relented slightly.

"I'm sorry," he says, shifting out of his Hound form to reach for her. Jesibelle clings to him as he lifts her, hugging her to his chest. He wondered how many of the Hounds out there were born from this woman in his lap. Or if any of them were even still alive after all the centuries. How many of them could be Kuma's brothers? Anzens? According to Luna, all of Akashi's were dead.

"I'm sorry," he repeats, arms tightening around her. As she finally begins to quiet, he wonders how in the hell any of them have survived like this for so long.

CHAPTER 39

Rebecca was frantic now that the anger wore off and the blood had dried. She killed an Angel. Snapped their neck between her jaws and relished in feeling their dying heartbeat. And only when Uriel's body sank into the dirt, becoming one with the earth once more, did the weight of what she'd done hit her.

"Silas we need to get her." She was running now, Silas matching pace with her even as a Hellcat.

"Agreed, but not like this. We need to let her settle herself." He said it so sweetly, so serene, yet Rebecca didn't know if Raven could. The state she was in had been world shuddering. Horns, scaled wings, and nothing but oily blackness rolling off of her. And it was Rebecca's fault. All of this was Rebecca's fault for following Mary's stupid plan.

"Change the course of your thoughts, my sweet." She felt Silas pass a hand over her fur even as they ran, and instantly the rush of panic eased a bit.

"If I didn't kill her—"

"I'm going to cut you off right there, because as she so eagerly displayed, Raven would have killed herself without hesitation. At least with you dealing the blow, it had purpose along with sacrifice."

"Is that supposed to make me feel better?"

"Hypothetically, yes." His chuckle made her spine tingle, and she fought the urge to roll her eyes.

They burst from the hole in the cave, the blinding white emptiness of what was once their home making a fresh pang of guilt ricochet through her. She had done this as well, the inability to control her power destroying everything in its path. She had never felt that consumed, that hopeless before. Was that how Raven felt all the time when dealing with her mixing powers?

"Well, would you look at that?" Pride dripped off of every word as Silas broke off from her, tearing towards the faintest black ripple in the dirt.

"What is it?" Rebecca asked, slowing to a trot, appraising the flapping edges of... air. What the hell was this?

"Oh, she's becoming something utterly surreal." Silas yanked one of the flapping corners wider, revealing the pitch of the shadow realm to them. Rebecca full on gaped at it.

"How..."

"Ask her when we get back." Silas was already halfway through the tear, causing her to leap in after him with a slight bit of panic. He snickered as his arms circled her, swinging up onto her back as she waded deeper into the realm, further down towards hell.

"This is insane," she whispered as she glanced behind them, seeing the tear now rippling with light of purgatory. Silas, perched on her back like a king on a throne, didn't reply until they emerged from another tear in the veil, this one just a few yards from the steps into the castle.

"When I reveal myself, should I do so dramatically, or with only a classic amount of bravado?" He asked as he slid off her. Though his words boast his usual charisma, his tone was dampening toward an unnerving seriousness that was rarely seen from him. Rebecca scowled.

"I said you should have weeks ago, and you still prolonged it. Just get it over with as quickly as possible, and try to avoid the death ray of a hit she's gonna throw for your head."

"Oh please," he chuckled. "It's not like this was our first secret or lie." He turned to march up the stairs, humming lightly, but Rebecca narrowed her eyes at his back.

"No, but it's the biggest. The worst."

He groaned, giving up the nonchalant parade and twisted to face her. "Fine. I will do it today, but not before she is settled. If that pleases you may we go?" He asked, gesturing towards the door above.

"And after you break your seal." Rebecca was a blur of darkness, racing ahead of him to block the door. "I agree she's unstable. All raw power with no control. While I know that appeals to you, I'm not letting you get yourself killed because you're an idiot and didn't break the seal first."

Silas scoffs, seeming offended that she would even suggest Raven could kill him.

"Very well my dear." He presses a kiss to the top of her head. "Now, you go and round up her brothers, and I'll find mine."

CHAPTER 40

Everything was slower than before. Every breath. Every step. Even my magic flowed through my body at a snail's pace instead of the rush I usually felt as I pushed open the doors to the old throne room.

It would be better this way. I would be stronger, and no longer get swept up in my emotions. I could become as formidable as Heaven feared I was. As dark as they accused. I would become the monster, if it meant protecting what I cherish. And this state would continue to numb me of the guilt which continuously weighed me down. My magic relished in that thought, a chord of freedom snapping loose from somewhere deep and buried.

I don't know why I'd fought it for so long, this power in me, this feeling of being absolutely uncontrollable. Beneath the curved claws on my fingers, my palms were staining with inky night. The kiss of lava and ice had me both sweating and shivering. And the pure golden ear cuff, my mother's shield, was making my skin go raw. I ripped it out, abandoning it on the floor. My scales would be my armor now.

As I prowled around the edge of the room, I studied my spiked shadow on the floor, more like a demon than a person. I came to a stop before the picture window, and pressed my forehead to the stained glass. It was a beautiful thing, but utterly useless.

Slowly I drew the other cuff from my ear, this one only having a slight prickle of pain. I spun the mechanism, the brilliant silver in the blade flashing before the metal began staining too, the obsidian laced within possessing it completely. It would only be used on Angels from now on anyway, so the more cursed, the more poisoned it was, the more effective its blows would be.

"You're descending into chaos." Vallen's voice echoed from behind me, and I turned to see his Hound making a graceful leap up onto the table to stare down at me. When I remained silent, he added, "This is exactly what you bargained your wings for, my dear. Tell me, where has your restraint gone?"

"Restraint got all those people killed." The setting sun covered me in a dappled rainbow from the window, the polar opposite of the darkness spewing from me in waves.

"More will die. More children, undoubtedly." He paused, seeming to weigh his words before proposing, "If we made the trade, and you handed over your Holy powers, I could detach and eliminate them myself. You would be able to step back, continue to protect those you love with your demonic half if you wish, but you could leave all this. And I would have my freedom."

The instinct to say no got clogged in my throat, because I was actually considering it. Be out of the war? No more deaths on my hands? No more throwing my loved ones in front of silver arrows?

I felt my wings unfurl, the remaining feathers shushing against my scales in both the most natural and twisted of sensations. Beneath my blackened fingertips, light was swirling in my veins again, the dull glow somehow piercing the shadows in the room. Two worlds colliding.

Would it tear me apart eventually? I could never be sure. But I was certain Vallen would uphold his end of the bargain. A piece of me would be gone, but we would be safe, without me having to sacrifice any more of my soul than I already had.

Before I could respond, something in me began shrieking, burning through my skin. My heart felt like it went aflame, and my fingers scratched against my chest. The imprint bond.

I cursed, dropping my blade to the floor before tearing the neckline of my shirt open to scratch at it. A faint violet light drifted from where it perched, accompanied by sparks of green as Akashi's emotions flooded me.

I whipped my head towards the door, feeling phantom strains in my muscles from his dead sprint up the stairs to reach me. Vallen watched on curiously as I snapped my fingers, and the two French doors morphed to pure stone, barricading us inside.

Then he winced as the very real chain between went taut, clattering against the stone floor. I paced, dragging my end with me, ignoring the feelings in my chest, drawing each breath from the ever-growing sense of blissful numbness as I dropped to my knees, caressing the metal.

"Your continuous resistance of him is no longer amusing, just appalling," Vallen murmurs, but his eyes were locked on my fingers which had begun to absently pick at the lock binding us together.

"You look like you're starving." I change the subject, my voice going silky with a tease just as the first resounding boom from Akashi came from beyond the stone walls. "You really crave my power that much?"

"I crave my freedom." Vallen's answer was instantaneous. His Hound shifted to human as he also slid to the floor, fisting the chain between his hands.

"You know what I crave?" I asked, eyes roving over his bare skin. He released a sound of disdain, cocking his head to the side.

"I'm not your lustful little vampire, Angel-born. He only wishes he could be as intimately familiar with you as I am." With a whoosh he invaded me, white flames prickling my skin as his voice echoed in my head, gutting me to the core.

"I know you're desperate to rid yourself of the feeling of those Hounds flesh tearing beneath your fingertips, but please don't toy with my freedom if you intend to give it to me."

I shuddered as a distinct, vulgar sense of pleasure shot through me at the memory. The numbness which was on the brink of taking me over caved in on itself, and I was once again left with nothing but self-loathing.

"You were so excited." Vallen's invisible hands traced down my forearms, coaxing my fingers back towards the lock on our chains. *"You finally shed those old habits which no longer serve you, and your mate looked about ready to drop to his knees and worship you for it."*

As if sensing the change in conversation, a vicious growl rumbled through the rock separating us. My eyes widened as tiny cracks appeared in the foundation, spiderwebbing upwards as Akashi's power repeatedly slammed into the stone.

"He will never stop pursuing you," Vallen chuckled, mouth hovering against

my ear. *"None of them will, I know you sense it. They await to see your full potential with anticipation, not disdain. So I'll ask clearly: which of us can you handle setting free? Me, or you?"*

I was about to snarl at him to stop, but suddenly, my head quieted for the first time in months as cold resolution washed through me. I knew I couldn't wholly spare my sister from this; she was going to be hunted just as much as I was until this war was over. But she didn't need to be locked down here with me. She could return to Purgatory, to her life and her city, and I would stay out of it as she wished.

When it came to my Hounds, I could protect them far more efficiently if my angelic magic was no longer a present risk to their safety. But changing to a full demon would put me at risk of dying under an Angels blade, which in turn would be a risk to one Hound in particular

The insistent thrumming against my chest slowly dulled to a light pulse, and as if in answer, Akashi's assault against the stone wall ceased. Absolute silence drowned the three of us as I forced my shaking fingers to drop the chain in my hands, and reach up to trace my imprinting mark.

"If I give you that half of my magic, is there a way to spare him from the consequences? A way he won't need to endure me changing into a demon?"

Vallen went deathly still, both his touch and power vanishing.

"You mean to sever the imprinting bond?"

I said nothing, turning back to the window. The darkness in me had stained the glass, and like a slow growing tumor it blurred the panes into a discolored mass.

"That will destroy him," Vallen argues, his tone now sounding more like a frantic protest. I smiled weakly.

"I'd rather that, than him be dragged down with me."

An explosion of power obliterated the stone molding over the doors, silencing us both. I drop to my knees, covering my head as rock and glass and bolts of green flame invade the space, somehow smothering my world of darkness faster than I created it.

"Don't you dare even think of trying it." Akashi's voice booms across the space towards me. I sweep my hand across the floor, summoning a fresh wall of stone to stand between us, but he eliminates this one with a single blast of his power.

I'm blinded by the surge of green flames. They climb the walls, engulfing the room and eating my shadows alive. Akashi strides through the wreckage with purpose, not even glancing at the utter chaos around him, at the power coming off him in waves.

Flames are pulsing off me now too, but the violet whips of them are quickly smothered by another pulse of his green magic. Shock like I've never felt before rushes through my veins and I'm rooted to the spot. I've never seen anyone beat my magic, not even my sister. I've seen them endure it yes, or dodge it, but not cancel it out with their own.

The floor beneath him explodes, and yards of my thorn covered vines sink into his skin. He doesn't even blink, just fucking smirks as my jaw drops. My heartbeat pounds in my skull as I watch my vines grow hazy, before they disappear in a breath of smoke against his skin.

"How are you doing that?" I whisper. The only answer he gives is releasing another whip of his power through the room, obliterating the fresh shadows which had sprung at his back from the corners.

Beyond him I can see Kuma skidding to a halt in the doorframe, Hikari right at his back. But Akashi draws my attention back to him as his fist lands on the blackened glass above my head.

"You might not believe I can, but I'll match you pace for pace." The mark on my chest flares with affirmation, our flames growing, merging as they dance against our skin.

Desperate now, I summon Vallen in the form of a small dagger, intending to shred the imprinting mark off my skin just as I shredded a hole through the world. This would free him of me, and obliterate whatever this twisted magic growing between us was. None of this was safe, and I was the problem.

But before I can plunge it into my skin Akashi grips my wrist, twisting it away, and steps directly into it. For a beat, neither of us moved. And then a flood of panic takes over.

"Oh my god, oh my god!" I release the blade as he leans back, his jaw working. Slowly, he grips the fiery hilt, and curses low as he yanks it out. I reach forward, tearing his shirt wider to reveal perfectly intact skin.

"What the fuck..." There's not a single drop of blood, not even a burn from the heat. "How is this possible?" My teeth are chattering so hard I can barely get the words out.

His hand tilts my chin up, his thumb slowly massaging my jaw until I finally look up at him. Something like victory shines in his eyes.

"I've said it a million times, Raven. We're entwined at the soul." He takes a breath before pressing his forehead to mine, voice lowering to a caress as he finally explains.

"I didn't imprint on you to trap you, and it wasn't some scheme or a trick to avoid the female Hounds. I did it so you wouldn't need to hold yourself back. Being your mate already shielded me from your powers, but the bond would ensure that you couldn't hurt me with them even if you genuinely tried."

"And you never thought to mention this before now?" I didn't know if I was feeling more terror or relief, but the growl that tore from me just made him laugh.

"I thought you'd already figured it out. I mean come on. On day one you cut me with a dagger that should have killed me, but it didn't. Right then I knew what you were to me." Before I could demand exact details on how it all worked, Vallen released an audible gag.

"If you ever feel the urge to test the truthfulness of his words again, please refrain from forcing me to penetrate the man." His disgust radiates around the room, and in my peripheral I can see his Hound incessantly grooming itself.

"That in and of itself makes no sense," I argue, mind reeling. "I didn't even strike you with my magic. Vallen isn't–"

"We're entwined down to the atom, Angel-born. In any other circumstance, I assure you I'd be able to perform to your full expectations." Akashi bites back a grin as he stoops to pick up my sword, spinning the mechanism so it shrinks back down into a shining black earring.

In the sudden silence, I'm intimately aware of him eating me with his eyes. Now that my shadows had dispersed, there's no hiding what I'd become. My horns were gone now, but I could still feel where scales met skin. My wings too remained morphed, glossy black feathers sitting in neat rows against my scales. My legs were clad in loose, silver trousers, and an open-backed tailcoat with embroidered roses clung to me. I could feel my tail shifting against the dark lapels of my coat nervously under the intensity of his gaze.

Slowly, his hands find my waist, urging me closer as he slides his knee between my legs. Then he shifts the jackets high collar to the side, momentarily exposing the scar on my throat and presses his mouth against it softly.

"So, my love, which is it?" His voice is painfully gentle now, caressing me in ways a touch never could as he gently secures the earring to my lobe. "Are you truly going mad and I need to intervene before you destroy yourself, or are you just scared and trying to run again?"

"Don't bother dignifying that ridiculous question with a response." Silas' annoyed voice suddenly pierces the quiet of the room. He's more brazen than my brothers, who still hesitated in the door, and is lounging against the table with a fresh bottle of wine, again.

"You're becoming an alcoholic," I mutter, glaring at him, and he flashes me a feline smile.

"I always pair a good drink with unfolding dramatics and my girl, you're a one man show." Akashi releases his grip on me so I can cross the room, surprising them both when I yank the bottle towards me and tip it back. With a gasp I shove it back across the table, eyes wide as I fight the urge to chug it.

"It's... how?" I ask, utterly perplexed and Silas leans back like a satisfied cat.

"O positive. The best."

"Enough." Rebecca's voice reaches my ears, and I instantly freeze.

I don't turn as I listen to her shove past my brothers and march for the table. Internally, I brace for another fight, but when she reaches my side she slams her palms down on the table to scowl at her mate instead.

"Break the seal Silas. Now."

CHAPTER 41

"Rebecca," Silas warns, assessing her as her eyes slide to me. She pointedly stares at Akashi's hands which had come to rest on my arms, but he doesn't move, remaining a pillar of strength at my back.

"My dear, this is a delicate–" Silas attempted once more but she cut him off.

"Can it." Her voice held more venom than I expected, and I glanced between the two, trying to read what was being left unsaid. Usually, he didn't possess a care in the world for what she was doing, but right now he looked like he was restraining himself from leaping over the table and dragging her from the room.

"What's going on is actually comically simple," she said before I could ask. Her pupils had narrowed to feline slits but other than that, it was like she was trying to hold all of her magic at bay.

Usually, she made a show of force. Flash her claws as a reminder or warning to listen, but as she slid her hands into her pockets and perched on the edge of the table, her vulnerability made my nerves race. Whatever they had to share was likely worse than anything else I'd learned over the past few months. And after Akashi's latest revelation, my patience for details was at an all time low.

"As the Devil's daughters, we possess a special little thing that other demonic creatures like the Hounds don't have," Rebecca started. Silas, though he hadn't lessened the severity of his gaze on her, remained quiet.

"Lucifers genes. That's why no other dark creature can hold a candle to us, in that respect. Top it off with the cocktail of our mothers powers, of course we would manifest something. The difference is, our bodies were bred to be able to withstand that amount of power. Not just anyone can possess magic, and have it not destroy them. The ability to wield it is something encoded in the blood; inherited." Her eyes glittered.

"And yet, if I somehow inherited whatever scraps of holy magic Lucifer still had, I wouldn't be able to withstand it. I already have too many warring powers to use any of them at full capacity, it's a miracle I've been able to do this much." She paused, before adding, "But what if there was someone else who was fit to wield holy magic with you?"

"Rebecca," Silas snapped, this time rising from his seat. She ignored him, bending at the waist to pluck the abandoned golden ear cuff off the floor that I'd tossed in my earlier frenzy. Wide-eyed, I watched as she pierced her own ear with the end, before securing it to her lobe as she continued.

"Gods, goddess's, demons, the whole lot of them overcomplicate the simplest things, and I'm sick of the games almost as much as you are."

My gaze slid from her to Silas as he rounded the table, his jaw prominently clenched, eyes burning as he glared at her. Beyond his facial expression he was the figurehead of poise and control, his body languid, his breaths even.

"Do you really think this is the best time?" He reached for her hand, but she swat him away.

"We're out of time. We were out of time even before they raided Purgatory," Becca countered. "And even if we had all the time in the world, everything has changed. Raven is my sister, Silas. Not a pawn. Even if that's what she began as."

"What?" I'm the one that asked, but Hikari and Kuma were the ones moving, shoving me behind them as Akashi's grip on me tightened.

"Boys, for hells sake," Becca wasn't visible to me anymore, but I could picture the look on her face as she released an exasperated sigh. "Mary already revealed the worst to her. Raven's creation was on purpose. Consensual. She wasn't a product of force which she was led to believe. The intention was always to use her as a tool in this war, whether it be for Lucifer or Mary or Gabriel, or a player they didn't know existed yet." I felt Akashi bristle behind me, his voice gruff in my ear.

"Is that true?"

By now, I had all but forgotten that dramatic revelation with my mother. All I could do was nod slowly in confirmation, apprehension coursing through me as Silas snarled.

"Their familial business was not ours to disclose."

"But your plan is," Rebecca hissed. "Especially since she obtained the source of God's Mark. She was once an object for you to obtain to gain retribution, but now she's transformed into the key to your revenge."

Silas went deathly still; I couldn't even hear his faint heartbeat. Then a cool laugh slipped out of him, eyes hardening into blackened rubies.

"Fine, have it your way." Shadows, disturbingly similar to my own, slunk from beneath the table, swirling around him on an unfelt breeze. I bristled, unconsciously calling upon Vallen, my veins instantly glimmering with his power.

"Silas." I could barely speak above a whisper. "Does this have to do with Gabriels original request of you? To hand over my sister and I?" My shot nerves wanted to tear his throat out as he gave a noncommitted shrugged.

"When you kill a God, Goddess, or a Demon," he said, lazily rolling his shoulders and cracking the ligaments like he had been holed up for centuries.

"Their power doesn't just disappear. It's absorbed, if the being is powerful enough to handle it. If the killer is too weak, or if they didn't inherit the correct genetic keys, it's returned to the natural cycle, and reborn." He lifted his gaze from mine to Akashi, who had once again begun to growl.

"I've been trying to get through to you both, but you're so young and obtuse at times, it really is infuriating." I blinked and he was directly in front of us. His breath washes over me like sleet, and for the first time since I'd met him, I was afraid.

"What the hell are you?" I asked, studying him anew.

"Ah, you feel it now, don't you?" His voice was like a purr. "Let's hope I'm not depleting Finnegan entirely; he still will be of use to you yet."

His hand closed around mine, and suddenly we were in darkness. I whirled around, panic thrumming through the mark on my chest as Akashi realized I had been dragged across the veil.

The Shadow Realm stood as a silent spectator, or a prison. Right now it felt like both. Silas released a relieved sigh, tilting his head back and drinking it in.

"It's been far too long since I've gotten a proper breath of this air."

"Silas," I could only say his name, too stunned to say anything else, and he chuckled.

"Relax, Raven. If this was some ultimate betrayal, you'd already be dead. You'll soon find I'm more capable of ending you than anyone else in our circle." He released my hand, the shadows clinging to him as he walked, gesturing to the space around us.

"Few beings in this world have the pleasure of getting to utilize this space like we do. Even fewer understand how it all works. That sword," he glanced over his shoulder at me, at the spark of white flame I had unconsciously manifested in my palm. "It's one of the many keys between realms. Our blood, another."

"What do you mean?" I asked, closing my hand slowly. The instinct to defend Vallen was all but screaming in my head. Even in the dull light, Silas' fangs glinted as he smiled, lowering his face to be level with mine.

"Vallen, like Lucifer, is yet another form of Heavens power. Hence why you were able to use him and open the door between worlds with ease."

"I don't know what you're—"

"I watched you do it." He cut me off, slamming me backwards into a wall of steel and knocking the breath out of me. His voice deepened to the tone of a predator who was running out of patience. "When Rebecca finally utilized all of what was hiding in her bloodline to set the world on fire, I watched you slice it open. Watched you hold it shut with your bare hands."

My brain was racing, trying to keep up. Flashes of memory. The desperation I felt as I tore a hole through the veil and forced everyone inside. The rush of my powers overlapping one another, gripping my loved ones with everything I had left.

"Your sister uses this place for travel, and for spying," he continues on. "But she's limited. Only able to utilize Lucifers unique manipulation of the magic. Beings like you and I use it for everything. For power. For creation, or sometimes for destruction."

As he spoke he yanked my hands forward. The shadows around us

426

instantly morphed, hardening into jewelry and bullets and coins that spilled over the edge of my palms before dissipating into puffs of smoke.

"What your sister insists I share, is my intention of utilizing your access to this realm to remain blissfully anonymous. I once was going to hand you over to Gabriel, so that I may go home." His grip on me loosened slightly, the word catching in his throat, and it struck me how little I actually knew about him. After a moment of composing himself he added, "But as your sister stated, everything has changed. Beings like you and I don't get to pursue our desires as flippantly as the rest."

"Beings like you and I?" I don't let him slip past it, locking gazes with him and he grins. Slowly, his hands track North from my knuckles to my shoulders.

"I am not just a vampire," he finally admitted, urging me to turn and face away from him. "And you are not just a demon. We can both enter and exit this realm, as well as many others, as often as we please. But only you can open the doors for everyone else."

Suddenly, he shoved my face against a wall of solid darkness, and I grunted as my fangs ripped into my lower lip. "Open a door, Raven," he all but commanded, adding more pressure against the back of my skull.

My hands were trembling as I forced them between me and the shadow wall, the flash of silver flames blinding me before I forced a crude cut through the world. Promptly, I topple forwards into the meeting hall, and land on my face. Vallen retreated back into my veins with a hiss as I roll over to glare at Silas, who elegantly ducks out of the rip behind me.

I couldn't stand the satisfied smirk on his face, so I looked away, eyes landing on Becca's hand as she reached down to haul me to my feet. Beyond her, Kuma and Hikari were gaping at the hole I'd torn in space. Only Akashi seemed completely at ease, his hand reaching out to grip the edge of the tear and spread it wider to peer inside.

"You're like her, aren't you?" He asked, eyes shifting to the vampire who had returned to the table.

"If only it were so simple. Rebecca, my dearest. You forced this exposition, you finish it," He drawled. With his normal attitude resumed, he plopped on a bench and reached for the abandoned bottle on the table.

"Silas Ebonar Hagan." That feline smile graced my sisters lips as she left my side to perch on his lap. "Once known to Heaven, as Silvanus."

"Silvanus?" Luna's voice had us all jumping, turning our heads toward the doors.

Her eyes, vacant and white, stared at the floor ahead of her, but the brilliant orbs of her spell pulsed with power. They became a blur of motion, a path of moonlight connecting her and Silas as she growled, "I should have known."

He only smiled wider, popping the cork and refilling his glass as she whispered, "So you're the one who killed Satan."

CHAPTER 42

"Instead of jumping me for my personal secrets, how about you ask our queen about her newest party trick that can locate our dearest Anzen, hmm?"

Rebecca smacked the glass out of Silas' hand before he could take a sip, and it shattered on the floor. The air rippled with tension, before he finally released one of the more dramatic sighs I've heard from him, and threw up his hands. "Oh, fine! But at least let me drink in peace," he grumbled, before taking a swig directly from the bottle.

We all took a seat then, Akashi dragging one of the benches over so he could lift my legs to rest over his. As Silas spoke, I folded a thread of flame back and forth between my hands, matching my pace to the cadence of his words.

Silas, or Silvanus, was a creature older than anyone here. Maybe older than Lucifer, if he were still alive. Nephilim. I'd heard of them, but like many creatures expressed only through faith and fairytales, had never seen one and had no reason to assume they were real. They were once Gods mightiest, and now they were the rejected. The Fallen.

Instantly, Kuma was calling bullshit, arguing and debating and cutting off Silas' explanations. However, they were quickly confirmed by an extremely irritated Luna. Frankly, her recognition of who he is was the only thing giving any merit to his claims.

"Gabriel had said they decided to eliminate your kind," she said lowly, making me pause.

I looked over at her for the first time since she'd entered. I hadn't seen her since after the battle. Though that had only been a few mere hours ago, it felt like a lifetime.

The glowing blue orbs of her soul-searching spell circled where she sat, like a moving shield. Her eyes, stained a milky white, flooded my gut with a mixture of rage and guilt that I didn't expect to vanish anytime soon. Despite her state, she was staring straight at Silas as if she could see all that he was, all that he'd done through the centuries.

"Gabriel says a lot if you think about it," his voice filtered into my ears, but I kept my gaze on my mother. "It's a rarity when he speaks truth."

"I'm assuming he doesn't know what you've done?" Luna arches a brow, "Or was it also part of your scheme. One Devil adopting another?"

"I still don't understand what the hell is happening here." Kuma's bitter voice popped up from the far end of the table. "Aren't Lucifer and Satan the same person?"

"No," Silas, Luna and I said in unison. Luna leaned back, eyes flicking toward me, which had me immediately staring down into my hands.

"There are many layers of Hell, which Raven has recently found out." I felt the tension in my body ease a degree at her words. At least for all his secrets, Silas wasn't lying. "Here. Purgatory. The Shadow Realm. Limbo. The list goes on. Do you truly think only a single demon lord held dominion over them all?"

"Lucifer was the first true Fallen Angel," I murmured, finding my voice. "He wasn't a Nephilim, but I'm assuming when he fell he became something like it. Hence why he was welcomed here."

"Welcomed might be a stretch, but he certainly wasn't challenged for the position he held." Silas ran his hand through his hair, the weariness I sometimes sensed he felt now plainly staining his face. "After all, why would demons get in the way of someone trying to dismantle the Silver City?"

"When did you do it?" Luna spoke again, leaning forwards on her elbows. "Had you already been cast out and sought to restore your power?"

"At first, no. I'd sought redemption." His smile was weak, words heavy with regret. "I, along with a few of my brothers, were offered forgiveness if we continued to pursue the work, and told we could go home after seeing to the errors of our ways. I specifically was an aide to convert the human world."

"And if they refused to convert they would burn at the stake." Finn materialized at his brothers side. A smile was on his face, but a cool rage I'd rarely seen from him made the air prickle with tension as he stared at his brother. "You ensured that by defiling them with Gods Mark yourself."

Becca instantly bristled, but didn't move. Silas's pale skin went even whiter before he straightened, eyes hardening along with his voice.

"That's correct."

"You burned people alive?" Accusation clung to my words, but his gaze slid to mine, amused.

"And you've torn their flesh from their bones." There was a flash of green in my peripheral, but Akashi remained silent.

"Those Hounds let innocents die." The words felt like knives in my throat. Who was I to sit here and try to simultaneously justify and condemn murder? Silas' eyes did not leave mine as he leaned forwards.

"And the Witches I burned killed what you could not." My blood chilled as he sat back, continuing without a hint of remorse.

"Though I am as enraged as you are, the children in Atlantis were not the first to die. And at the time, Heavens were mine to protect. To a degree they still are. And I assume you feel similarly

434

considering you didn't slaughter the ones you stumbled across on your latest visit."

I hadn't told anyone of the Angel children. Not even Akashi. Silas flashed me another pained smile before moving to rise from his seat, but Finns hand on his shoulder forced him back down.

"I wanted a fresh slate for her and for us." Finn spoke through gritted teeth. "It was foolish of me to think that since she had grown up so sheltered from what she was, that she would remain that way forever. Or at least for long enough that all of this would unfold differently."

"What do you think I was trying to do?" Luna snapped. "This all would have progressed differently had you just left her be."

"Gabriel was growing impatient, and would have acted on his own," Silas argued. "Besides, she's been set on determining her own fate since her birth. Not even Mary has been able to control every aspect of her life."

"Silas," I interrupted what I could tell was becoming a contest of will, and repeated Luna's earlier question. "When, or how, did you inherit Satan's power?" Silas gave me a look which told me he would rather be buried alive than answer that question, but before he could avoid it a second time, Finn spoke.

"When he lit the torch that burned my mother." I felt myself stop breathing.

"Your mother was Satan?"

"Yes." His voice was dead serious in his reply. "Silas, like you, directly inherited her power after killing her. But for some reason, he's never used it."

"Why didn't you kill him?" When the only memories I possessed of Mary were of the night she was taken from me, revenge was all I could think about. I couldn't comprehend how Finn was able to live with Silas for God knows how long, let alone call him his brother.

"Because," Finn's grip on Silas' shoulder tightened the slightest bit, "she was cruel."

So much hung on that one word. He relinquished his grip on his brother to finally take a seat. Silas though was instantly up to pace, leaving my sister to help herself to his forgotten drink.

"Now that all cards are on the table, shall we get started on a new plan?

I for one would appreciate not being handed over due to some overemotional reaction to necessary secrets." His tone was clipped, and I tried not to take offense at the implication. At this point, I was too exhausted to kick his ass anyway.

"Not all the cards," Akashi finally spoke. His eyes were on Silas, reassessing him as a potential threat once again. "I won't speak for everyone, but I'm quite curious as to what God's Mark could be." Silas released a noise of exasperation.

"Always obsessed with the smallest of details." He seemed to glitch in space for a moment, disappearing to just reappear seconds later with an apple perched in his palm. With no explanation, but a surplus of bravado, he sank his teeth into it. His fangs sank so deep that juices ran down his wrist when he pulled it back.

"There you have it." He dumped the mutilated fruit on the table in front of Akashi and crossed his arms. "The Nephilim, a race cursed with the thirst for blood. Blessed by Gabriel who provided us with a way to quench it, so long as we used the gift to mark a sinners soul. It effectively barred them from rising after death to the supposed comforts of the Silver City. That enough dramatics for you?"

The more he spoke, the less I could explain why I still trusted him, or Finn for that matter. Since they came into my life, things have gone from stressful to downright dangerous. There was no way of knowing what exactly was motivating them to assist me now rather than use me for one thing or another.

"I also wanted to use you in the beginning." Becca spoke up, as if reading my mind. "To get my revenge. To help Silas get his. I didn't care if you wound up dead, so long as my future was secure. That's why I didn't argue with you when you told me what I needed to do." She averted her gaze from me.

"Somewhere along the way though, I started to care for you. I don't know when or why. I didn't even realize it until I drew that blade across your neck. All I could think over and over was 'what did I do?' I didn't expect the immediate agony." Each Hound in the room growled, and she actually flinched.

"Silas and I aren't imprinted, so my changed emotions held no sway over him. He's decided independently of me to be an ally now, rather than use you. I need you to know that." Silas snorted.

"Even if I still intended to use her, I couldn't turn her over in the pitiful state we found her without tarnishing my reputation. And as a fellow Devil, I simply can't allow her to remain so weak." Humor laced the words, but after receiving a glare from both of us he rolled his eyes, quietly adding, "Though, irritatingly enough, I've formed what I hope is an obvious attachment to you."

"And Finn's been disturbingly obsessed with you since I've known him," Rebecca went on, causing the accused to sink further in his seat. "I'd be willing to bet he would do anything you said."

"That's been made clear." I agreed, ignoring the feeling of Akashi's eyes burning into the side of my head.

"What I'm trying to say is, I don't expect everyone to believe us. The Hounds had always been right. At the start, it was all an act to deceive you. And it was working, because you were so desperate to avenge Mary."

Becca stopped talking when I stood, quickly rounding the table to reach her side. She leaned back slightly, looking nervous for the first time since I'd known her, and went stiff as my arms circled her, crushing her to me.

"I'm exhausted," I admitted, dropping my forehead to her shoulder. "I'm beyond exhausted. At this point my soul is almost sapped dry. So please stop. The three of you have had so many opportunities to kill me, and even if you weren't powerful enough to do it yourself, there's not a single doubt in my mind that my family would be dead just to hurt me in the only way you could." Her thin arms had wrapped around me by then, and I could feel her shuddering against me, so I didn't move, anchoring us both.

"I'm not mad at you. I don't distrust you. I can't, there's no time for it. I can't predict what's going to happen to us, or what I'm going to turn into throughout this," my voice catches in my throat. By now, I was addressing everyone in the room.

"But I'm done fighting it. I am both. So, if you need to use me, use me. If you want to love me, love me. I'm going to fall apart in a million more ways. I don't know what pieces of me are needed, and I need you to help me make the right choices. Starting with this one."

I pull back from my sister, giving her the respect to not look at the tears that I know are on her face. It takes little effort to summon the flaming sword, the energy of it coursing through me, quieting all that's in my head.

"Vallen?" I murmur aloud, and immediately feel his invisible hands caressing their way down my spine, fingers tracing the slits in my back making my eyes flutter shut.

"Yes Angel-born?" He purrs, sending a rush through my veins.

"One of these day's you'll need to admit you enjoy being wielded by me."

The world glitters at the edges as he flares brighter, and I can imagine his smile, as we tear the veil apart once more to bring the silent weight of Limbo bearing down on us.

CHAPTER 43

"Don't,"

My brothers had started moving instantaneously. The worry, the adrenaline, the need to dive in and find him. The four of us were all feeling the same things, but I wasn't about to let our combined desperation allow them to launch themselves into a void they wouldn't find their way back from.

I turned, meeting Silas' gaze over Akashi's shoulder. "Care to join me?" His lips spread into a knowing smile.

"I thought you would never ask."

"Raven," Akashi grabs my arm, his fear rippling through me.

"Breathe." I guide his free hand to rest on my chest, skin on skin with my mark. Then I slip my hand under the hem of his shirt, finding his own and press my palm to it. "I'm not dying, and I won't be there alone. I'm going to find our brother." I promise against his lips, and I can feel the reluctance in his grip as I step away.

"Make sure they don't do anything desperate or stupid while I'm gone?" I ask. A blue orb of power drifts across the floor, rising to dance around my shoulders as Luna slowly crosses to me, and I reach out to grip her hand.

"They wouldn't dare to try it while their mother is in such a state." A half-smile quirks her mouth, both humoring and paining me. Of course she wouldn't want an ounce of sympathy, and it's about time I stopped forcing my emotions onto everyone else.

Her hand follows my arm up to cup my face, and I let her give me a rare kiss on the cheek before guiding her to Hikari's side. Then I turn and take the hand Silas offers. He's already halfway through the veil, holding the edge up over his head so I can duck through.

"Angel!" I glance back at Finn, but make the last step over the threshold.

"I'll be back," I promise again, before Silas lets the edge above us fall shut. I will Vallen into my cupped palm, and a wave of him caresses the torn edges of the word, sewing it back together so nothing can sneak out.

"So, tell me." Silas' voice sounds further away even though we walk side by side. "How does one shift from a complete meltdown to a savior complex within a 20-minute span?"

"If you're this funny the whole trip, I might just need to knock you out when we get back," I grumble, drawing a laugh from him.

"Well, at the very least all this drama finally pushed your sister into gutting that damned Angel." I halted.

"Uriel's dead?"

"Oh undoubtedly." A spark of relief coursed through me. Well, that was one less thing to handle at least.

"I have to ask," I hesitated, afraid of the answer, but he arched a brow, waiting. "Months ago, your emotional monologue about originally failing to rescue me..." A grimace crosses his features.

"I will admit that was part of our façade. It was based on the truth. I did fail to get you at first, but it wasn't for your benefit."

"Obviously." I rolled my eyes. "But how does masking your powers and using mine benefit you? At this point it seems like a lot of wasted effort."

"On the contrary, I've been able to keep Gabriel in the dark about my true abilities. So I'd say my plans have turned out quite successful, even though the elements surrounding them have changed drastically."

"Were you avoiding my position? Not wanting to be used by them to end the war?" He snorts, looking down at me.

"You really think Gabriel wants this war to end? He wiped out a branch of his own kind to ensure it continued on. I'm not the only Nephilim which remains with the new craving of revenge over redemption." His tone grew dark. "And remaining in Heavens good graces was an easy way to obtain otherwise carefully guarded information. That advantage has obviously been lost now, but at least he only thinks I'm continuing to rebel. We might get the jump on him yet."

I purse my lips, having to agree. Two of us with this power would give us quite an advantage. That is, if he ever decided to utilize his to whatever their full extent was.

The air behind us shifts, catching my attention. Of course there's not a sound in this place, just the never-ending nothingness, but I feel eyes on us. Goosebumps cover my flesh as I raise my arm, stopping him.

"Don't move."

Before he can even react I feel something wrapping around us, but I can't tell if it's the same being I stumbled across my last time here. Whatever it is, it's highly curious. Silas now floated in the air above me, and I jogged to keep up as whatever it is spins him slowly off into the dark.

Witch Killer. The words crash through the silence, loud enough to make me clamp my hands over my ears. Fury ripples through the never-ending blackness, and the shadows seem to come alive as it demands, *What is an Angel doing in its company?*

"Well to be fair, I've killed a few dozen people myself, so I'm not exactly pure." The air becomes pressurized as a hiss rolls through the dark.

The Creator did not say you would be a sinner when you returned.

"Ah, so it is you." My eyes search the dark. "I remember you."

The world hums around us, pride swelling through the space, before Silas lands with a smack on the ground in front of me. A head of night slithers from the dark above him, scaled like a serpent. Black pits for eyes stare me down, mouth gaping to inhale sharply before pulling away.

There are many here who would wish for him to join them in the fire. The creature floats over Silas, who smartly, remains on his knees as it begins to circle him. His restraint is short lived as he opens his mouth.

"That'd be a shame, as I've wound up being the very thing a few of them chose to worship." The creature hisses at his snide comment, a forked tongue dripping with venom darting out in annoyance.

And the innocents? The women who were forced to stand to burn for nothing? Instantly, the smirk fell off Silas' face.

"A shameful misjudgment on my part." Though remorse clung to the words, the creature just hummed again, shaking its head viciously.

Unacceptable.

A tail strikes from the shadows, cording around him so tightly I hear a few of his bones crack.

"Wait," I say, drawing the creatures gaze back to me. "I won't argue in his favor, but I am searching for someone else who is here."

You seek the Hound who bleeds golden blood. It was a statement, not a question. I force myself to nod.

"He's my younger brother, and sacrificed himself to this realm without realizing he could leave it."

You are not supposed to come and go from this place. There are few exceptions.

"Then let's propose a trade." Silas gasps for a breath as the tail wrapping around him adds pressure, and the creatures black eyes seem to glow with curiosity.

You come and go as a whole. There is nothing fragmented which you could possibly give me.

I fight the urge to look at Silas, who I can feel staring at me as if he knows exactly what I plan to do. I lift my hand, pointing at him, and the air around us swells like the sea, lifting me off my feet once more.

"I see how much you crave to keep him here. A place he's been dodging for far too long."

"Raven." Silas' voice is strained, but pure rage penetrates the word.

"Silvanus," I narrow my gaze at him, feeling my lips curl. "Don't tell me after all you've revealed that you thought I would be utterly forgiving? You were going to use me. In fact, you are right now to be here." His eyes flared scarlet, and I could damn near taste the power he was forcing back down. The serpent watched on as I crossed the space to him, sliding my fingertips under his chin to force his gaze to meet mine.

"If you thought we were just going to continue on with me playing puppet for you, then you're not the man I thought you were. So," I slide my gaze back to the

creature, arching a brow in question. It
instantly spread its scaled lips into what I
assumed was a smile.

Acceptable.

Silas said nothing before the world
plunged into darkness, but I felt the
curses from his anger pelting my skin. I
lost my footing, caught in a surge of
power. This realm seemed to function and
breathe on its own, as if it were tangibly
alive. For the second time, I felt an
insistent longing to stay here. I twisted
through the dark, hands spreading before
me, searching for a grip.

*Your brother lies just beyond your
reach. You must let yourself be lost, to be
taken to him. We will not trap you.*

I didn't question it, just spread my
wings for balance. The next wave of
pressure made each feather swell whole,
hurtling me backwards through the dark.
I squeezed my eyes shut, just breathing,
just trying to keep a sense of what was up
and down. And then a sudden warmth
through the cold made me gasp.

My eyes flew open, wings flaring to
snap me to a stop. There was nothing but
absolute silence here. Silence, and

warmth. Like the front porch of the cottage on a true spring day.

"Anzen?" Nothing stirred in the gray. Nothing visible anyway, but that warmth I felt multiplied tenfold, and then my fingers were caressing what I knew was auburn fur.

I couldn't see him, but I felt his bulk curling around me, his growl reverberating through my chest as I finally drew Vallen from my veins. We were the only source of light in this otherwise empty realm. As I swung the blade to open the door, Anzens doe eyes met mine in the dark.

CHAPTER 44

Our entrance lacked the elegance I wished for, mainly because Anzens Hound was deadweight against me. He was awake, but delirious to all hell. I used my shadows to help manage some of the weight, but at the end of the day, I was carrying a three-ton Hellhound on my back.

Kuma forced his upper body through the tear in the veil, helping me drag our brother across the threshold. As soon as I was out, Hikari materialized at my other side, coaxing me away so Akashi could bring Luna close enough to grab onto Anzen. Her hands dug into his shoulders, clinging to him and speaking gently as he fought to stay steady on his feet.

Clearly, he'd noticed her eyes. The strained whine he released gave it away, but my focus has drifted to the women across the room. By now, Mary and Jesibelle had joined the rest of the group.

My mother didn't even glance at me as she fell to her knees, a sob tearing through her at the sight of Anzen. The reaction from her felt like a knife through my gut. So, she was capable of love and concern. Just not when it came to me.

Anzen though was oblivious to her, so I just clenched my jaw and bit my tongue, refusing to cause another scene. Turning my back towards her, my gaze was instantly captured by my sister's.

"Where's Silas?"

Fuck.

The question was casual enough, but the discreet sheen of ice coating the floor under the table revealed the anxiety she was keeping at bay. I was saved from what I was sure to be a mess of a response by Anzen suddenly lunging forward, teeth snapping.

"Okay, okay, easy, let's just talk!" Finn flew across the room, easily keeping a safe distance from my brother. Despite his state, Anzen righted himself from where he fell, and roared with a force that made the stained-glass rattle.

"I get that our last meeting wasn't exactly a pleasure," Finn started, but Anzen lunged for him again. Never before had I seen him so vicious, and considering no one moved to intervene, I think we were all in equal states of shock.

"Traitor." His voice penetrated all of our heads, I'm sure. "Saving my mother's life does not absolve you of what you've done."

By now, Finn had his arms fully raised above his head in a complete surrender, releasing a panicked laugh as Anzen stalked towards him. Finding my wits, I turned to see Akashi lounging back in my seat at the table, grinning like he'd just won the lottery.

"Aren't you going to do something?" I snapped. He shrugged towards me, before tossing his feet up on the polished wood.

"Hey, who am I to get in the way of a loved one's revenge?"

"You're incorrigible," I mutter, starting across the room.

"Finn's had this coming for a while," Akashi called at my back. "Plus, Anzen's an unsworn Alpha. He wouldn't listen to me even if I tried to make him."

With everything going on, I'd forgotten about that. Jesibelle, Mary and

Luna had found a safe space between Hikari and Kuma, the latter's face pinched with worry. Anzen's fury had only grown in the few seconds that had gone by, and right when I got between them Finn jerked forwards, before slumping forwards against me unconscious.

"What the fuck?" I snapped, lowering him down with a groan. Rebecca just dropped the gun she'd pistol whipped him with before shoving her finger in my face.

"Raven, where the fuck is Silas?" My irritation overflowed at the question.

"You know exactly where he is."

She didn't like that answer, power sparking in her eyes. I smirked, lowering my voice to warn softly, "I'd be careful if I were you. If you blow this place up with another celestial outburst, he'll have nowhere to come back to."

"You fucking left him in there?" She moved to shove me, but I grabbed her wrists, vines of fire circling her arms and forcing her still.

"All he has do is stop using me like he so brazenly admitted to, and use his own damn power to walk out of there." She opened her mouth to argue but I cut her off. "He's got nothing to salvage from his relationship with Heaven, and frankly, I could really use the back up."

"He hid his power, splitting it between him and another vessel!" My flames are hissing against her frost so I release her, but she doesn't come for me again. She runs both her hands through her hair as she turns away, panic lacing her voice. "He can't just call on all of it like you without additional risks."

"How about you share those risks so I can help mitigate them?" She gave me a cool glare.

"Anzen, will you please tell your sister to get my mate out of Limbo?" She asked, dodging the subject.

"With pleasure. If you can convince her to move so I can rid us all of that pest." I heard Akashi snort as I whirled to gape at Anzen, gaze still locked on Finn.

"Unfortunately, I can't." Becca's voice was bitter as she turned away.

"And why would that be?" Anzen growled again, and this time I grabbed him by the scruff of his neck, not trusting him in this state to not attack her with her back turned.

"Because Finn's the vessel." Her words had my grip on Anzen instantly loosening, and I raised my free hand to my head feeling an oncoming headache.

"Becca, I swear to God—"

"Silas absorbed Satan's power when he lit her up, yes. But Finn was her literal child. Like us. Like me, actually," she corrected, kneeling by his side. "His body was built to withstand it because it was built in her womb. So, Silas hid it there. Most of it, anyway."

I feel my skin prickle with apprehension. Was that a factor as to why Finn was trying to drain him during the first battle?

"Would Silas have to kill him in order to reclaim it?" I ask warily.

"It would be the easiest way to break the seal, yes." She doesn't deny it.

"Sounds good to me," Anzen huffs, and Akashi grunts a sound of affirmation. My stomach flips but other than that I don't react.

Silas cares for his brother deeply, that was especially evident considering what he's done. However, I don't know how his anger at my actions or the desperation to get out of Limbo would affect the future choices he makes.

"If I go back in there and get him, is there a less murderous way for him to take the power back?"

"Of course," her gaze slides back to mine. "So if you've had fun making your point, go get him before I go do it myself."

That had me moving, knowing for a fact she would toss herself through that tear in the void even though she couldn't come back from it. If it were Akashi, I'd do it too.

"Wait, we're letting him live?" Anzen cuts me off, blocking my route with his body. He looks equally pissed off as confused.

"We unfortunately do that a lot around here." The chair scrapes roughly on the floor as Akashi finally pushes back and gets to his feet.

Silently, he and Anzen study one another, two Alphas sizing each other up. I can actually see Anzen bristle when

Akashi releases a fraction of his power from whatever lock he keeps it under, and his aura fills the room. While everyone else braces for yet another fight to break out, I just used the distraction to brush past my youngest brother and keep heading for the tear in the veil.

"Don't let your mate hurt him!" Mary appeared at my side, her nails digging into my wrist in a death grip. I glared at her.

"His name is Akashi. And if you want to argue with the Commander of the Hellhounds be my guest, but I intend to let them work it out for themselves." My words held no compassion, and I yanked my arm away so hard she actually stumbled.

"There's nothing to work out because I don't want his stupid job." Despite the tension in the air, Anzen's voice was filled with conviction. I glanced back to see he hadn't dropped his head in subservience like the others had, but he wasn't exactly challenging Akashi either.

"With all due respect," he added, sounding downright sarcastic if anything, "I dare say that my job of keeping Raven alive is far too difficult for me to take on another demanding role."

"Hey," I frowned. "I'm not that difficult." Well, that was the wrong thing to say because everyone, including Jesibelle, had instant arguments to voice at the statement.

"Alright, alright, Jesus." It was my turn to throw up my hands. "Can I go now? I kind of have to sweet talk Silas out of ripping my head off before bringing him back, and I don't know how long that's gonna take."

"I can't let you do that." Anzen lunged between me Limbo again, more adamantly than before. "Each time you pass through, you run a higher risk of not returning."

"I dare say I'll be fine. Whatever that thing in Limbo is likes me," I remind him, stubbornly trying to pass him again but he blocks me with a single step.

"You think that it'll still like you after taking away the prize you just left it?" He challenged, and I could feel another icy glare coming from my sister.

"I'll figure it out," I mutter. We were wasting time. Anzen had to be brought up to speed on the past months, Silas had to be powered up, Finn had to be *woken* up, and the war was still far from over.

I turned to tell Mary to coax her favored child out of my way so I could do *my* job, but she'd disappeared. A second ago she was at my side, but now I couldn't see her anywhere. While everyone else continued to argue, I slowly turned to gaze around the room. My eyes snagged on the space behind my sister, to the spot Finn had been lying in which was now empty.

"No..." Anzen wasn't prepared for the blast of power I knocked him aside with, and even if he had been his body was not in a state to deal with me. As soon as he was out of my way, I saw them.

Mary stood at the very edge of the veil, terror shining in her eyes as Finn caressed her arms. His gaze met mine, but his mouth kept moving, reciting a whispered spell which kept everyone besides me from moving.

"It's a curse of your bloodline, I hear," he purrs to Mary, eyes gleaming. "And as far as I'm aware, you have yet to visit Limbo, putting you at the lowest risk of getting stuck for eternity. Isn't that right?" She flinched as he pressed his face to her neck, inhaling sharply.

"After all this time, your blood is still somehow so pure. Because you've always had your daughter to dirty her hands for you, yes?"

"Finn." I was frozen to the spot, unsure if I was trapped under one of his spells or if my shock was just that great.

"Raven…" Mary's voice shook as violently as her body making Finn release a dark chuckle.

"Oh no, that's not an option. This time, you'll be the one to sacrifice for her instead." He lowered his voice then, the mocking humor turning cold and resolute. "I will not see my Angel harmed because of you again."

She didn't say anything else. Didn't even struggle as he pushed her to tumble headfirst into the paralyzing darkness of Limbo.

"Rave…" Becca was right behind me but sounded far away as my senses honed directly onto Finn, who just slid his hands into his pockets with nonchalance.

"Little Bird," Akashi's voice pierced through whatever tunnel-visioned existence I had been in, and only then did I realize that the stained glass behind us had completely melted under the force of my grief.

CHAPTER 45

Grief was the word. It was the only thing tangible enough to carry the complex meaning of rage and pain and heartache as one. Loss that I didn't care about, but made me sick to my stomach all the same.

My claws were digging into Finn's skull, wanting to rip Silas's power from him myself so that he could never wield it again. It took both Akashi and Rebecca to drag me off him, screaming like a mad woman.

Akashi was encapsulated by a green mirage, my powers bouncing off him harmlessly as I raged. Becca was cursing though, unable to withstand the strikes of Holy Power I was no longer in control of. She released me for her own safety, choosing instead to drag Finn from the room by his neck.

"So peculiar," Vallen mused, perched on the edge of the table like a vulture. "I thought we hated her? I thought we resented the woman who'd abandoned us to this fate?"

I was losing my shit and had absolutely no meritable reason as to why. Anzen was alive. Silas would come back. Finn would live. A new plan would be made. I wasn't alone in this anymore.

And Mary...

Another enraged scream tore from my throat. Most of my life was fueled by misplaced vengeance for her. And she bet on it, to ensure that I, the cursed savior, performed to her every expectation. As deplorable as his actions were, Finn was right in his taunts. I was just her plan, her tool, her object to sacrifice so that she may get the results she wanted without risking herself.

And for a brief moment, I loved him for throwing her into the void. I loved him for not letting me sacrifice myself again for someone who did not value me enough to protect me. I loved him for doing for me what I could not do for myself. And I wanted to kill him for it.

I don't think I'll ever be completely beyond this, these visceral, emotional reactions that take control. At least not without the rush of numbness currently threading through my veins, the demonic urge to obliterate empathy and personal care from my system, which actually helped center me and catch my breath.

Besides Akashi, Anzen seemed to be the only one unperturbed by my fit. He'd shifted at some point, and was currently yanking on the clothes Kuma threw at him.

"Who even was she?" He asked, and instantly I was choking on air again. Akashi cursed, shifting me in his arms to press his palm to my mark again, the ebb and flow of the bond evening me out.

"Only the woman who bore you." Vallen had his eyes glued to my brother, pupils blown wide. Fascination and curiosity thrummed off him as he slid off the table. He circled my brother, humming with satisfaction, but Anzen returned his interest with a glare.

"Please tell me I'm hallucinating, and that this creature didn't break out of the ice?"

"You two know each other?" I asked.

"Intimately," Vallen cooed.

"Unfortunately," Anzen grumbled. On top of everything else, this was officially too much. I had to steady myself against the table as my vision began to blur, and slowly sank onto one of the benches while fighting the urge to vomit.

"We can't just leave that standing open, can we?" Kuma interjected, drawing our attention away from the pair. He was toeing the edge of the veil, peeking into Limbo's darkness with a frown.

I didn't feel like I should shut it, but at the same time Silas shouldn't need the door open to get out. Especially since Mary should be able to find another avenue for him to escape just as I had on my first visit there. Vallen seemed to have a similar thought process, finally dragging his attention off my brother long enough to trace his fingers along the edge of the tear, sealing it closed himself.

"So what now?" Hikari broke the silence in the room, but I didn't have an answer.

Vallen was slowly creeping towards Anzen once again, and to give everyone some reprieve from the tension bouncing between the two, I yanked our chain taut. There was a sizzling protest of white flames on my fingers as I drew him back to me, but after a final pop of sparks, he settled.

Anzen visibly relaxed with him gone, but his eyes lingered on the shimmer of magic still clinging to my skin. A flurry of emotions crossed his face as he lifted his gaze to mine.

"He'll sap you dry eventually." The words were cold, but not unkind. "He won't hesitate to steal an avenue for his freedom, so be careful how much trust you give him."

"He's already had the opportunity to," I admitted, and Anzen's brows drew together in confusion. "Long story short, I gave him full access to my power when I had to throw all the Hounds into the Shadow Realm."

Anzen grit his teeth, before roughly swiping a hand through his hair, and it struck me how much he's changed. His hair had grown long enough to curl at the shoulders, and though he hadn't grown in height, his body had swelled with muscle and power I was certain wasn't there before.

"How did you do it?" I asked, and his eyes snapped back to mine. "How did you suppress that you were an Alpha?

Didn't it hurt?" I could feel the weight of the others interest; Akashi especially was practically vibrating with the need to know.

"Lucifer," Anzen muttered, averting his gaze. In my peripheral I noticed Luna stiffen. "He tied my power to this place. The longer or farther I'm away from it, the weaker I am." Suddenly he barked a laugh. "Actually, I guess that won't be the case anymore."

"What do you mean?" Luna asked, worry staining the words. Anzen grimaced, but gestured towards me.

"As long as I'm close to Raven, I should be fine. Because somehow, that wretched thing got inside her."

"Your tied to Vallen?" I asked the question slowly, each word deliberate. Anzen bared his teeth at the name, but said nothing.

"Oh my god." I dropped my head into my hands, mind racing.

The night the Hounds found me I had killed one of them. That's what got this whole ball rolling, and none of us at the time even realized it. And I had made the stupidest, most miscalculated assumption based off what Akashi and I had done.

"Anzen," I ground out, not looking up at him. "Did I kill your mate the night you rescued me?"

"No," his voice was flat in his reply. "And before you ask, he wasn't the Hound I imprinted on either. His name was Salem, and he wasn't on our side."

He paused, crossing the room to squat in front of me, his voice gentling. "You actually saved my life that night, because he was going to kill me. I didn't think you remembered that."

Vallen's desperation beat against the rising nausea, and I released my grip on him, letting him out. Akashi was there in an instant, dragging me away as Vallen's Hound materialized behind Anzen. He instantly bristled under the weight of his gaze without even turning around. Vallen also didn't move, his edges flickering wildly like he was nervous. Or excited.

"There's no possible way," Luna breathed out, but I was shaking my head, already knowing.

Lucifer used to be an Angel, and came here after he'd stolen Eden's Flame. Vallen had already disclosed enough to know he was once that power, before transforming over time into the Hellfire. To Lucifer he was just a source of power to draw from, to make his Hounds stronger by giving them magic.

But Vallen had become sentient, and like my brother was a mix of Heaven and Hell. So not only was it possible, but it was done.

"Another secret you couldn't bother to share?" I bit out at Vallen. He dared to press closer to Anzen, who for all the world looked like he wanted to tear the Hounds throat out. Vallen chuckled, the sound like the finest silk.

"Did I fail to mention the imprinting mark on your brothers skin happens to match mine?"

EPILOGUE

"What the fuck were you thinking?"

Rebecca hurls Finn against the stone face of the cliff, her hands still shaking with the mixture of her shock and fear. After seeing the look on her sister's face, she dragged the vampire as far from her as she could before he finally teleported out of her grip. The last time she'd seen that look on Ravens face, she'd torn a group of men apart with her bare hands. If she repeated the action with Finn, there would be nothing left for Silas to salvage. If Mary found him.

"I was thinking that we had wasted enough time playing games." Finn's voice turned rough. "You and my brother truly thought I was oblivious to what's been buried in my blood?"

His question caught her off guard, shutting her mouth before the next insult could fly out of it. Satisfied by her silence he leaned forwards.

"You did a wonderful job remaining quiet about it for your mate, but I'm not

472

the naive child he once rescued." He exhales a laugh, a scowl crossing his face. "Now, restraining her power, and my own magic for that matter, to manifest as similar gifts was a clever move to fool the masses. But it wasn't clever enough to blind me to what he inherited after her death."

Rebecca felt her teeth grinding. Many years ago, she expressed her concerns about Finn catching on for the very same reason. To the supernatural world, as long as they displayed it with consistency, the brother's powers wouldn't raise any red flags. One could manipulate a person's movements with their name, another with ancient spells. The same gift with different methods, because it was derived from the same source.

From what she was told, from the beginning there was no fooling Finn about his heritage. It was clear he knew who and what his mother was. However, Silas neglected to mention what he inherited from her death, and purposely left it unsaid to avoid the event of Finn trying to steal it for himself.

In order to sooth Gabriels annoyance at not burning the boy, and to

not raise suspicions, Silas decided to turn
Finn into a creature which mimicked his
way of life as a Nephilim: a vampire. This
visually added another ally to Heavens
crusade, as well as explain away the
frustrations of Finn's now limited magic.

But Rebecca had always known
what Silas had hidden. That during
Finn's transition, Silas used his feedings
as a way to slowly transfer the power he
inherited, hiding it away until future use.
Furthermore, the limit on the magic they
wielded was self-inflicted, taught and
tethered by Silas to ensure the whole of it
didn't flood either of them, making them
too powerful to control. If Heaven realized
what luck they had, having one of their
own burn a Devil and gain their power…
she didn't want to imagine it.

"I've always known he had access
to it." Finn's voice shocked Rebecca back
to the present. Pure exhaustion had
replaced the annoyed look on his face,
and he released a strained groan, running
a hand down his face. "Perhaps this is
why I crave Raven so much. She's the
only other being I know who is so
painfully aware of those trying to fool her,
and being incapable of stopping them."

"We weren't trying to fool you," she said, truly apologetic. "Silas was afraid if you knew the extent of it, you would do something drastic. Especially if it were for Ravens sake."

"Fair enough," Finn admitted quietly. "Though, might I ask what to expect upon his return?"

"Freedom." The voice behind her was damningly soft. And dangerous. They both turned, eyes catching on a ripple of shadows at the base of the stairs which was steadily growing.

"That was fast," Becca murmured, relief flooding her as her mates scent hit her nose. There was no way of knowing if Mary had found him, but as Silas emerged from the frothing shadows, it was clear he was using his own power to do so.

He was as pristine as ever. The pallor of his skin was somehow even fairer than before, but his once ruby eyes now shone darker, like polished garnet. His hair had grown too, thick black waves spilling down his back and flapping like a cloak as he stalked up the steps.

It was an effort to not batter him with questions as she surveyed him for any injuries, and a downright pain to remain rooted to her spot. The last thing they needed right now was for him to fully snap, and by the look on his face, anything could set him off.

"Freedom," Finn repeated, sounding skeptical. Though he exhibited a bridled anxiety, he made no move to retreat and dared to add, "Making the description glamourous or dramatic does not change that you plan to kill me."

"You wish to wield the full extent of your magic again, yes?" Silas punctuated the question with the crack of his fist against the stone next to Finns head, looming over him. Finn's eyes flared, shock crossing his features in such a childlike way that Silas chuckled. "Of course, all your magic is still there. It's just buried beneath mine."

There was the sudden sound of shredding fabric, and Silas tossed Finn's shirt over his shoulder unceremoniously. All Rebecca could do was gawk at the two of them as her mate leaned into Finns neck, inhaling with the force of someone who was drowning.

"You won't truly die," he mumbled against his skin. "And even better for you, once you receive Gods Mark, you'll never be separated from your Deviless, even in death."

Finn was breathing rapidly now, his eyes flashing towards Rebecca in both question and desperation. She quickly averted her gaze, pretending to study her claws to ignore the pounding in her head.

"Don't look at me. You were the one complaining about him wasting time a second ago," she reminded him.

"Oh, were you?" Silas slowly brushed the hair off Finn's neck, fully caging him in now. "Frankly, I'm too starved and enraged to pretend you were wrong. I have waited too long, for both me and you. It's time I give back what I have taken from you, and take back what's mine."

Finn jolted as Silas' fangs pierced his throat, one hand flying up to grip his shoulder as his knees buckled. Silas groaned at the first rush of power, his body trembling from the instant high. He grew hungrier with each gulp, biting deeper, not holding himself back. His body was beginning to warm after centuries of cold, his heart beginning to race in his chest like a freed beast.

His arms maneuvered to cradled Finn as he began to wilt, easing him slowly down to the ground until he was fully hunched over him like an animal tearing into its prey. And when Finn's veins ran dry, Silas pulled back with a gasp.

He shuddered violently for breath, his face and his neck stained a brilliant red. Rebecca stared down at them wide-eyed. At Finn's pale body, still as a corpse. At her mate, an awakening predator, pushing to its feet.

"You just said you wouldn't kill him," she whispers, her nerves showing for the first time in years as Silas turns towards her, eyes wholly black.

"Rest assured, Finnegan will wake. That's what she's for." He wipes his mouth with the back of his hand as he stands, eyes returning to the growing swell of blackness below them.

"Should I assume I've been brought along to give life to the boy?" It was the silken voice of a woman echoing from the dark. Silas grins.

"Giving life is your specialty."

There's the faintest haze of light, and at first, Rebecca thinks it's her sister emerging from the layers of shadows. But this woman dons the silver armor of Heavens legion, and though her dark hair is braided the same, her eyes resemble the warm tones of the earth. Rebecca wants to scream, but her throat clogs as the woman kneels over Finns body, painting his pale lips with the golden blood dripping off her fingers.

Silas hums, returning his attention to Rebecca. And her pulse. He eliminates the space between them in less than a breath.

"What's happening?" She manages to get out, straining to see over his shoulder but he cages her in. The world dims at the edges as the shadows clinging to him bloom into full darkness, isolating them from the outside.

"At the moment I'm most concerned with you, mate. I've been waiting to have you at my best since you tracked me down."

ACKNOWLEDGEMENTS

As always, the first person I would like to thank is my husband. The phrase 'thank-you' honestly isn't enough anymore. It doesn't cover the extent of the support he gives each time I'm down the rabbit hole. Or just walking and talking in daily life. My love, you give me confidence that I feel blessed to have.

Throughout the journey of this book I have met so many fantastic people in the indie community. Whether it be someone I've been working with for a few years, or if you're new to my chaotic system, know I am deeply grateful to have you in my circle.

And to you the reader. You're the ones who make this magic possible. The writers of the world may come up with amazing ideas, but you are the ones who breathe life into our creations. Thank you for your time and your passion.

With grace, love, and respect,
NIGHTSHADE